ANNA HODGES OGINSKY

The Soluna's Way

Brighton, Michigan

First paperback edition October 2020

Cover design and interior illustration by Carole Chevalier
Page layout design and formatting by Ines Monnet
Author photograph © Christina Kafkakis

ISBN 978-1-7350877-8-8 (paperback)
ISBN 978-1-7350877-7-1 (ebook)

Library of Congress Control Number: 2020912157

First published in the United States of America by All Heart Press, LLC.

All Heart Press is part of Heartmonic Holdings, LLC. Heartmonic is a good works enterprise. Its mission is to promote meaningful endeavors that center around art and community. In short, we seek to Make Awesome Things and Make Things Awesome.

www.allheartpress.com

This book is for my young ones—Sophia, Alexander, and James.
And to all the young ones. The future is in good hands.

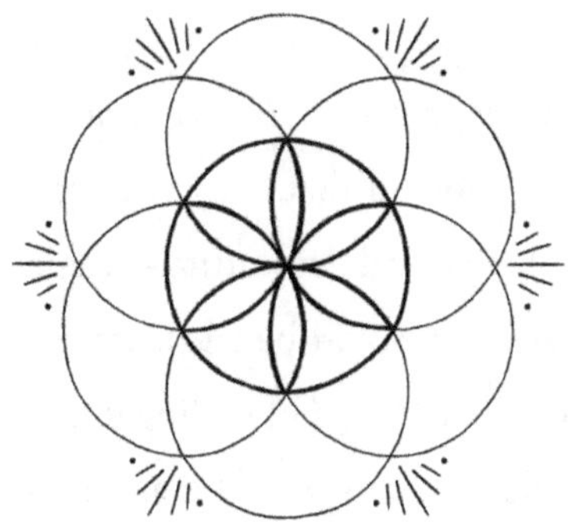

CHAPTER 1

AYLA PLOPPED DOWN next to the creek with a loud sigh. She peered over the small hill leading into the creek, trailing her fingers back and forth through the water, and strained to remember every detail of the day. She wanted to memorize everything that happened, but she couldn't recall anything before the argument she had with her mom.

That morning, she'd gotten dressed in her new dark red sweater and favorite black leggings with the cool zigzag stitching up the sides. She'd pulled on her tall brown UGGs and stood in front of the full-length mirror in her parents' bedroom. If her insides were going to be shredded into pieces that day, she at least wanted to feel comfortable on the outside.

Her mom appeared, firing questions. "Ayla, what is that? What are you wearing?"

"It's my new top," she responded, pulling her shoulders back. "Red. Grandpa's favorite."

"I laid out a dress on your bed. *That* is what you will wear."

"I won't be comfortable in that." It was a stretch for Ayla to wear anything outside of her typical daily attire—leggings, a T-shirt, maybe a hoodie. Surely a sweater would be adequate for a funeral. Plus, she would wear her hair down instead of pulling it into a ponytail—her attempt to look extra fancy. Pretty good for an ordinary twelve-year-old.

"Grandpa liked you in dresses, Ayla," her mom said. "Please wear the dress out of respect for him."

"But *I* don't like dresses."

"Honey, sometimes we have to do things we don't like. Plus, I know Grandpa would appreciate it."

"What about being true to myself? You always say *be true to you.*" Ayla knew her mother's favorite response to all of Ayla's doubts about what to do in any situation would hold at least some weight in this argument.

Her mom let out a long exhale. "I hear you, honey. I do. I always want you to be true to you. Believe me." She paused. "But what if honoring your grandfather in this way would allow you to honor him *and* be true to you? He loved you so much. He loved seeing you in dresses."

Trickery. Ayla knew she wasn't going to win this one. She rolled her eyes and headed back to her bedroom to change her clothes.

Later, Ayla tried to sit still in the cold, hard church pew without fidgeting. She listened as Pastor Godfrey recalled the story of her grandfather's long, happy life. He talked about how Grandpa George came from humble beginnings and how he was a self-made man.

Ayla got distracted halfway through the eulogy as she wracked her brain for an early memory of her grandpa. One that didn't involve caked-on makeup, a body without breath, or a neatly pressed suit. One that didn't force Grandma Ettie into silence. A memory where there were no whispers, no tear-filled eyes, and no sadness.

Nothing. No memories. Ayla was empty.

She wondered what Grandpa George would think of his funeral service. Would he approve? He knew a good pecan pie from a bad one and a proper necktie knot from a sloppy one. Would he know she had spent hours at the dining room table, helping her grandma and mom flip through books of old family photos to choose just the right ones for display? Births, graduations, weddings, celebrations. His Chevy, the lake house, their last Christmas as a family. They tried to tell the story of his entire life in a stack of photos. Did he see Grandma Ettie's eyes fill with tears when Connor handed her the freshly printed programs?

She had so many questions. She sat at the creek now, the place she liked to go when questions overwhelmed her. When she didn't know what to do next. Sometimes at the quiet of the creekside, she found answers. She hoped that would be the case now.

She scooped up a few small rocks and dropped them, one by one, into the water. She watched as the water rippled in circles and remembered her mom doing the same thing many times—most recently on one of the last days of summer vacation. On that day, Ayla had wanted to go to the lake with friends, but Grandma Ettie had invited her to some luncheon for old people. She'd been pouting by the creek when her mom found her there and settled down on the ground next to her.

"One act of kindness, Ayla Bug—one simple act," her mother said as she dropped stones into the water, one by one. She pointed to the first ripple. "You choose to attend Grandma's luncheon, and you make her day. She's then happy at the luncheon because she gets to brag about her granddaughter with you *right there* in front of her friends."

Her mother's eyes grew big with enthusiasm as she pointed to the next fading ripple. "Then Grandma's happiness ripples out to her guests. Their happiness ripples out to *their* families. And so on. The ripple keeps going. It goes on and on and on, all because you said yes. All because you agreed to help."

Ayla liked the idea of making a difference, but she rarely knew *how* to make a difference. She wondered what it would take to brighten Grandma Ettie's day now. How many luncheons would Ayla need to attend to bring back the sparkle in her grandma's eyes?

A branch cracked nearby. Ayla dropped the remaining rocks in her hand and lay flat on the ground, her arms and legs splayed. She didn't want to get up from her sanctuary by the creek, yet she knew she should get back inside to see if her mom needed help with anything.

She thought she heard a whisper coming from the trees.

"Hello?" she called out. "Connor, is that you? You know I hate it when you sneak up on me, Connor! Hello?"

Silence. She rolled over to look up at her house on the top of the hill that led to the creek, expecting to see her brother, Connor, sneaking away. But when she turned around, her house was gone.

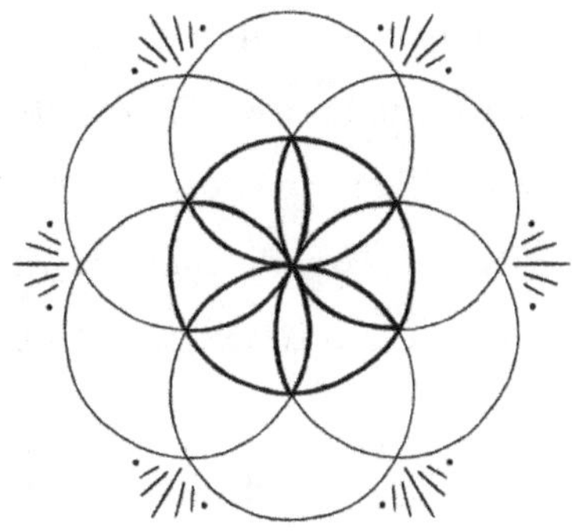

CHAPTER 2

"Don't be afraid."

Ayla didn't recognize the soft voice that floated toward her.

"I mean, I know that might seem hard right now, under the circumstances," the voice continued, "but you're safe. You don't need to be afraid."

The words hung in the air around Ayla like a long-held secret.

She turned her head to follow the voice back to an opening in the trees by the creek. Her eyes landed on a girl who was about her height and probably her age too. The girl looked familiar, but there was something strange about her. A boy, taller and probably older, stood next to her, and he also felt familiar yet strange. She noticed their eyes were kind.

They wore brightly colored tunics, his the color of a ripe orange and hers longer and covered with emerald-green and magenta swirls. He wore loose gray pants with brown hiking boots, and she wore emerald-green leggings with tall brown boots.

Sensible, but a little out there, thought Ayla. Still, their clothing looked comfortable, and she appreciated that. Comfort was her guiding fashion principle.

The girl's dark brown hair was piled on top of her head in a sloppy bun. Ayla noticed some strands were braided and woven into the bun. She also noticed the girl's hair was extraordinarily shiny. The boy's sand-colored hair was straight, cut to about chin length, and a tad shaggy.

"We're glad you made it. Thank you for coming." The girl smiled warmly at Ayla. Her eyes were the color of blueberries.

Ayla felt like she knew this girl, but she didn't know how. She also felt safe, even though she had no idea where her house had gone or what else was happening. Maybe she was asleep? She loved the feeling of this dream and was curious to see where it would go next. If this was a dream, she didn't want to wake up.

The boy reminded Ayla of an earthier, more rugged version of her brother, Connor. Connor liked to hike, and hiking boots were his footwear of choice, but Ayla couldn't imagine him wearing a tunic—or such long hair.

"Hello, Ayla," the boy said.

She wondered how he knew her name. She wondered if she should be scared. She thought maybe she did feel a little uneasy after all.

"Ayla, I'm Prem," the boy continued. "This is my sister, Mina."

Prem's voice sounded like a deep note on the piano. His voice made her heart hum.

Ayla turned to meet Mina's eyes. "Am I dreaming?" She decided it would be best to get straight to the truth of the matter.

"No, Ayla, you're not dreaming," Prem said. "This is real. We invited you here because we need your help, and you were open, thankfully, so you came—"

"Our mother is waiting for us, Ayla," Mina interrupted, glaring at Prem as if he had said too much. "*She* will explain everything. Are you hungry?"

Ayla's tummy rumbled at the mention of hunger. She hadn't eaten much after the funeral.

When Ayla stood up, Mina took her hand and gave it a small, reassuring squeeze that sent warm chills throughout Ayla's body. Warm chills? So far, these two people and this new place felt like a—what was that word? A paradox? Yes. Strange yet familiar. Chilly but warm.

Ayla would typically launch into a million questions at a moment like this. Prem said they needed her help, but she was used to feeling mostly unhelpful. She often felt cringey, like she didn't fit in. Right now, though, she couldn't find the words to even form a question. And the quiet she felt in place of her questions was oddly comforting.

As they walked, Ayla noticed a small tattoo near Mina's left wrist. It looked like a flower, with the outline of just six narrow petals. *Isn't she too young for a tattoo?* She tried to see if Prem had one too, but he was walking too fast.

The girls tried to keep up with Prem's long strides. The sound of dead leaves crackling beneath their feet filled the air.

The surrounding area looked a lot like home, yet the grass grew in deeper shades of green than she had ever seen. The dead brown leaves were deeper in color too, as if their lives before they fell from the branches had been richer and even more meaningful than the lives of the leaves around her house at home. She could smell things in the air she didn't recall smelling before. She caught whiffs of a stronger, more robust scent of grass and tree bark. She breathed in powerful wafts of soil and air, and something sweet, apples maybe, with cinnamon, cooking in the distance.

Once they made it to the top of the hill, where Ayla's house would have been, there was a different house, one she had never seen before. Its roof looked like one giant solar panel. The house glowed from within.

"This is our home, Ayla," Mina said, breaking the silence. Mina's eyes filled with tears. She looked closely at Ayla, whose eyes also filled with tears, as if they were responding to Mina's.

"Oh gosh," Ayla said. "I'm such a baby. I'm sorry. I don't know why I'm crying." She wiped her eyes with her hands.

Mina and Prem smiled at Ayla. "It's okay," they said softly and in unison.

"I guess it's been a long day," Ayla said.

"No explanation needed." Prem patted her on the shoulder and stepped forward to open the door to the house.

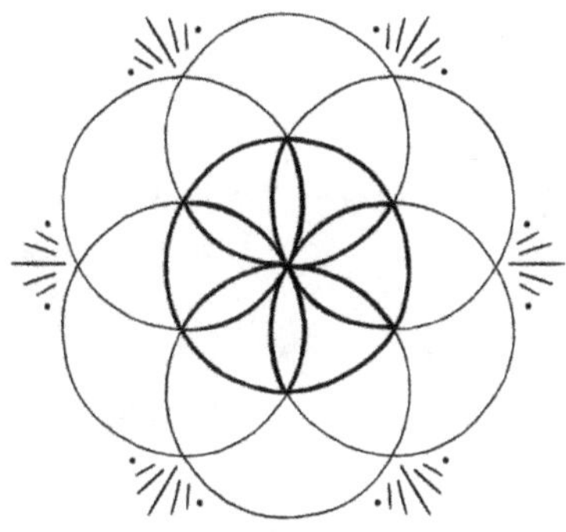

CHAPTER 3

A WOMAN CAME to the door with open arms and a toothy smile. She looked like an angel. Light emanated from her bright green eyes, and her dark brown hair fell in curls down her back. She wore a tunic and leggings too, in shades of white and cream, and looked like she'd just come in from a walk on the beach on a breezy summer night.

"I'm Noor Star," the woman said. "Mina and Prem are my children."

Noor wrapped Ayla in a tight hug, and she could feel Noor's heart beat against her chest like a drum from the drumline at school. With each thump of Noor's heart, Ayla felt a sense of calm settle into her own body. This strange angel-woman was pumping peace directly into Ayla's heart. But how?

Ayla's chest tingled as the woman pulled away and held Ayla at arm's length—just like Grandpa always did before he remarked on how much she had grown since the last time he saw her. "There are many ways to grow, Ayla Bug," he would say. "This time you grew even prettier!"

"Ayla," Noor said, "thank you for being here with us." Her eyes, too, filled with tears.

"I don't know how I got here," Ayla started, not wanting to cry again. "So, while I appreciate your warm welcome, I, uh, well, I guess I'm not sure I deserve your thanks."

She felt like she was stumbling over the words in her head as she tried to speak them.

"Where am I?" she finally asked. *Are you sure it's me you want to help you?* she thought but didn't ask.

"Well, hmm." Noor squinted into Ayla's eyes like she was looking for something lost there. "I guess it wouldn't hurt to be straight right from the start." After a deep breath and a long pause, Noor continued, "You are on a planet called Eema. Eema is like Earth, where you are from, in a galaxy that is like the Milky Way."

"Eema and Earth are twins," Mina said, studying Ayla's face closely.

Ayla's eyes lit up when she remembered Connor's fascination with parallel universes two years ago, when he was in seventh grade.

"Yes! There you go!" Noor said, noticing the spark of connection in Ayla's eyes. She laughed. "You're getting it!"

Then more tears formed in Noor's eyes. "I . . . I wasn't sure how we would communicate—telepathically, by talking, or in some other way. I was unsure what the limitations would be. I honestly wasn't even sure we *could* communicate. This is incredible. So, yes. Eema is Earth's twin.

At one point, Earth and Eema were one. Then came a turning point in time, where a choice was to be made. Earth took one path, and Eema formed to take another."

Ayla didn't quite follow Noor's train of thought. "So, what you're saying is, I somehow traveled through space without realizing it, and now I'm in a parallel universe on Earth's twin?"

"Well, that is certainly a start." Noor pulled her in for another hug. "You should know that no matter what, you are going to be okay here, dear. You *are* okay. Let's have something to eat, and I'll explain more later."

Ayla felt that warm tingle run through her body again. And while she was dumbfounded, hungry, and still wondering why she didn't feel more uneasy than she did, she also felt like she could trust Noor when she said she was okay. Despite all logic telling her otherwise, she *felt* okay. That seemed like a good enough reason not to panic.

Noor released her and led her to the table, where they each pulled out a chair and sat down. In the next moment, another angel-like being—a very tall man—came through a door from what must have been the kitchen. His hair was probably as long as Prem's, maybe longer, but he had it pulled back in a ponytail. He moved like he walked on air rather than the floor.

The man smiled at Ayla and nodded in her direction as he set down the tray of food he carried.

"Welcome," he said quietly, the vibrations of his voice bouncing around the room. "I'm Bodhi, their father." He winked in the direction of Mina and Prem. "We are happy you're here."

Ayla smiled slowly, noting Bodhi's deep brown eyes and the dark curls that escaped from his ponytail.

But as she smiled, she became distracted by her thoughts. She felt comfortable with Bodhi, Noor, Prem, and Mina, despite the highly unlikely but seemingly true fact that she'd been whisked into a parallel universe and was now sitting at a table with this group of strange but familiar people who seemed more like angelic beings than humans.

She couldn't comprehend how she had left her family, traveled through space, met these strangers, and was just okay with it all. It made absolutely no sense. But she didn't feel her chest tighten like she normally did when she arrived in new places. Her stomach wasn't in knots, and her palms weren't sweating. She felt as comfortable as she did at home with her own family, maybe even more comfortable than she felt with her own family sometimes. Her comfort in this unusual setting seemed even stranger than the situation itself.

She was almost dizzy with contentment, in fact. So this had to be a dream. But she was still curious and didn't mind staying in the dream. The dream was, after all, a welcome distraction from Grandpa George being gone, Grandma Ettie's seemingly bottomless well of pain, and her mother's heaviness since Grandpa George's death.

She felt like light bulbs were shining in every cell of her body.

"Ayla?" Mina's voice interrupted Ayla's assessment of her situation. "This is a lot to take in, we know. Is it okay if it doesn't all make sense right away? Maybe eat some food and have some rest."

Mina's words startled Ayla. Was it okay if none of this made sense? For as long as she could remember, she had spent most of her waking moments trying to make sense of her parents, her brother, her grandparents, her friends, *herself*. And in this beyond-strange experience, these new people were asking if it was okay if she didn't make sense of it all. Could she stop with all the thinking and let it be okay, at least for now?

As these thoughts crossed her mind, she was met with smiles around the table, as if Mina, Prem, Noor, and Bodhi were right there in her brain, hearing the conversation she was having with herself.

"Can you read my mind?" she asked, looking around the table to meet the eyes of every member of this Star family.

"Well, not exactly," Prem said.

Ayla looked at Prem in disbelief. "You seem to know what I'm thinking without me saying it, though. You *must* be reading my mind."

"Ayla, has your family ever had a dog as a pet?" he asked.

"Well, yeah. We've always had a dog. We're dog people," Ayla said. *That* was something she was sure of.

"Okay, good. Have you ever noticed how dogs hear sounds that humans don't hear?" Prem looked at Noor, and when she nodded, he continued, "You know, sounds that are on a higher frequency than normal?"

"Yes," Ayla said. She could picture the way her family's new puppy, Apollo, stopped whatever he was doing as soon as he heard a sound. Sometimes she heard the sound a few seconds later, and sometimes she never quite heard it.

"Okay, well, think of it like this," Prem continued. "Your thoughts are on a higher frequency than the words that come out of your mouth.

We aren't reading your mind like you read a story—word for word, thought for thought. We can't do that . . . yet. But we *can* tune in to your mind's frequency. So, in a way, we can sense what you are thinking."

"That defies all logic," Ayla said. She felt like she was arguing with her brother.

Mina giggled and raised her eyebrows. "Again, can it just not make sense?"

"Listen, dear," Noor said, her voice calm. "On Earth, you mainly communicate your thoughts with your voice, right?"

Ayla nodded.

"Here, we communicate with our whole selves. It means we have a better chance of understanding each other because we exchange signals on different levels."

For some reason, this explanation satisfied Ayla. She felt her body relax. And she decided, just like Mina suggested, that she didn't need to know exactly how it worked to trust that it *could* work. Besides, she was glad they couldn't read her mind.

"Eat." Noor smiled again, which caused Ayla's body to shiver like the warm, unexpected shiver she felt when someone whispered in her ear.

The food on Ayla's plate was, again, a contradiction. It looked simple: roasted golden potatoes, sautéed spinach, and something in a milk-chocolate-colored sauce. But as simple as it looked, it tasted complex. Each bite she took set off a new burst of flavor in her mouth. It was the most delicious meal she had ever eaten.

For dessert, Bodhi had made apple crisp with vanilla ice cream. Each bite Ayla took dissolved in her mouth, leaving behind the most delectable apple-y, cinnamon-y, rich vanilla flavor. She silently begged the flavors to last inside her mouth for as long as possible.

As she took the last bite on her plate, Ayla's eyes grew heavy. She yawned, realizing she was enjoying her food so much, she'd stopped listening to the conversation.

"Ayla? You must be exhausted. Space travel will do that to you," Bodhi said, winking. "Would you like Mina to show you to bed?"

Before Ayla could answer, Mina stood and took her hand. They walked from the dinner table to a bedroom in another part of the home in a blur. *I don't care what they say. This could very well be a dream*, she thought as she climbed into bed.

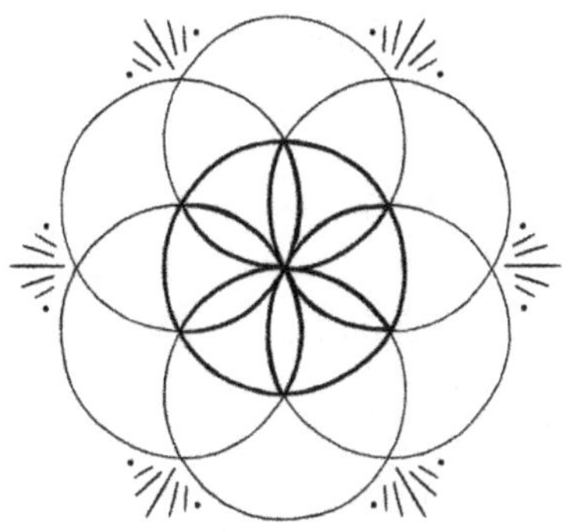

CHAPTER 4

The next morning, a twinkling sound like wind chimes woke Ayla. She had forgotten where she was. She looked around the strange room for something familiar, something to jostle her memory. Then a whiff of apples filled her nose, and the events of the night before came back to her.

She nestled deeper into the warm, soft blankets that cradled her. Each piece of bedding was meticulous in appearance but still broken in like an old favorite. In the morning light, the room looked like a spread in a futuristic home-and-garden magazine. Crisp, clean lines surrounded her. The room was airy, decorated with different textures in varying shades of white: cloud white bedding, paper white walls, and a marshmallow white chair in the corner of the room. It was unlike any room Ayla had ever seen in person.

She rolled out of bed wearing the same clothes she had changed into after Grandpa George's funeral. It had been such a relief to finally slip into her new red tunic and her favorite leggings after being trapped in that awful black dress all day.

She noticed a fresh set of brightly colored clothes placed neatly on a chair in the corner of the room, but she didn't feel like changing. She walked through the door and wasn't sure where to go next. She followed the scent of the apples.

"Good morning?" Ayla asked once she found her way to the kitchen. Noor was bent over a pot on the stove, stirring and smelling the mixture inside the pot.

"Good morning, dear!" Noor's face lit up. "I'm making applesauce. I thought it would be a tasty addition to our oatmeal. Are you hungry? Did you sleep well? Would you like to take a shower?"

Even in her otherworldly body, Noor acted like a typical mother, flooding Ayla with questions. Ayla wasn't sure which question to answer first, or if she even needed to answer any of them.

"Well, yes, I slept very well," she began. "I don't know when I last slept that deeply."

Ayla stopped. She was suddenly very worried about the ramifications of falling asleep, then waking up in a dream. Could she sleep in a dream? This was feeling less and less like a dream.

"Um, Noor?" Ayla asked, grappling with the reality that she wasn't dreaming at all. "What about my family? Will they be worried I'm gone? We just buried Grandpa yesterday . . ." Her voice trailed off as tears began to form in her eyes.

"Oh my," Noor started. "Right. Okay. So, I'm terribly sorry about your grandfather. That he . . . *passed away*, as you say it. Oh, Ayla, there are so many things you just don't know. Things people on Earth just don't know."

"What kind of things?"

"Like what it really means to live—or die—as humans. Or in human *bodies*, I guess would be the more accurate way to say that." Noor shook her head like a little kid trying to shake water out of her ear.

"The relationship we have here with space and time—and with our bodies too—it is all much different than the relationships you have on Earth," Noor continued. "But we have a window to work with, having you here, and I do hope it is a big enough window. We can't be sure because, well, you are the first to come here. Others have come to Eema in the past, from what I understand, but you are the first to come *right* here, where we live. At least, as far as we know."

Noor paused, nodding her head. Ayla was completely confused.

"I think we can make it work within this window, though. I trust we can," Noor murmured. "But to answer your question, as far as your family knows, you are still by the creek in your backyard. They aren't any more worried about you now than they would be otherwise. You need have no apprehension about that at all."

Noor seemed less calm this morning. More frazzled. More like Ayla's own mother.

Despite her confusion, Ayla felt even more at ease now than she did last night. It felt like a full belly, a good night's sleep, a fun day with family, a sky full of stars, and a favorite song all rolled into one. Ayla had a sense—an inexplicable sense—that everything was okay and that it was going to be okay and that it always was okay. This place felt *good* to her.

After breakfast, Bodhi asked Ayla if she was ready for an adventure. She, Mina, and Prem piled into the family car with Bodhi—at least, Ayla decided to think of it as a car, even though it didn't look much like the cars at home. It reminded her of Grace's dad's Jeep, except it had no wheels. It operated a lot like an airplane, but it didn't have wings either. Was it a spaceship? She wasn't sure. Riding in the space Jeep made her feel like she was floating in the air. Her belly had that little tickle it got when her dad drove too fast over a hill.

She peeked out the window and watched the scenery speed by below. That was it! Instead of the sensation of moving, like she felt in a car or plane, the sensation was one of stillness while everything raced by on the ground. It was a smooth ride, as Grandpa George used to say about his Chevy.

They slowed down as they approached an area that looked like her city's own quaint downtown area. Everything looked crisp and clean, but the brick buildings appeared much older than the Stars' home. The space Jeep hovered over a large building that resembled her grandparents' church downtown. It was over 100 years old and a treasure in her town. An old cemetery sat behind it, and there were huge, old trees all around it as well.

"Here we are!" Bodhi's eyes lit up like a child's eyes, and he smiled eagerly. "This, my dear child, is the home of the Collective Chronicles, where I spend most of my days. Isn't it lovely?"

Ayla nodded while Mina and Prem rolled their eyes, which made Ayla giggle. In so many ways, she felt right at home with this family.

Bodhi landed and parked the space Jeep. When they all stepped out to walk toward the church-like building, the rich autumn smells filled Ayla's nose. It reminded her of Connor's description of the first time he wore his eyeglasses. He had stared out the window all the way home from the optometrist, marveling at the new details he hadn't seen before. Leaves on trees, words on signs—he was in complete awe.

Ayla felt that way with all her senses here. Everything she touched, tasted, smelled, and saw felt more pronounced. Even the sounds were so different, she almost didn't recognize words she'd heard spoken her entire life. It was like listening to a song in her earbuds for months, then hearing it live in concert. She felt a tug at her heart at the thought of home yet also sensed home was not that far away.

As Bodhi approached the door of the building, Ayla noticed a red laser scan on his face, then Prem's, then Mina's, and then her own. The use of this high-tech light seemed out of place in such an old building.

The door unlocked, and Bodhi crossed the threshold, holding the door open for them. Lights illuminated what appeared to be a marble hall. The grandeur of the marble also seemed out of place in the building, which felt old and even a little rickety. She expected to see a lot of wood like she would see in a creaky old library. She spotted the flower-like symbol she'd noticed on Mina's forearm carved into some of the marble walls.

"Ayla," Bodhi said, cutting into her thoughts, "remember when Mina asked whether you could accept that there would be things you might not understand while you are here?" His expression had changed from one of great, almost childlike enthusiasm to that of a serious teacher explaining concepts that would definitely be on the exam.

Ayla nodded, wondering what he was gleaning from her thoughts while also sensing the weight of this moment and watching him carefully.

"From here on out," he continued, "it is important to remember that things—*all* things—are not always what they seem."

He turned and motioned for the children to follow him down a long hall. They passed glass cases built into the walls that held old tools, bowls, and wooden eating utensils displayed like historical artifacts in a museum.

When they turned a corner, Bodhi waved his arm over his head, left to right, like a windshield wiper. The marble walls completely disappeared.

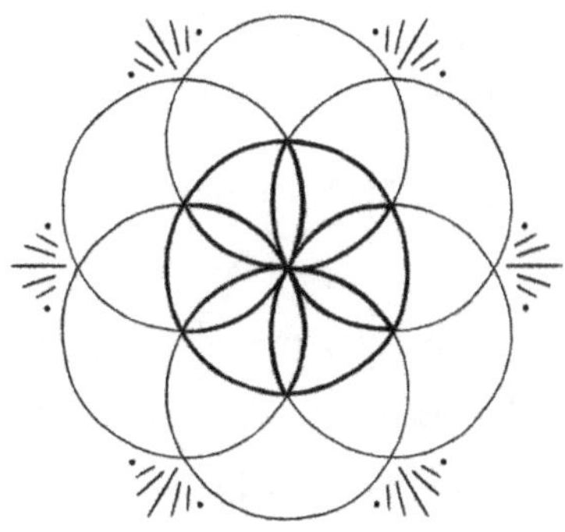

CHAPTER 5

ONCE THE MARBLE walls were gone, the inside of the building looked more like what Ayla had expected of the old building. The exterior walls were lined with bookcases that ran from the floor to a high ceiling that appeared to have been built just like her grandparents' church. Maybe it *was* once a church?

Every bookcase was filled with books. Some books looked very old, and some looked more current. Each book had that same symbol from Mina's forearm engraved on its spine. But what Ayla could not have anticipated were the floor-to-ceiling, computer-like display screens that sat directly in front of the bookcases. The screens were mostly transparent, with little lights flashing sporadically across them. Ayla's mouth hung open as her eyes raced from side to side, wall to wall, floor to ceiling, and ceiling to wall, trying to take it all in. She felt like her head was going to explode.

"What is this?" Ayla asked, spinning around to lock eyes with Mina.

Mina appeared to be as surprised as Ayla felt. "Dad, I—we—it's been so long. I don't remember any of this."

"Yeah, Dad," Prem added. "None of this looks familiar to me either."

Bodhi swiped his arm again, and what looked like a weather map appeared on one of the screens. It was just like the map Ayla saw on the morning news every day before school when her mom checked the weather—just like the map of the United States Ayla had always known as home. She let out a breath she didn't realize she had been holding.

"Ayla, we aren't sure how long you can stay here with us," Bodhi said. "This is all new and unknown to us. We have theories—well, we *had* theories. Some of what we predicted has happened, and there are other variables we didn't expect."

Bodhi paused and looked carefully at each of them. "Prem and Mina, this part of the Collective Chronicles is normally hidden, as you may have guessed. It has been in development for some time now. Our former colleague, Seth, helped us get it started, but he has since moved on to other work. Outside of Seth, only our close colleagues from the Circle of the Ways even know this exists."

He watched their faces closely, trying to read their reactions. "I know I can trust you. I'm not worried about that," he said, "but there are people—the Circle of the Ways, to be exact—who wouldn't approve of my bringing you here. They aren't all happy we invited Ayla. They didn't think it wise to explore that kind of travel between universes."

Invited? Ayla thought. *I must have missed that invitation. I don't remember sending an RSVP.*

"I guess what I'm trying to say is that we need to be very careful here," Bodhi said. "Do you understand?"

He again studied their faces. They nodded.

Ayla opened her mouth to ask a question. She had so many questions. She wondered about the invitation and the Circle of the Ways—what was that? What did it mean that some people didn't approve of her being there? She wondered about the timing. And the symbol. The questions buzzed around like the tiny bugs that swarmed her head on the beach in late summer.

When she caught Bodhi's eyes, she didn't know where to start. But before she could say anything, she somehow *felt* his answer, and her questions faded. The old, familiar anxious feeling she felt rising in her chest subsided. A small voice inside her asked her to be still, to listen.

Bodhi passed his hand over what would be Texas on the map, and little red blurs appeared along its coast. "These red areas indicate tornadoes that have recently struck in the South, which is this area here."

"Tornadoes?" Prem and Mina asked in unison.

"Right," Bodhi started. "A tornado is a storm. They're destructive. We've never experienced anything like that here on Eema. We've never seen a tornado or endured any weather that could compare to the magnitude of one. Here on our planet, we have clouds, rain . . . " His voice trailed off.

"So, this is the *South*?" Ayla pointed to the area that looked like Texas. "Then where are we located on this map?"

Bodhi pointed to what looked like her home state of Michigan.

"And this area that includes us," Bodhi waved his hand over the northern part of the map "this is the North."

Okay, so north and south, just like Earth, Ayla thought. Bodhi nodded in agreement with her thoughts.

"Ayla, on Earth you experience tornadoes, do you not?"

When Ayla nodded, he continued, "You—well, I guess it's more accurate to say *your people*—your people have made choices. Choices that impact your weather. According to our calculations, your planet will experience some of the worst weather in its history in the coming years."

He paused, as if searching the space above the screen for the next thing to say.

In the silence, Ayla's hands began to shake. She felt a lump forming in her throat. "How—what?" Tears filled her eyes, and Mina reached out, lightly rubbing Ayla's back.

Questions swarmed in her head again. She found it hard to decipher what had been said and what was happening in the room, in her body—in her life!

She remembered the morning her mother told her Grandpa George was gone. Dead. Everything she relied upon in her life shifted like the ground in an earthquake in that moment. She didn't even believe her mom at first. She couldn't picture life without her Grandpa George. With each hour, then each day after his death, she began to learn how to live without him and how to live, instead, with a heartbroken grandma and mother.

This felt similar, like she was at the start of learning a whole new way of life.

"Ayla, what you and your people know on Earth is a very small part of what there is to know," Mina whispered. "There is so much more out there—out here." Mina waved her arms in the air. "You've never heard of us, right? *But we know you.* We know Earth. We study it here. From what I understand, on Earth you study *world* history. We keep going, beyond our world, and even beyond yours."

Ayla let out another burst of breath. "But why? Why do you study Earth if you're here in another galaxy?"

"We inhabit Earth as much as we inhabit our own planet," Prem said. "We're all part of this one big, much bigger, thing together. It is bigger than you can imagine, Ayla. Even we cannot possibly fathom its breadth and depth. We know it is all connected, even if we cannot explain why or how."

Prem stopped talking and watched Ayla.

"Okay," Ayla said, nodding slowly. "Go on."

"We know it helps us to know as much as we can about you and your land and your people," Prem said, "even if we cannot possibly know everything."

He touched her shoulder, which then became warm. As it warmed, her body relaxed. Her mind felt like a tornado had swept right through it. In the rest of her body, she felt calm.

"Ayla, we understand that you and your people know fear, right?" Bodhi waited until Ayla nodded.

"We haven't had the same experience with fear here," he continued, speaking slowly and calmly. "But this—these tornadoes. They scare us. We are genuinely scared. We're not prepared, and we cannot know how to respond because we've never experienced anything like this."

"I'm afraid I don't know how to help you," Ayla said softly, shaking her head. "I know hardly anything about weather patterns or outer space or parallel universes. *We're all connected* sounds bananas to me, to be honest. I'm—I'm probably not your girl here."

"But you *are*, Ayla Bug," Bodhi said, closing his eyes. "You *are* our girl."

A dam broke in Ayla's mind, and it flooded with images. She saw her mom, her dad, Connor. Grandpa George and Grandma Ettie. Grace and Amanda. Her bedroom at home, her sit spot by the creek, her school, her downtown, the mitten shape of Michigan, the United States, the world map, Planet Earth. She saw other faces—faces of many colors and bodies of many shapes. Some were familiar, and some she didn't recognize. She saw it all. The images swirled and swirled until they morphed into colors and then the colors swirled quickly together. Then the colors slowed.

She saw the creek again. Then she saw Mina, Prem, Noor, and Bodhi. She saw the weather map. She felt the terror one might feel in the face of a tornado. All at once, she felt and saw the fear creeping into Bodhi and his family and spreading out into this place and this time. The fear that was new to these new friends of hers was not new to her. It was a part of her. It always had been. She was born with it. She saw the fear like a string, weaving between the images of the people here and the land here, and then the string extended. It wrapped around this planet that looked like Earth but was called Eema, and then it moved into what must be outer space. It extended on and on, then wrapped around her planet, her Earth, her land, and her people.

Being connected *sounded* fruity, but it *felt* right, now that she could see it so vividly. On some level beyond what her mind could conceive, Ayla felt that connection. She wanted to be their girl. She wanted to help.

"Okay then," Bodhi said, opening his eyes and smiling at Ayla. "Let's get started."

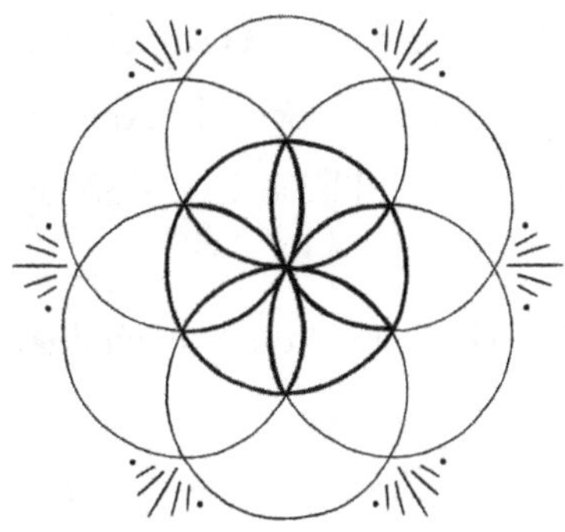

CHAPTER 6

AYLA WATCHED THE scenery as Bodhi drove the space Jeep through the streets to the restaurant where the group would meet Noor for lunch.

This town bore an uncanny yet comforting resemblance to her hometown. It was updated in some ways, like a new version of a familiar app on her phone. It wasn't quite futuristic, but it looked cleaner than the town where she lived. The lines along the buildings seemed crisper, the sidewalks newer, and the whole area fresher, even though she could tell it wasn't new. The landscape made the place seem more advanced than, or ahead of, Ayla's hometown.

Most of the buildings had unique characteristics, but one type seemed to repeat again and again. At first it looked like the one-room schoolhouse Ayla's class visited at Greenfield Village in fourth grade. Each was built with stone along the bottom of the outside walls and dark wood siding along the rest of it. But as she continued to see many of these buildings, she noticed they were much bigger than a one-room schoolhouse. And even though they looked the same, Ayla sensed that they weren't *exactly* the same, like a chain store or a restaurant would be at home.

"What *is* that?" Ayla pointed out the window. "I think I've seen, like, five of them!"

"Oh, that's one of the Mother's Tables," Mina said.

"But it's a building, not a table. Why are there so many?" Ayla asked. She noticed each of the buildings had the flower-like symbol carved into it.

The space Jeep hovered over a parking lot, and Bodhi landed it swiftly. He pushed a button near the steering column, and the low hum of the motor stopped. He let out a deep breath and turned toward Ayla.

"Each of those buildings represents a different set of Ways," he said. "The buildings look the same on the outside, as a sign of unity, but on the inside, they are more distinct—except for the actual Mother's Table inside. That's the same in every building. It's a basic table, really. Nothing unusual. The building gets its name from the table."

"What are the Ways again? Did you tell me that already?"

"I mentioned the Circle of the Ways, Ayla." Bodhi smiled at Ayla reassuringly.

Ayla was nervous about not being able to remember all that she was learning. She tried to recall what had come up just that day. The Collective Chronicles was where Bodhi took them. The Circle of the

Ways was—she wasn't sure what. Now there were the Mother's Tables and different sets of Ways. What did it all mean?

"You're picking up more than you think, Ayla," Bodhi said.

"This place feels familiar to me. It feels like home, in an odd way, even though it's different than anywhere I've ever been." Ayla didn't want to sound dumb.

"Well, it's familiar because, as a parallel universe, our universe is kind of like a twin of your universe." Prem had kept quiet most of the morning. The sound of his voice surprised Ayla.

"Prem," Bodhi said, "we're not sure—"

"*What?*" Ayla yelled, her eyes as big as plums. Of all the conversations she'd had with Connor about parallel universes, she'd never thought about what that *truly* meant. Thinking of Eema as Earth's twin blew her mind. The synapses in her brain were firing faster than she could comprehend.

"Just think of it this way, Ayla," Mina said, reaching for Ayla's hand and giving it a gentle squeeze. "An infinite number of universes, including the ones that contain your Earth and our Eema, were made from the same cosmic materials at the same time. We think of Earth and Eema, and the universes they belong to, like twins made in the same likeness. Each universe went a separate way, and their people made different choices, so we're different in a lot of ways, but we are similar too. It makes sense that Eema would feel familiar to you.

"Let me tell you about the people of the First Ways, Ayla. I think it might help." Mina smiled reassuringly.

Ayla listened as Mina began the story of the First Ways. The people of the First Ways sounded a lot like the Native Americans from home. They lived off the land, which they deeply revered. Animals were teachers. Plants were medicine. The people worked together to gather food and help each other build homes. They took care of each other.

Then one day, New People showed up on the land. They had come from other lands. Their ways were different than those of the First Ways. When they arrived, they tried to learn from the people of the First Ways, but together, both groups faced many challenges. The New People didn't share the same reverence for the land and all the wonders it provided, like food and medicine. They were hasty and impatient. Rather than working with the First People and learning from them, and rather than waiting for the seeds they planted together to grow, the New People wanted to take over the land and do things their own way. The New People brought what were now known as Old Ways. As tensions grew between the First People and the New People, a Mother of the First Ways stepped forward and invited everyone to gather together. She asked her children to build her a long table that all the people—the First People and the New People—could sit around together.

About a week after the Mother issued her invitation, the First People came together with the New People. The Mother and her sisters had prepared an incredible feast for everyone. The brightly colored food was cooked over fires to perfection. As everyone ate, the Mother shared her observations with all of them. She described how the First People lived and had been living for as long as she could remember. She described how her mother and grandmothers told stories about how they lived and how they continued to adapt and learn the longer they lived. She described how the New People had arrived and how they didn't want to work together but wanted to take over the land. She then asked the New People why they came.

A woman from the New People spoke up and said they were told this land was a place of unfathomable potential and possibility. They were told they would become land owners and that from the land they could gain riches by selling its natural resources. Many of them felt stifled by the authorities and the rules and the religions of the lands from which they came. They believed there must be another way to live, one that would allow them more choices and more freedom than they had in their original lands. More than anything, they had come here to explore the land and to find out if what they had been told was true.

The Mother listened as the woman talked about the promises that were made about the land and the difficulties the New People left behind.

After a while, the Mother said softly, "You are becoming the rulers you left behind."

The woman looked surprised.

The Mother continued, "You want us, the First People here on this land, to follow your rules like you were expected to follow the rules from your first land. In doing so, you are creating here the very same circumstances you say you came to leave behind."

Everyone who was gathered around the Mother's Table was silent as the Mother continued, her voice rising as she spoke.

"If you truly want to break away from the Old Ways you left behind and live in a land of possibility," she said, "you yourselves must let go of your old ways of doing things. You must be open to *our* ways, the First Ways of this land."

The group stayed at the table several days. Food and drinks were replenished. What the New People realized as they sat together, sharing stories and eating meals, was that it was difficult to let go of their Old Ways. The Old Ways were as much a part of them as their arms and legs, their blood and their organs.

Later, when she thought the rest of the New People couldn't hear her speak, the woman who spoke for the New People shared with the Mother that they didn't want to abandon some aspects of their old land. They held some of the rituals that were part of their lives as sacred, and they wanted to continue practicing them.

The Mother and the woman stayed up through the night while the rest of the group slept. They cried and laughed together. By the end of three days, they were holding hands and leaning into each other like sisters.

Together, they created a Chronicle of Other Ways. This Chronicle would serve as the rule of the land for many years to come. The Chronicle was beautifully written and held dear by all the people. While the First People could continue living their lives as they always had, the New People learned from them. The New People learned to hunt and how to honor the land and its resources. The New People shared some of their practices with the First People, and some of the First People enjoyed learning new ways to honor each other and the Great Spirit-like Being that the New People referred to as *God.*

As more New People arrived on the land over time, all the people were invited to gather around the Mother's Table again. Each time, a new Mother would extend the invitation and a new, larger table would be built to gather the growing group of people. Anyone who didn't agree to gather was asked to leave the land. Some left, but some stayed and eventually agreed to attend the gatherings.

What transpired over time were many Chronicles of Other Ways. No one set of Ways could be sustained as the rule. Instead, the groups would gather and discuss the differences in their Ways until they could reach agreements about how to live together as one tribe and see each other as sisters and brothers.

Each group built its own gathering place, where it could practice integrating its Ways with the Ways of the land. Each group was given its own Mother's Table, which was built just like the original table. The original table was kept at a large community gathering place.

Eventually, there were no First People or New People. They were all simply known as *people.*

And even though new groups of people arrived there to that day, it had been a very long time since a gathering at the original Mother's Table had taken place. The people still came together frequently for other kinds of gatherings, festivals, and celebrations, but there hadn't been a gathering at the Mother's Table in many, many years.

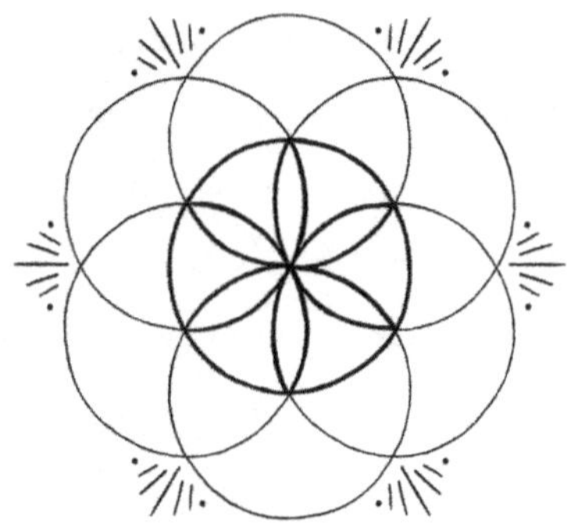

CHAPTER 7

AYLA CHEWED SLOWLY as she reviewed Mina's story in her mind. By this time, they were seated at a table in the restaurant where they came for lunch, although Ayla hardly remembered arriving at the restaurant or getting seated, so lost was she in her thoughts.

The story sounded so simple, and she could easily see the connection to what she knew of America's history. But could it have happened—that rather than taking over the Native Americans' land, the settlers who came to America could have learned to live alongside their new neighbors? Knowing what little she had learned in school about the brutal truth of what had happened when settlers arrived in America, Ayla couldn't imagine how it could have gone a different way.

"Mina?" Ayla turned to Mina, who sat right next to her. When Mina looked at Ayla, she continued, "Mina, you said you've studied Earth, right? And my people? The Americans? You've studied us?"

"Yes, Ayla. We study Earth and its people in our schools."

"Well, here's the thing. We didn't quite get it right when the New People came to America. We were all about taking over the land and killing the First People. We were at war from the moment we stepped foot on the land, maybe even before we arrived."

Ayla stopped. Even though she knew the way her history read was a far cry from ideal or even humane, she felt protective of it in a small way. It was still *her* story somehow. She was overcome with a deep sadness, a sense of mourning for what could have been and what was instead.

Noor noticed the girls' quiet conversation and reached across the table to touch Ayla's arm. Ayla pulled away.

"I don't think I should be here," Ayla said. "I want to go home." Her eyes filled with tears once again.

"Ayla, please try to consider the possibility that this *is* your home," Noor said. "Your stories are our stories just as much as they are yours. And the same is true for our stories. They are yours. There's no *us* versus *you* here."

Noor's voice was so soft, and she spoke with such kindness that hearing from her felt like a soothing balm on Ayla's tender heart.

"I want to help you," Ayla started, "but, well, I don't even know what I'm expected to do. I know time is an issue here, and it's going to take me forever to learn all there is to learn. And then what? I still don't even know anything about tornadoes."

Noor pulled out something from her purse that resembled an iPad. She laid it in front of Ayla and waved her hand over it. The weather map they'd seen at the Collective appeared on the screen.

Noor pointed to the area on the map that was hit by tornadoes.

"Listen very carefully, Ayla. I'm sure Bodhi told you these tornadoes are unlike anything we've ever seen on our planet. Bodhi and his team have been working to figure out why we would be having them now. They have a hypothesis that involves you, in a way, and that is why we invited you. We think that is why you said yes too."

"You *didn't* invite me. I *didn't* say yes," Ayla said. She was growing tired and felt like her head might explode.

"You did not receive an invitation like you are accustomed to, no. That is true," Noor said. "But in our way, we sent an invitation. You did not accept it like you are accustomed to accepting invitations either. However, we know you accepted it because you stayed *open*."

Noor sounded convincing, but Ayla just felt more confused. *Open? What was that all about?* But this time when Noor reached out for Ayla's arm, Ayla left it for Noor to touch. Her warm touch made Ayla's arm tingle. The explosion going off in her head faded, her heart softened, and within seconds, her entire body felt calm.

"When you touch me, I feel so calm," Ayla said.

Noor took a deep breath. "Touch is one of the ways we communicate here. You do the same on Earth. It is just different here." Noor stopped. With her hand on Ayla's arm and her eyes locked with Ayla's eyes, she said, "Shall we slow down a bit, Ayla?"

Ayla nodded.

Noor smiled. "If you can trust this feeling you have now—the peaceful feeling—and stay open, just as you are now, remembering that not everything will sound logical or make sense the way it does to you on Earth, I know you will continue to feel at ease with us."

Ayla went back to her lunch. Again, she appreciated the richness in flavor of ordinary foods like the ones she ate at home. A sandwich, fruit, water with lemon.

She wanted so badly to be able to take in each new piece of information as it came without letting it affect her. She wanted to be helpful. She wanted to believe in this strange but familiar mission on which she found herself. Her body was relaxed; it was her mind that kept running in all directions. Her mind was agitated.

Out of nowhere, she remembered what her mom had shared about eating mindfully: Bite. Taste. Chew. Swallow. She focused all of her attention on eating the food in front of her. *Bite. Taste. Chew. Swallow. Bite. Taste. Chew. Swallow.*

Once Ayla fell into a rhythm, Noor began speaking again.

"Ayla, here we know that space—outer space—is much bigger than most of the people on Earth believe it to be. Can we start there?"

Bite. Taste. Chew. Swallow. Ayla nodded.

"Okay, good!" Noor's demeanor lightened. "And here we know that Earth is our twin planet. We know that we—both you *and* us—live in twin universes, or parallel universes. Are you following?"

"Yes. We talked about that earlier."

Once again, Ayla's thoughts began to rise. *Bite. Taste. Chew. Swallow.* She focused, and the thoughts subsided.

"Great. Okay," Noor said. "So, while these two universes seem separate, we know that in some way they are also connected—the same, even."

Noor raised her eyebrows. Ayla nodded. Then, just as Noor was about to begin speaking again, Bodhi jumped in.

"The hypothesis is that because we are connected, because we are the same, the choices you've made on Earth have impacted us here. Now Earth finds itself in troubling times. Do you know what I'm referring to, Ayla?"

Ayla's head began to ache as images of the Native Americans and the New People who came to America returned. She saw war, blood, guns, death, fighting, fighting, fighting. She saw slaves. War. War. War. Her heart grew heavy. Protestors. War. Technology. The climate. War. Hungry, angry, hardworking people. Things she didn't always understand but heard her parents talk about. Or argue about. All kinds of people fighting each other for power over each other. Saying hateful things to each other. Always saying, saying, saying, and *not listening*. Chaos.

And President Shad. The man who, at the very least, was credited for making her mother's life a living hell, as she heard her mother say repeatedly. She said he was evil. Helen Stone had been consumed with making sure Mr. Shad would never be elected president in all the days leading up to the election and had been crushed by his victory ever since. The election changed her. Then Grandpa George died. Grandpa

George, who had voted for President Shad and was outraged by his daughter's outspokenness against him.

Along with the images in her mind, the feeling in her heart spread to her stomach and her throat. It all felt like one big, heavy mess.

"Um, I think so," Ayla finally said with a sigh. "I understand Earth is in turmoil. At least, that's what my mother tells me. I really don't know all the details, to be honest. Which seems ridiculous, since Mina knows all about Eema *and* Earth, but I can feel it in the air. I hear it in the news. I feel the tension. And earlier, Bodhi, you talked about fear. My people? In America? A lot of people are afraid right now, afraid for the future."

Ayla felt defeated and depleted, and it was only lunchtime.

"Before we go on, you need to know something, Ayla." Noor seemed to be pleading with her. "You need to know you are not alone in this. This isn't a situation where anyone is against you. We truly are in this together. Do you understand that?"

"I guess. I'm going to try to understand. Or to believe you, anyway."

"So, because everything appears to be spiraling out of control on Earth," Bodhi continued, "we believe Earth cannot contain its own chaos. And so, the chaos that originated on Earth is now beginning to spiral toward us here on Eema."

Bodhi stopped. Mina and Prem's eyes opened wide.

"We can't go back and erase anything that happened on Earth," Ayla said slowly. "Most people there don't even understand what's happening. It's like everything was fine one day, or at least mostly fine, or at least we *thought* it was fine. Then *bam!* It feels like the whole world is falling apart. How can we possibly fix it? Especially from here?"

"If our hypothesis is right," Bodhi said, a glimmer in his eyes and a trace of the childlike enthusiasm he showed earlier in the day returning, "and what is happening on Earth is having an impact here on Eema, then what is happening *here* can have a similar impact on Earth. Meaning, if we can restore peace and order *here*, that will help to restore peace and order *there*. That's how we fix it!" Bodhi took a deep breath before he continued. "On the flip side—as far as we can tell, the last time there was this much chaos moving back and forth and all through space and time . . . well, the big bang happened."

"The big bang?" Ayla immediately thought of Connor. He'd gone through a phase where he wouldn't shut up about the big bang.

"Right." Bodhi nodded. "That is what you call it on Earth. I know countless people have studied it, and there are numerous conclusions drawn from that study. Now, the moments before the big bang? Well, those are an even bigger mystery. What we know is that whatever was happening in time and space before the big bang caused the big bang. You, your people, know a little bit about what was created by the big bang, and we know even more than that. But what we don't know, what neither of us know, is what was destroyed. We don't know what the big bang destroyed."

"So, let me get this straight," Prem said. "If this chaos continues, you think . . ."

"We think, or we suspect," Bodhi said, taking a deep breath, "that the worlds—ours, Ayla's, and everything in between—will be no more. And we're not willing to take that chance."

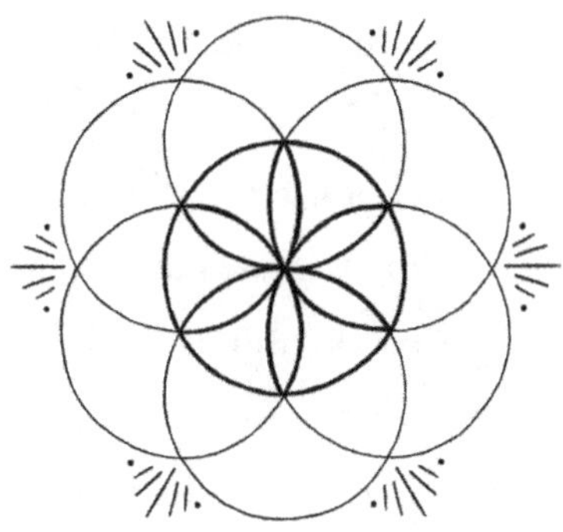

CHAPTER 8

AYLA SPENT THE next several days—or weeks; she couldn't be sure—at the Collective Chronicles, working alongside Bodhi and the Circle of the Ways, who appeared to be his co-workers. Mina and Prem spent their days in school.

Noor visited often to catch up on the latest developments with the Circle and to fuel them with her delectable cookies. She was famous for her oatmeal walnut chocolate chip cookies, which were almost identical to Ayla's mother's famous oatmeal pecan chocolate chip cookies. Like so many other things in this strange but familiar place, Ayla was comforted by the similarity between them, even if cookies were a small thing compared to space travel and tornadoes.

Bodhi's team members had a presence much like his and Noor's. Simply stated, they were absolutely gorgeous beings. When they walked, they glided, much like the space Jeeps they drove around town. They even appeared to walk on air sometimes. The shades of their skin varied from deep black to brown to beige to varying shades of white. Their eyes were multiple shades of brown and blue and green and appeared to carry many lifetimes of stories inside them. Some might be classified as full-bodied, and some were as wispy as wheat blowing in the wind.

Ayla wasn't able to tell whether some of them were men or women, and sometimes one might seem to be both a man and a woman at once. Their loose-fitting clothes were similar to the tunics, leggings, and yoga pants that Mina, Prem, Noor, and Bodhi wore—but instead of wearing neutral shades, like Noor preferred, they wore bright colors and unpredictable patterns that rarely seemed to go together at first glance.

The qualities that distinguished people from each other here didn't seem to be an issue like it was at home. Yet every person she met was unique in a way she couldn't articulate. Ayla was fascinated by the people and the way they worked together like different musical instruments in one big symphony. They glided by and around each other with ease, finished each other's sentences, and spontaneously hummed the same tune together at times. If there was any dissent among the members of Bodhi's team, Ayla didn't pick up on it.

She sat in front of screens most days, watching movies from the Chronicles. Each story that could be seen on the screen corresponded with a story, or chapter, in a book on the shelves behind the screens.

The first story Ayla watched was about the Mother's Table. Then she watched another story about each of the new groups of people who came to the land. She watched stories about different areas on

Eema. Every once in a while, Bodhi would pause the stories to check in with Ayla.

"Well, what do you think?" he asked at one point. "Is it helpful to see how we reached this point?"

"It is," Ayla said. "I guess I'm kind of sad, though. I mean, if the United States had just followed the same path you did here, maybe we wouldn't be so angry at each other now. I don't understand how your First People convinced the New People not to just obliterate them and take their land."

Bodhi waved an arm in the air toward the largest screen. The Mother's Table story displayed on the screen. He clicked through until he reached the point where all the people had gathered around the table for the first time.

"Ayla, tell me what you see here."

He turned toward Ayla with a furrowed brow. He appeared to be concentrating deeply on Ayla's face.

"Well, I see the people," she said. "The table. They're outside. That food looks delicious . . . ?" Her voice trailed off.

"But what do you *see*, Ayla? Look at their faces."

Ayla sensed a tinge of urgency in Bodhi's voice. They were just trying to figure out how to save the world, after all. No big deal, right?

She stared at each face on the screen, spending a few seconds on each one and at least a minute on the Mother's face. Then she started over from the beginning and studied each face again. The longer she looked, the less able she felt to form a conclusion about the faces. At the same time, she felt a sense of dread rise from her belly to her throat.

Then a surge of energy burst from her stomach through her chest and into her throat. "They look scared!" she yelled.

"Exactly!" Bodhi nodded his head excitedly. "They *were* scared, Ayla. From what I understand, they were terrified."

"Is that how it happened, then? Were the New People afraid of the First People? Were they afraid of each other?" Ayla was confident she had figured it out.

"Ayla, they weren't afraid of each other—not as fellow humans. They were afraid because they were in a situation neither group had anticipated or experienced before in their lives. They didn't know how any of this would turn out. They were just doing their best, in the same way *your* people did *their* best."

"Geez, that was our best?" Ayla sighed deeply. "We really got it all wrong. They *were* there first. We've been afraid of each other ever since."

"Let's get some fresh air, shall we?"

Bodhi led Ayla out the door. As they walked, he said, "Ayla, are you familiar with evolution?"

"Yeah, I guess. Well, sort of."

"Okay, well, it's really important that you understand that each of our planets has evolved in different ways. There isn't a right or wrong way to evolve—it is *all* evolution, or just growth, really. Your people and our people, each group was born to learn different lessons, and we are both evolving, or growing, as we learn."

"I wish I had been born here, then." Ayla looked down at her feet as they walked. Bodhi shared her own father's enthusiasm for history and evolution, and she found that comforting.

"Ayla, what is comparison?"

The question surprised her. It was the same question her mom always asked her at home.

"What? How do you know to even ask me that?"

"It's from a book in the Collective Chronicles. One of *your* Chronicles. Theodore Roosevelt said it, right? 'Comparison is the thief of joy.' I know Helen, your mother, refers to it often."

Ayla's mouth dropped open. "Wait, what? *My* Chronicles? You have *my* Chronicles here?"

"Ayla, yes. That is how we came to know you. The Collective holds *all* the stories. Every single story of every living thing. It's hard to fathom, but they're all there."

Bodhi said this like he would say something as obvious as "You have a nose on your face, Ayla."

Seemingly out of nowhere, Noor appeared on the path ahead of them. She walked toward Ayla and Bodhi and took Ayla's hand in hers.

"What Bodhi is trying to say," Noor began, "is that even though your way, or the ways of your people, do not appear to have been the *right* way as you see it now, the ways were not wrong, Ayla. Wondering what would have been or even speculating on what the two groups were thinking at any given time is futile. You will only become frustrated if you continue that line of thinking."

Noor smiled her reassuring smile as Ayla's skin tingled with warmth from her touch.

"Maybe that's enough today," Noor said as she turned to Bodhi.

Bodhi nodded and turned toward Ayla. "I apologize, Ayla. I probably shouldn't have mentioned your Chronicles. I can see how that could be unsettling to you."

"It's okay," Ayla said. "I mean, I like hearing these things. It's very sci-fi and interesting. But it's so different to be *living* sci-fi, not just reading about it. You know?" She looked from Bodhi to Noor. "And then all the stories I've seen here. Everything looks so dreamy. Like an advertisement for what could have been. Maybe I'm just trying to make sense of things again—things that don't really have explanations."

Ayla searched their faces for some hint, any hint, that she was still okay.

"You are taking in a great deal of information, and you are handling it all very well, my dear," Noor said as she again squeezed Ayla's hand in hers. "When you feel distraught, just remember you are here because you carry wisdom we do not have. So, clearly, you and your people couldn't have taken a path that was entirely wrong."

"What could I possibly know that you don't?" Ayla asked. "You have the Chronicles!"

"What we have come to know for sure, dear, even with the Chronicles, is that living an experience is not the same as reading about it or even witnessing it," Noor said. "You have developed something out of your experience—the dilemmas of your land—that we have not developed here. *You are resilient.* And now we are in trouble, and we are not prepared."

Something in Noor shifted as she spoke. Her body looked stiff, and her words were more carefully chosen.

Resilient. Resilient. Resilient. Ayla repeated the word in her head. It sounded like a protective shield. *Resilient.* Was she resilient? She vaguely remembered hearing that word at one time, but right now she wasn't even sure what it meant.

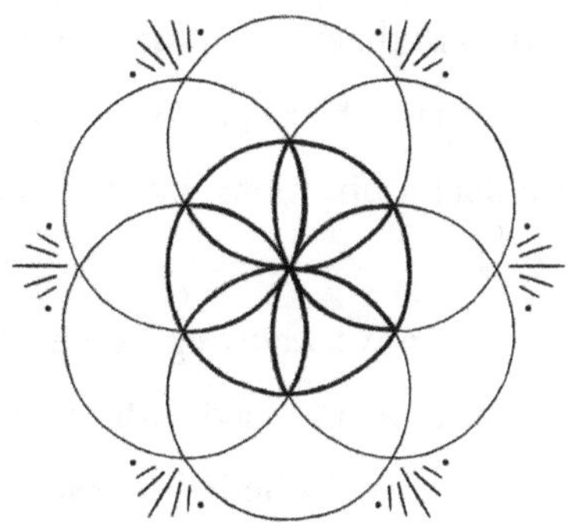

CHAPTER 9

Ayla woke up the next morning with the previous day's conversation with Noor and Bodhi running through her head. She felt slightly betrayed that they had seen her Chronicles—that they even *had* her Chronicles. They knew so much about her, and she knew so little about them. But she continued to find comfort in the way they made her feel—like she was home, even though she wasn't. That she belonged, even though she didn't. That she was one of them, even though she was from an entirely different planet.

Then again, even this whole other planet felt familiar.

She noticed how everything seemed to flow so smoothly here. The way Bodhi's team floated gracefully like ballerinas as they worked alongside each other. The way Bodhi and Noor communicated with each other, often without words. They were synchronized in their conversations and motions and sometimes seemed like one person instead of two. It was very different than the frenzied starts and stops her own parents had in their marriage. Her parents were the opposite of that, always going off in different directions, like they were living two different lives.

She started to feel defensive, knowing Bodhi and Noor had probably watched her parents as they argued with each other. What would Bodhi and Noor make of that? Nobody here ever argued. When Ayla had mentioned that to Bodhi, he'd said, "Your people spend much of their energy innovating *things* and little energy innovating *people*." What did that even mean? Whenever she thought about it, she felt annoyed. Her mom's entire life was dedicated to innovating people! She was a social worker, for the love of God. And it was hard work.

Ayla remembered watching her mom's anxiety level rise after President Shad was elected. His campaign had promised to make devastating cuts to the budgets that funded the programs her mother's clients relied upon. Helen Stone had been livid. It wasn't just anger she expressed, though. It was also sadness. She was sad for her clients who would be impacted by the budget cuts.

"They'll be fine," Ayla's dad had said during family dinner that week. "Let's not ruin the night with politics."

Ayla watched as her mother took a deep breath and let it out through her mouth. She had shared many times that trying to express her concerns to Ayla's dad was useless because his concerns were so different. But that night it was like she forgot everything she normally did to keep the peace.

"Philip, this isn't a conversation about politics," Helen began. "It's a conversation about *people*. Real, living, breathing people. People who will suffer *because of politics*."

Helen was shaking at that point, and Ayla was torn between her parents. No, she didn't want to talk politics if it meant her parents would argue. But yes, she did care about her mom and her mom's clients.

"The problem with this country," Helen continued, "is that every issue is discussed in the context of political views—and in politics, everything is reduced to two sides. But in reality, there are many sides. I couldn't care less about those two sides, Philip—the people who are arguing for the sake of being right and proving the other side wrong. I *do* care about the people who are impacted by the arguments. I care deeply about them."

Helen excused herself from the dining room table and went into the kitchen.

"I care about them too," Philip said under his breath. "I just care more right now about other things . . ." His voice trailed off.

Ayla and Connor stared at their plates. Their parents were always talking to each other or yelling at each other, but Ayla couldn't recall a time when they ever actually *listened* to each other.

Ayla got up and walked into the kitchen to find her mom sitting on the floor, rubbing Apollo the puppy's belly. She looked up at Ayla and wiped her eyes of tears.

"Just keeping it real, Bug." She sniffed. That was what she always said when Ayla or Connor saw her upset. She believed in showing her children a full range of what she called "normal, natural human emotions," and yet she didn't always seem comfortable *experiencing* these emotions.

Helen took a deep breath and returned to her usual state of full composure. She smiled at Ayla and reached for her hand.

Ayla settled in next to her mom and scratched Apollo behind his ears. "Are you okay, Mom?" she asked. "Dad said he cares about your clients. I think he does. I do too. I'm worried about them. Do you think they'll be okay?"

"Oh, honey, I love that you care so deeply," Helen said. "I guess the truth is, we just can't know. I imagine the proposed budget cuts will hurt my clients, and some have already voiced concerns. I don't like to see them so afraid. We've faced similar cuts in the past, though, and somehow we've managed. The agency is resourceful. The people we serve are resilient." Helen nodded as if convincing herself that what she said was true.

"I'm not sure what that means, Mom," Ayla said. "Resilient?"

"It means that in the face of difficulty, you keep going. You don't let the difficulty break you or define you. And when it does overwhelm you, you eventually bounce back." Helen seemed to be giving herself a pep talk as she answered Ayla.

"So, if something bad happens to your clients, they'll be okay?" Ayla asked. "They're resilient?"

"Right. Ultimately, they'll be okay. But the thing is, Bug, I want them to be *more* than okay. There are enough resources for *all* of us to be okay. The budget cuts are a setback. But yes, I think they will be okay."

"It must be hard to know what to care about when you're an adult."

Helen laughed. "Yes, Bug. It's really hard to know what to care about. Well, actually, knowing what to care about isn't as hard as knowing where to invest your energy. There are lots of things I care about that I know I just can't tackle right now."

Helen lifted Ayla's chin and looked into her eyes. She gave her a quick kiss on the nose. "I love you so much, Bug. I'm so proud of you."

"What can't you tackle, Mom? You always tell me I can do anything. Can't you do anything too?"

"Oh, honey, just things. Things I'd rather not weigh you down with." Helen half-smiled at her daughter, the way she did when she wanted to indicate the conversation was over without actually saying it was over.

Ayla missed her mom. She was glad to remember their conversation about resilience, though. That was something she felt her people could be proud of—their resilience—even though they appeared to have gotten off to what she thought was a disastrous start from Day One.

Even so, Ayla was beginning to see how whether it was a good start or a bad start was a matter of perspective. Obviously, it was a devastating start for the Native Americans who already lived on the land. The settlers did exactly what they came to do, and they thought they had every right to take over the land. Now, hundreds of years later, she had no doubt it was a bad start. And so many people in her country cared about different things.

Even though it was hard to admit, there were many sides to the story right from the beginning. There had to be some valuable lesson in all of that.

She rolled onto her side, tucked her hand under her cheek, and closed her eyes. Before too long, the door to her bedroom creaked open and she heard footsteps.

"Still sleeping, Ayla?" Noor whispered near Ayla's ear.

"Mm-hmm." Ayla felt herself drifting in and out of sleep.

She sensed Noor and Bodhi standing there, watching her breathe in the same way she knew her parents had sneaked into her bedroom to watch her breathe since the day she was born.

"I don't know if we did the right thing bringing her here, Noor," Bodhi said. "I'm not sure she knows what she's doing."

"The truth is, none of us know what we're doing," Noor said.

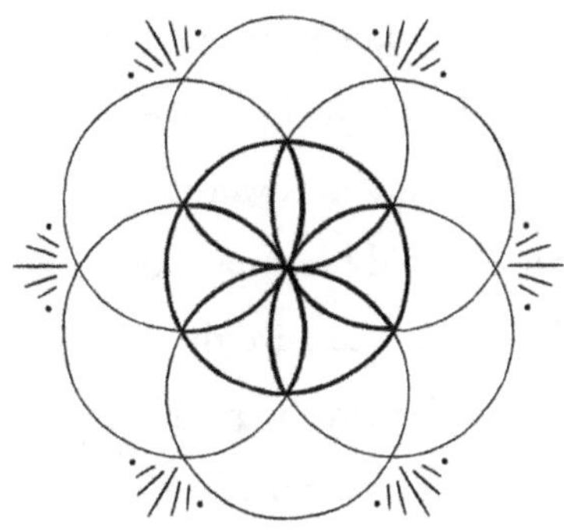

CHAPTER 10

RATHER THAN ENTERING the Collective as soon as they arrived the next morning, Bodhi led Ayla around to the back of the building and through a line of tall cedar trees that Ayla didn't recall seeing before. Mina and Prem, who were home from school that day, headed into the building.

Just beyond the trees, the members of the Circle formed an actual circle, sitting cross-legged on blankets that looked like the yoga blankets Ayla's mom used at home. There was just enough space for Bodhi and Ayla to slip in and complete the circle.

Ayla looked around, surprised to see Noor sitting there. She also saw a few faces she didn't recognize.

Sitting in the circle, looking around at faces both familiar and unfamiliar, Ayla was struck again by how comfortable she felt here.

Her surroundings were so similar to home, but the people, even those with faces she had come to know, were different. It felt a lot like the time her family hosted Thanksgiving dinner and the house filled with people she didn't know. It was awkward when they remarked on how much she had grown and told her what a beautiful young woman she had become, but she didn't recognize them. It was the same house as any other day, and even though the people in the house seemed like strangers to her, she was still at home.

Ayla was still struggling to describe the people on Eema. She would start to settle on words that she thought she could use to describe them, and shortly thereafter the words seemed inadequate. Perhaps the words one would use to describe these people didn't even exist in Ayla's vocabulary.

"Thank you all for gathering here today."

Noor's voice startled Ayla, bringing her attention back to the circle and the serene people sitting around it. Yes! *Serene*. That was the perfect word to describe the people here.

"As some of you know, the Collective was broken into last night," Noor said. "It appears that everything is where it belongs; however, we have not yet had enough time to verify that all the Chronicles are in place. That could take several days, maybe longer. At this time, I would like to offer each of you the opportunity to share any information you might have about the break-in."

Noor stopped talking and closed her eyes.

When she opened her eyes, she turned to meet the gaze of a gentle-looking figure who was seated next to her. They locked eyes as time stretched in front of them. Only a few moments must have passed, but it seemed like hours. Noor continued around the circle, meeting the eyes of each person seated there.

Ayla's head was spinning. A break-in? How could these peaceful, seemingly perfect people orchestrate a break-in? How did they even know what that was?

Bodhi reached over and placed his hand on her knee. Ayla welcomed the warmth that came with Bodhi's touch and took a deep breath as her body relaxed. But while her body relaxed, her mind kept spinning. Bodhi hadn't yet said a word to the group. Why was Noor leading this circle? Wasn't Bodhi in charge here?

"Noor is the Mother, Ayla," Bodhi whispered. "She is our leader, the Mother of our people."

Whoa, Ayla thought. *Noor is the Mother?*

"So, she's like your president or something?" Ayla felt an urgent need to sort this information into something she could better understand.

"Something like that," Bodhi said. "She is our leader."

Bodhi stopped talking as Noor's eyes came closer to meeting his. Their eyes locked. They nodded at each other, and then Noor's eyes met Ayla's eyes.

"Thank you for being here, Ayla," Noor said, closing her eyes and nodding her head.

Then she said to the group, "I look forward to hearing from any of you who can help with more information. As you all know, there are very few people who even have access to the Collective, and even fewer know exactly what is stored here."

Noor looked at a man in the circle named Ishwa who was, hands down, the most gorgeous being Ayla had ever laid eyes upon. Then she looked at a person called Nell, who had an angelic presence. Ayla wasn't sure whether Nell was a man or a woman.

"In fact, as you all know," Noor continued, "the only people who know exactly what Chronicles we keep are sitting in this circle. Well, except for our former Circle member, Seth."

Noor paused. She sat silent for a few seconds, her face strained, as if she was trying to calculate a difficult equation. Then her attention snapped back to the circle.

"But anyway. It is important that we keep these Chronicles from the community. You are our trusted comrades. Again, I look forward to hearing from you."

Noor stood, and the others stood also. A few clusters of people formed, and those in the small groups began to speak to each other in quiet whispers.

"I don't understand, Bodhi," Ayla said. "If you know what I'm thinking and when I'm thinking it, why don't you know what the person who broke into the Collective is thinking? If they were here in the circle, wouldn't you and Noor know it was them?"

Bodhi took Ayla's hands in his, causing her to feel calm once again. He must have sensed she was feeling overwhelmed as soon as she started in with all her questions. He was silent for a moment before he spoke.

"Do you remember when we told you we could invite you here because you were open, Ayla?"

"Yes. I don't know what you meant by that, but I do remember."

"Well, we knew you were open because we have been following your Chronicles. We knew your heart, so to speak."

"Not really following," Ayla said.

Bodhi tried again. "Okay, so, you were open because your Grandpa George had just passed away. When someone on Earth who is a tenderhearted being like yourself loses a loved one, their heart literally opens. The opening creates space for other things to enter. When we said you were open, that was the literal meaning. Your heart opened when Grandpa George passed."

Ayla stared at Bodhi. Grandpa George had died of a heart attack. His heart breaking caused her heart to open? Was his heart open? Was that why it broke? Was she going to die too?

"Oh, Ayla, I know this is confusing to you," Bodhi said. "It's hard to explain because you have always known your heart and your mind to function in a specific way, and I have known the same, but the ways we've known those things are just, well, different."

Bodhi watched Ayla closely for any sign of understanding.

"So I'm not going to die because my heart is open?" Ayla said.

"No, absolutely not. You are not in any danger of dying. But what about an open mind—do you understand the concept of an open mind?"

"Yes. An open mind is open to new ideas. Got it."

"Okay, great!" Bodhi was excited. "So, if your open mind means you are open to new ways of thinking, imagine that your open heart means you are open to new ways of being, of feeling, of experiencing the world around you. Can you picture that?"

"Yes! Oh, sorry. I guess I was taking you literally with the open heart thing."

"No, it's fine. This is good. So, your heart was open, and we knew your story. We knew you had a good heart and a good mind, and we knew you cared about people. You care about people in a unique way, Ayla. It is one thing to care about people, it is another to be willing to do things that show you care. You could say, simply, we felt like we really knew you."

Bodhi watched Ayla again, and she nodded. She was following his words. She felt excited, the feeling of being known delighted her.

"Good," Bodhi continued. "You were open, we knew your story, and we invited you here—and you came. You're still open here with us now, so we can sense with our hearts and through your heart what you're feeling. We can sense when you are tense or scared. And sometimes those sensations can be translated into words we can say to you to check in."

Ayla nodded.

"The people here, though?" he continued, speaking slowly and softly. "The ones around the circle we think are responsible for the break-in? Ayla, it appears that they have *closed*."

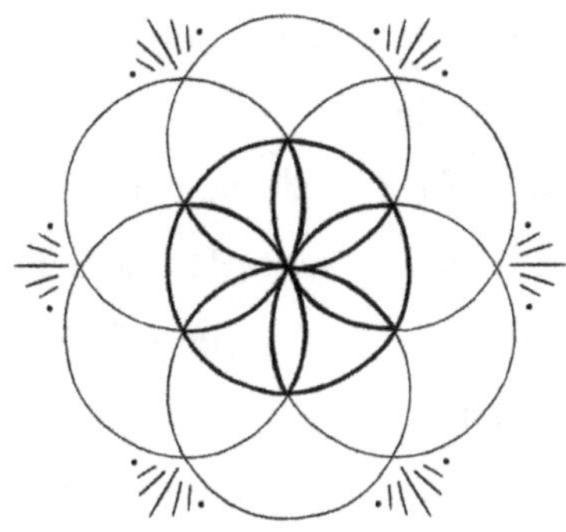

CHAPTER 11

Bodhi spoke the words with great remorse. It was the same tone her mom had used when she told Ayla that Grandpa George had died. Like it was the worst possible thing to ever happen in the history of time. Even worse than the potential end of the world, she supposed.

The air around them felt heavy.

"Were they always closed?" Ayla asked.

Noor had joined Ayla and Bodhi outside, which allowed Bodhi to go into the Collective to check on Prem and Mina while Noor and Ayla continued their conversation.

"No, Ayla," Noor said. "That is part of why this is so troubling. We, the people here, have stayed open since our origin." Tears formed on the edges of her eyes. "Being open is what has allowed us to reach agreements since the very first conversation around the first Mother's Table. Being open is the only way we know."

"How did they close, then?"

"We don't know. We're baffled. We don't know how they closed, and we don't know if they even *wanted* to close. Perhaps it was an accident. We have no idea how this happened." Noor spoke in a hushed tone, not quite a whisper.

"Of course you don't know how this happened!" A strange, uninvited voice cut through their conversation.

Noor and Ayla turned to meet the fiery gaze of Ishwa. Ayla was mesmerized by the fire in his eyes, which she suspected was not a good thing but made him even more attractive—if that was possible.

"You don't know how it happened, but I guarantee you it has something to do with *her*." Ishwa turned to stare Ayla in the face.

She felt like she was melting into the ground, undoubtedly from the fire radiating from his eyes. He moved closer to Noor, and Noor and Ayla shrunk in his looming presence.

"You have no evidence of that, Ishwa," Noor said calmly and with the sound of complete confidence.

He stepped back slightly, still looming, his physical presence overwhelming, and all Ayla could think was, *Why did Bodhi leave? Where is he now? Or Prem?*

"Back off, Ishwa!" It was Mina's voice that came from behind. Ayla doubted Ishwa would respond with anything other than more fire, more looming.

Ishwa took a step back.

"There is no need to make false accusations about Ayla." Mina stopped to take a breath before she continued speaking. "She is here to help us, Ishwa. She shouldn't be blamed for anything, let alone this. We should be thanking her."

Ishwa looked from Mina to Noor before his eyes settled on Ayla, burning holes through her entire body. Then he touched Ayla's arm and hissed, "*Thank you*," in a way that implied he didn't really mean to thank her before he turned and walked away.

Again, Ayla's head was spinning. She was shocked Ishwa had touched her. Where he'd laid his hand, she felt a burning sensation that had the exact opposite effect of the touches she'd experienced from Noor and her family. Instead of calming her, his touch made her squirm.

She silently berated herself for thinking Bodhi or Prem should come to the rescue, when it was Mina who came and told Ishwa to back off. Why did she think it would have to be a man?

Noor laughed gently. "Don't be so hard on yourself, Ayla."

"I feel stupid."

"You're not stupid!" Mina said firmly. "But why do you feel that way?"

"Gosh, I don't even know how to explain it," Ayla said. "I just wish I wasn't so surprised by all of you. I wish I understood you like you seem to understand me. You do things so differently here. So *evenly*. At home, despite how hard we try, the men make more of our decisions. The men overrule us *all the time*. Here, you all rule together. It's like whether you're a man or a woman doesn't even matter to you."

Ayla's voice trailed off as her head continued to spin.

"Well, you're right, I guess," Mina said. "I've never really paid attention to whether someone is a man or a woman or both or neither. But Ayla, of course you're going to be surprised. It's different here than it is on your planet. It's not what you're used to. Mom is right. Don't be so hard on yourself."

"I just don't want to let you down, Mina. I don't want to let any of you down."

Ayla turned toward Noor, who appeared to be listening intently to the girls as they spoke but also seemed preoccupied.

"What is it, Mom?" Mina asked.

"The members of the Circle who are closed—they trouble me," Noor said. "I'm not sure how to confront them. I wonder if they closed intentionally and if we can help them reopen."

Noor looked at Ayla. "According to all the calculations Bodhi and his team made and all the scenarios we ran together, there was no reason to suspect your arrival would disrupt the flow of either of our universes. However, I'm not blind to the possibility that creating a portal through which someone from Earth could travel here could be dangerous. It's been done before, but it isn't something we do regularly. I want you to feel safe here, but I am no longer confident I can make you feel safe."

The thoughts in Noor's head appeared to be jumping around like Ayla's thoughts usually did. Mina was silent. Was she waiting for Ayla to talk, or Noor? Ayla looked from Noor to Mina, not sure what to say or what to do.

"Ayla, Mina, I think it's time to return to the Collective," Noor said to the girls, who were both relieved to hear her speak. "Ayla, there's something I want you to see. That is, if you are willing."

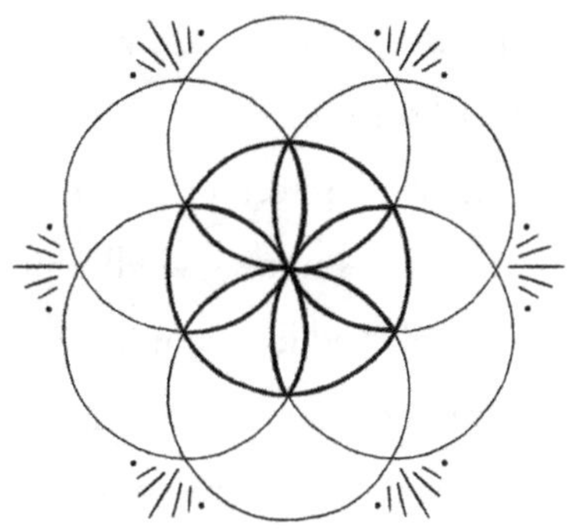

CHAPTER 12

As soon as the story appeared on the screen, Ayla recognized the scene. She and one of her besties, Grace, were sitting close to each other on the gorgeous, soft-colored quilt Grace's grandmama had made. "Each stitch sewn by my loving hands," her grandmama was quick to remind the girls whenever she saw them. Grace would roll her eyes behind her grandmama's back, which made Ayla laugh every time.

Ayla went soft at the sight of Grace and the quilt. But at the same time, her memories of that night made her chest tighten.

"Do you remember this night, Ayla?" Noor asked softly.

She did. It would be hard to forget. It was the night of Grace's Back to School Bash. Ayla hadn't thought she would be able to attend because she had to help her mom and grandma get ready for the funeral, but she was able to arrive late, after most of the other kids had gone home.

Noor wrapped her arm around Ayla as the Chronicle began to play. "Ayla, this was the night we knew you were the one, the one who could help us with Eema," she said.

Ayla watched herself on the screen in awe and in dread. She was so unlike Grace, who was simply stunning—tall, thin, and graceful, just like her name suggested. Ayla had long admired Grace's smooth, chocolate brown skin and deep brown eyes. Now, as they both grew closer to womanhood, she was even more in awe of Grace's beauty.

The best thing about Grace, though, was that she had no idea how beautiful she was. She didn't try or even seem to care that she was beautiful. Ayla suspected that might make Grace even *more* beautiful—if that was possible.

Then Ayla caught herself and felt guilty for getting caught up in Grace's appearance when what happened that night may have changed the course of Grace's life altogether.

"It isn't your fault, Grace," Ayla was saying on the screen.

She squirmed when she heard her voice projected from the speakers around the room. It sounded different than it did in her own head.

Ayla and Grace were sitting side by side, as close as two people can possibly sit without one being in the other's lap. Grace's head was bowed. She had just had an *encounter*, as she had decided to call it, with Ryan Davis.

Ayla had known Ryan since she was in kindergarten and he was in second grade—Connor's grade. Ryan had always given her the creeps, at least since she caught him picking his nose on the playground. Picking his nose was no big deal—everyone picked their nose, or so Connor told her—but seeing Ryan bury his boogers in different spots all over the playground made her queasy. He called it buried treasure.

For as long as Ayla had known Ryan, he'd acted as if every little bit of him was some kind of treasure. When he came to her house to visit Connor, he stared at her when he thought she wasn't looking. That *really* creeped her out.

Grace thought he was funny, and since she was nice to everyone and he lived in her neighborhood, she had invited him to her party. And just like the creep he was, he came. Most freshmen wouldn't be caught dead at a middle school party.

"He hugged me so hard. I couldn't breathe, Ayla," Grace was saying. "He said he wanted to kiss me—"

Grace stopped talking and clasped her hand over her mouth. She then burst into tears. Ayla pulled her friend into a hug and held her as she cried.

"Nobody will believe me either," Grace said. "Why did I even follow him in here? I should have said no way."

Grace's body shook as she cried and tried to catch her breath at the same time. As soon as she seemed close to calming down, she gasped and began crying again.

Ayla's eyes also filled with tears. "Grace, I believe you," she said.

Ayla watched as she and Grace cried together on the screen. She listened as they eventually caught their breath, stopped crying, and blew their noses. She noticed Grace had picked up a corner of her grandmama's quilt and rubbed her thumb on it again and again. She hadn't even noticed Grace touching the blanket that night.

She listened as they decided what to do next.

"We can't tell anyone, Ayla," Grace said. "My dad didn't even want me to have a party with boys. He'll keep me locked up in this house until I'm ancient if he knows what happened. Besides, Ryan didn't hurt me. Really. I'm fine. Nothing really happened. It's okay."

Ayla knew that wasn't true. She could tell Grace wasn't okay. A hard, poisonous pit formed in her stomach. If they couldn't tell Grace's parents, she knew they could tell her mom. Helen Stone would know what to do.

"Please, Ayla," Grace pleaded with fresh tears in her eyes. "Please don't ever say a word about this again—to anyone. If it comes up, we'll just call it the *encounter*. Okay?"

Ayla thought they should tell their friend Amanda, especially because Amanda would know right away something was wrong when she saw them. But Grace knew Amanda would confront Ryan, and she was afraid Amanda might take it further than that. She was capable of just about anything when she was angry.

When it was clear there was no way Grace would tell Amanda what happened, Ayla asked if *she* could say something to Ryan. She wanted to threaten him in some way. Grace refused, though, and Ayla reluctantly agreed to Grace's wishes. When the girls saw each other at school that Monday, it was as if nothing had ever happened.

But when Ayla saw Ryan walk into her house a few days later with Connor, she felt her blood begin to boil. When Connor went to the bathroom, she couldn't stop herself from marching right up to Ryan.

She broke rules spoken and unspoken in that moment. She normally didn't say much to Connor's friends, and he didn't say much to hers. It was just easier that way, an agreement between brother and sister. More importantly she had promised Grace, and a friend breaking a promise to her beloved friend was definitely not acceptable.

As Ayla approached Ryan, she tried to meet his eyes, even though he was about a head taller than her. He seemed like an even bigger giant in that moment. Her hands trembled. He had the same smug look he always had on his face, and that infuriated Ayla.

"I don't know what kind of person you really are," Ayla started, whispering so he could hear her but nobody else could. "I don't know what happened to you that would make you force yourself onto someone without her consent. But what you did—*it is not okay*. You're not allowed to touch Grace *ever again*. Do you understand?"

Ryan jerked back, turned, and walked away, toward Connor's bedroom. Having him in her home made her so uncomfortable, she couldn't settle the rest of the night. Luckily, he hadn't been back since then.

Ayla stared at the screen, her blood racing through her veins as if she was right there with Ryan again. She couldn't move, so she just stared until she realized she was holding her breath. She let it out slowly.

"That was it, Ayla," Noor said as she stopped the Chronicle. "That's how we knew you could help us."

"Oh, you mean when I betrayed my friend? That's what settled it?" Ayla asked. Her heart felt like it was on fire.

"Ayla, you did something very brave there," Bodhi said. "And very kind. You could have said a lot of different things to Grace or Ryan. You could have made many different choices."

"That was just a glitch," Ayla said. "It tells you nothing about me. Nothing good, anyway. I promised Grace I wouldn't say anything. I still feel horrible about betraying her trust."

She sighed. Here she was, on another planet in a different time and with strangers, and she was watching herself betray her friend. She didn't realize how good it had felt not to have to think about the things that were happening at home. This Chronicle brought it all back: the stress her mom was under, the tension between her parents, the loss of Grandpa George, and this thing, the *encounter*, that had happened with Grace.

A heavy weight formed in her chest. She wanted out. She wanted air. She wanted to be free of all of this weird science, space travel, and tornado business. She was not fit for this. She couldn't even help her friend!

"I want to go home—for real this time." Ayla looked from Noor to Bodhi to Prem and then Mina, secretly hoping they would beg her to stay.

"Ayla, you can go," Noor said, her voice strained. "If you really want to, we can figure that out."

"But your degree of openness!" Bodhi blurted out. "It's so high!"

"Bodhi!" Noor spun to look at him. "Ayla needs space. Don't pressure her. Don't make this even more difficult than it already is."

"She needs to see this, Noor." Bodhi swiped his arm in the air like a windshield wiper, making the Chronicle disappear. After a few hand signals, a chart appeared in its place.

"Look," Bodhi said and pointed to the first column on the chart.

Impact on Openness	Ideal	Ayla
Age	Adolescence	Twelve (*perfect*)
Seeing	Beyond what is obvious	Beyond what is obvious
Listening	With deep concentration	With low distraction rate
Responding	With compassion	With compassion
Life Event (on Earth)	Death of a loved one, life-threatening illness, other major life event	Loss of Grandpa George
Other	Innate knowing, trusting	Good intuition
CANDIDATE MATCH		**100%**

"In my research of human development on Earth," Bodhi started, "outside of infants, who are—"

"Who aren't good for much," Prem interrupted.

Mina and Ayla giggled. Ayla noted how nice it was to have them around. She missed her friends, and even her brother.

"Dad is wild about Earth's history, Ayla," Prem said, eyebrows raised. Then he lowered his voice to a whisper. "It's a little strange."

"Thank you, Prem," Bodhi smirked. Then he continued, with a hint of pride, "It's true, Ayla. I have been studying Earth's history for a long time.

"From what I can tell, outside of infants who are born open, fresh from the source, children and adolescents are next in ideal openness. Children haven't developed the same discernment as adolescents, though. Sometimes they can't tell the difference between what is real and what is imagined. Adolescents can typically tell the difference and, ideally, can appreciate or at least acknowledge both, which allows them to stay open. Most adults on Earth have closed completely or have closed in certain areas."

Ayla was fascinated.

Bodhi went on. "You have the ability, Ayla, to see beyond what is obvious. You see what is obvious, and you know there is more. We believe we need that quality in a helper here.

"You listen closely when you are engaged in a conversation, which, from what we've observed, is a truly rare trait in humans on Earth at this time. In our study of openness, we determined that deep, active listening is crucial for problem-solving."

Bodhi sounded like her dad did when he used his work voice. He was more businesslike than dad-like when he explained things in those moments, especially when discussing history.

"You also have the ability to see the soft sides—or the circles, really. Throughout Earth's history, mostly two sides were represented in every story and every conflict. We talked about that, right?"

Bodhi nodded toward Ayla, waiting for her to affirm, and then kept going.

"In the beginning of America, even, that was not ideal, but people were used to reducing difficult situations to a divergence between two sides, and that strategy has remained at the center of most relationships and conflicts among groups on Earth.

"At this point, though, in your overall Earth Chronicle, circumstances have evolved past a two-sided story. Stories are actually circular. No sides. A lot of different variables present at once. People need to catch up to the stories.

"A lot of your people are looking for two sides, fighting for two sides, and not seeing the circles. Unlike you, Ayla. You *are* seeing what lies between the two sides, in the soft, circular space. You follow?"

Bodhi stopped for a breath. He took a drink of water.

"I think so," Ayla nodded. "But I know a lot of people who see . . . circles. I'm not the only one. You could have asked any of them for help."

"Right. That is true. But you have a gift. You listened to Grace, and you believed her." Bodhi's voice got louder. "And then you gave Ryan the benefit of the doubt."

"Huh?" Ayla didn't comprehend what Bodhi was saying. She had been focused on her betrayal of Grace.

"Ayla, you acknowledged there was something in Ryan's past that made him think it was okay to hurt Grace. You didn't just blame him for hurting her. A lot of circle seers still take sides."

Bodhi said each of his words with such determination, as if he was a lawyer proving a case in a courtroom.

"Oh," Ayla said, starting to feel hot again. "Well, I'm definitely on Grace's side."

"Right. But instead of lashing out at Ryan, you showed him compassion. You made space for the possibility that he somehow didn't see that what he did was wrong. You may be on Grace's side, and you let Ryan know what he did was not acceptable, but you also didn't make him feel little. You treated him like a fellow human.

"That is becoming rarer in your society. The urge to be right or to belittle others is overwhelming your people."

Bodhi sounded like he was finished.

But then he continued, "So, each of these factors adds to your openness. Then Grandpa George's death, as we've already discussed, opened you even further. That loss guaranteed you would stay open for a while longer, at least.

"We concluded we needed someone who was open but could also relate to those who are closed. Someone like us."

Bodhi stopped, but it sounded like he wanted to say more.

"And?" Ayla asked.

"And you are one of us, Ayla," Noor said. "So we chose you."

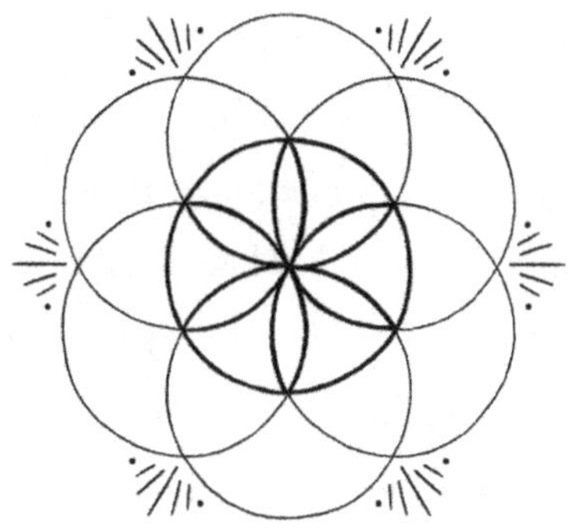

CHAPTER 13

ONCE AYLA SAW a glimpse of her own Chronicle, she wanted to see more. She wanted to see all of Earth's Chronicles, from the very beginning.

She watched the screens for days. Much of the time, she felt sick to her stomach. She hated the feelings that bubbled up as she watched the story of her land, her planet, her home—Earth. There was more violence than she ever knew. More suffering, more torture, and more pain. She felt robbed of the truth of what had transpired. She felt betrayed by those who came before her. She felt sad. Angry.

On one of the first nights of watching, she didn't rest well. She dreamt of Genghis Khan's face on her Grandpa George's body. She watched as the awful Genghis Khan/Grandpa George figure defeated his opponent's warriors. She woke up feeling like she had betrayed her grandpa. She didn't understand how she could possibly have seen him in that way, as a terror to those around him.

The next night, Noor filled the bathtub with water, rose petals, and essential oils. Ayla soaked while sipping warm chamomile tea from a sturdy ceramic mug. Noor and Mina checked in on Ayla while she bathed, sang to her, and helped her get cozy before bed. They followed the same ritual each night after that.

Prem and Bodhi were even kinder than usual to her, giving Noor and the girls space to nurture each other and making delicious, nourishing meals each night. The contrast between the scenes she watched on the screen during the day and the warm tenderness they showed her each night comforted her.

It was hard for her to face the screens each day, but she didn't want to stop watching. She closed her eyes at some points and turned down the volume too. She followed Noor's lead and fast-forwarded through the stories when she had a sense of how they would end. She rewound and replayed conversations where negotiations were being made.

In the beginning, Ayla felt distraught as soon as a confrontation would begin between two groups or people. When she listened closely to what was said, though, she always felt there must be more to the story.

"Exactly," Noor said as they exchanged insights about the scenes. "In studying the history of Earth, I have observed how it is always two sides fighting against each other. No one should ever have to choose just one side, Ayla. Humans weren't meant to be so rigid. Humans were made to mimic the Earth, to be soft and flexible, like the Earth is in its roundness—with no sides. Here, we see ourselves as one people representing many perspectives within the whole. And we see you as one of us also. Earth and all of your people, Eema and ours—it is all one."

Noor reminded Ayla so much of her own mother, who was also curious about the ways of the world and who also had a gift for seeing beyond what was in front of her. Maybe in another time or in another place, Helen Stone would have been less burdened by her work and instead energized by it, as Noor appeared to be.

Mostly, Ayla kept watching the Chronicles because for each horrific, heartbreaking story, there were at least eleven others that restored her faith in the world she knew as home. She watched in awe as communities came together after disasters to help each other. She listened as leaders instilled hope through their speeches and deeds. She saw women, men, and even children rise again and again to stand up against evil and to speak truth to power. Even the horrible, legendary Genghis Khan surprised her by being one of the first leaders to accept other religions alongside his own. For every person who seemed determined to destroy the world, there were many, many more who worked each day to save it.

Ayla was fascinated by the dance between good and evil. Good always took the lead, but evil stole the show with its vast presence. And all the while, the people—her people—stumbled along, trying to make sense of it all while living their lives, which were often so hard. It was a miracle anyone had energy left to do anything outside whatever it took to get through each day. Ayla was mesmerized by these stories. Some felt familiar to her because she had read about them or learned about them in school. Others were new and seemed more like fiction. She knew nobody could know all the history of the Earth, and yet it troubled her that she knew so little.

At one point, she fled the room after a disturbing story about the Salem witch trials. She needed air—and she ran into Ishwa in the hallway. Her skin burned where her head connected with his hard chest.

"You shouldn't be here, Ayla," he hissed in her ear. "You carry the disease of your barbaric people." He turned and walked away just as Noor appeared in the hallway.

"Are you okay, Ayla?" Noor asked.

Ayla was moved by the obvious concern in Noor's eyes. As the burning sensation faded from her skin, she was hit with exhaustion from the day's work.

"I am," she said. "I wish he didn't hate me so much, though."

"He doesn't hate you, Ayla Bug. He's afraid of you. He doesn't understand why you're here."

"I don't blame him," Ayla said under her breath, suddenly irritated. "I'm really just a kid still, Noor. I heard Bodhi talking to Nell about the tornadoes and the damage they're causing in the South. He said the people there are confused. I can't help with that. And I especially can't help if I'm just sitting here all day, every day."

"Ayla, the tornadoes are causing people in the South to turn on each other. You've noticed in the Earth Chronicles the way your people, dating back to the beginning of time, come together in difficult times and look out for each other. They *help* each other. We do not understand why the same is not happening here."

Noor's normally soft expression turned harder with each word she spoke. Her brow furrowed.

"Well, I don't understand it either," Ayla said. "It appears, according to the Chronicles, that you did everything perfectly. I'm not sure how we Earthlings screwed up so much in so many ways but managed to get that one thing right."

Noor looked at Ayla for several minutes before saying anything.

"You know, Ayla," she finally said, "sometimes events occur in our lives that we cannot explain. Like the tornadoes here. We don't know why, after all these years, we are now experiencing tornadoes for the first time. We don't understand why the people in the South appear to be turning on each other. Do you think we did everything perfectly and now we—how do you say it?—*screwed up?*"

"No," Ayla said, avoiding Noor's gaze. "I guess not."

"Well then, Ayla, what if we *had* screwed up? What if somehow, without even knowing it, we caused the tornadoes? Would you hold that against us? Would you blame us for this situation we find ourselves in?"

"Well, if you didn't *know* you screwed up, or if you didn't *try* to screw up, I'm not sure you would be at fault." Ayla looked up, feeling hopeful again.

"Ayla, what we are talking about now is that soft, circular space, where there are no sides," Noor said, touching her on the arm. "It is a space between, where there are no crystal clear explanations for why a situation has occurred. It is where we can't be sure we are making the right choices or the wrong choices because there is no map that shows us which way is the best way through this. We do not know how we got here, and we do not know where we are headed. All we can do is trust that, moving forward, knowing what we know now, we will do what is right."

Noor held Ayla's hands in hers. "I trust that bringing you here to Eema to help us was right. And I think you know *here*"—Noor lifted her right hand and placed it over her heart—"that you can make a difference, even though we may not fully understand why or how. You can help. You can help save all of us."

Ayla nodded. She could feel some truth in Noor's plea. Even though none of this made sense, it felt right to be here, and she knew she wanted to make a difference here. She also hoped her efforts, whatever they may be, could ripple right out of Eema and onto Earth, where she knew so many people were hurting in the soft space between what was obviously right and wrong.

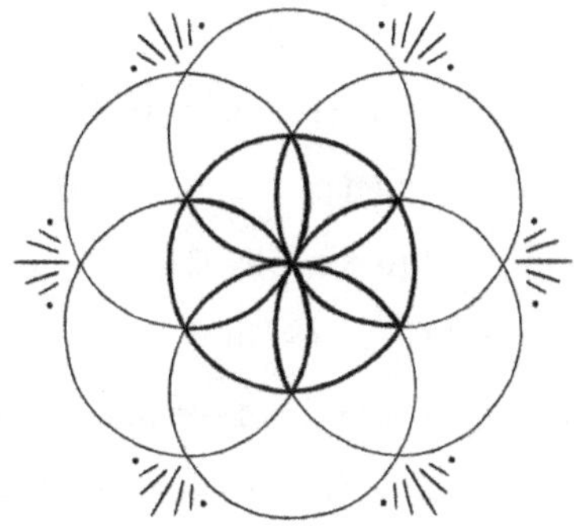

CHAPTER 14

Ayla woke the next morning feeling cranky, maybe even a little hopeless again. She wanted to believe she could help Noor and Bodhi. She even felt competent, like given her experience and her personality, she could somehow find a way to help. Yet a little voice inside her head insisted she was wrong. The voice persisted with the questions, *Why you? Who do you think you are?* It then chimed in with, *You know nothing about any of this.*

As hard as she tried, Ayla couldn't think of an adequate response. Chronicles spun through her head like the tornadoes spun in the South, leaving questions in their wake. She didn't think she had the answers she needed to make a difference, and as much as she wanted to believe she could do it anyway, she was scared.

Ayla pulled out the sketchbook she had asked Mina to borrow. She grabbed a pencil and drew two circles side by side. She wrote *Earth* on the first circle and *Eema* on the second. Somehow, just seeing the two circles side by side helped her relax. Her mom had told her that she was a visual learner. She needed to see things.

She then made a third circle that intersected the first two and started a list: *land, trees, animals, humans, food, love, connection*. These were the first things she could think of that Earth and Eema shared in common. These were such simple things—the simplest.

And what about *faith?* She added it with a question mark at the end.

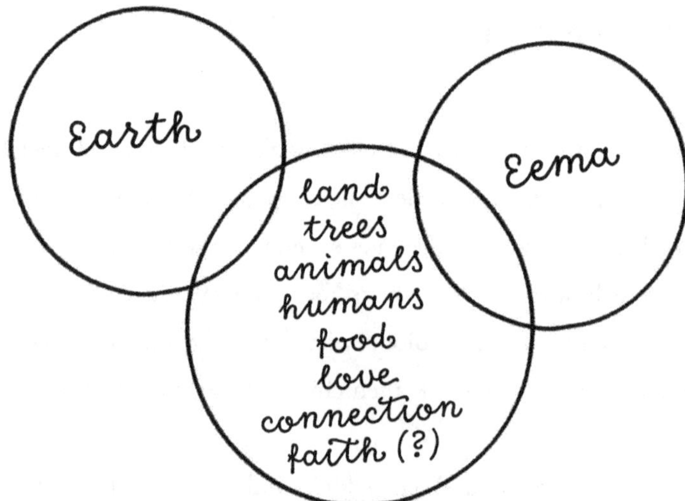

If only she had a dollar for every time she'd heard Grandma Ettie and Connor argue about God. Connor, as a scientist, believed the big bang created Earth. Grandma Ettie believed God created Earth and everything in it. Connor wouldn't budge. Neither would Grandma Ettie.

Ayla would listen, not saying a word, wondering if there was something in between Grandma Ettie's God and Connor's science that was the truth. Something like the soft space Noor talked about. She had wondered if maybe God initiated the big bang. That seemed insane to her now that she was here on Eema, now that Bodhi had told her chaos probably caused the big bang. *But what was before that?* That was Ayla's question now. Where was God in all of this?

When Connor probed her, Grandma Ettie didn't have to actually say it to show how sure she was that she was right about God and His Word and her belief that anyone with dissimilar beliefs was wrong. "I'll pray on it," she often said when there was a problem or a question about anything. It was her last-resort answer to anything. Ayla wasn't sure exactly what Grandma Ettie was praying *on*, and rarely did she come back to the conversation to follow up with a conclusion.

"I'll get back to you on that one, Ettie," Ayla's mom would say in a deep voice, pretending to be God, whenever Grandma Ettie said she'd pray on it.

Ayla smiled. Again, she wondered what her family would think of her in this strange but familiar place called Eema. She missed them but also felt grateful to be away for a while, to catch a break from the constant tension and to not have to think about Grandpa George and how his death was almost like a new person in the family, a new thing to tend to and to try to get along with.

So, this was it. All she could come up with for now was a short and simple list of what these two similar but different places had in common. She suspected that knowing how these two planets were the same would help her figure out how they were different too. Beyond the obvious differences, there was something that happened here that didn't happen at home, and vice versa—something that caused her people to help each other and these people to turn on each other.

Ayla drew more circles around the original circles as she became even more lost in the forest of thoughts taking root in her brain. Eventually, she noticed the group of circles looked similar to the flower-like design on Mina's forearm. She had seen it many different times since arriving on Eema, but she hadn't worked up the courage to ask anyone what it meant.

"Ayla? Are you up?" Mina's excited voice was followed by a knock on Ayla's door.

"Yes, I'm up!" Ayla exclaimed, trying to match Mina's enthusiasm. "Come on in!"

She pulled her covers over her lap, covering her sketch. She wasn't ready for Mina to see it. Not yet, anyway.

"Hey, guess what, Ayla!" Mina could not contain her excitement as she burst through the door.

"What is it?" She had never seen Mina, or anyone here, filled with such obvious enthusiasm.

"Ayla! It's tonight! The Embody Festival! Oh my goodness, I cannot *wait* for you to see it. You are going to *love* it!"

If it wasn't for gravity, Mina would be floating to the ceiling. She was barely touching the floor as it was.

"You're in for a real treat, Ayla. We're so excited to share it with you!"

With that, Mina jumped into bed with Ayla and gave her a big hug.

Ayla was not one to resist a good hug. She leaned into Mina's excitement, hoping some of it would rub off on her.

"What is this? A festival? What is this festival you speak of?" Ayla tried to sound like she had official business with Mina. In all the seriousness since her arrival, she had forgotten how fun it was to be goofy with her friends.

"Well," Mina began, "I really can't explain it. It started years and years ago. Almost at the beginning of time, I think. It was in this junglelike area. Maybe it was tropical? Or maybe in a forest? Really lush, that's for sure. And there was a group of elders, of women, who went through . . . what is that word? Menopause? They went through menopause all at the same time."

"*Menopause?* Are you kidding me, Mina?"

Mina looked offended. "Kidding you? No. This is a true story, Ayla."

Ayla looked doubtful, but Mina continued.

"Okay, see, that's the thing," Mina said. "They didn't *know* it was menopause. That's your word anyway—we would never call it that. Anyway, they were scared when they realized that they would no longer have moons—"

"Uh, do you mean periods?" Ayla asked, rolling her eyes. "*Of course* you call them moons."

"What else would we call them? They coordinate with the *moon*! Just listen, Ayla."

"Okay." Ayla snuggled back into Mina and listened.

"The elders were scared. They were afraid that once all the women stopped having moons, then humans would cease to exist. They thought it was the end of time, Ayla. The women all moved away from their village together. They felt shunned, but really, they were the ones turning away from the others in the village. Nobody told them to leave—they just left!"

The girls adjusted their bodies and sank further into each other.

"Each night, they sat beneath the moon and sobbed because the world was ending," Mina continued. "One of the women suggested they ask the moon how to tell everyone the end was near. They spent a few days writing lyrics for a song they would sing to the moon. They rejected pages and pages of lyrics before they finally came up with the right words. And on the night they sang their song, *the moon flickered, Ayla*!" Mina's eyes were as big as moons as she said this.

Ayla enjoyed the storytelling here on Eema. Even the simplest, most basic stories had an air of mystery to them. They were magical. But as much as she liked hearing Mina tell this story, she just couldn't imagine it. It was a little *too* unreal for her.

"The moon flickered?" she asked, scrunching up her nose.

"Ayla, I know it sounds unlikely to you, but please just bear with me. This is how it happened. The moon *flickered.* And then the women heard a deep voice speak to them. It was a woman's voice, and they were convinced it was the moon's voice."

"The moon spoke to them? And she was a woman?" Ayla's eyebrows rose at the end of her question. Again, she was doubtful, but also more intrigued.

"The voice said, 'This is not the end of humanity, dear ones.' It sounded like a grandmother's voice." Mina lowered her voice a few octaves to sound more like the moon that night. "'Fear not. Humanity will continue. Your bodies are changing. The next generation of women are now the Mothers. You are now the crones.'"

"*Crones?*" Ayla asked.

"Yes, Ayla!" Mina's excitement was back in full force. "Crones are wise women. Physically, their bodies could no longer bear children, so they were called upon to—get this—*hold our stories*!"

"*Mina!*" Ayla yelled. "You don't have to yell!"

The two girls burst into laughter.

"Sorry, Ayla. This is just one of the best—days—of—the—year." Mina moved as close as she could get to Ayla's face until their noses were barely a centimeter away from each other. Then she drew back and continued her story.

"The women who gathered beneath the moon went back to their village and began collecting stories. They talked to everyone—women, men, and children. They even talked to animals and plants and trees. Every living thing has a story, Ayla." Mina whispered those last words like she was sharing a long-held secret.

"As wise women, it was up to them to hold the stories," she said, "to carry the stories for the village. It's how the Chronicles started, really. The stories are so important to us. So, it's a pretty big deal—the festival. It's where we celebrate the wise women. At the Embody Festival. Tonight."

Mina impressed upon Ayla the importance of the night by speaking slowly and nodding after each sentence.

"Why is it called the Embody Festival?" Ayla wondered.

"Well, you know how babies are carried in the womb, right?"

Mina waited for Ayla's nod.

"Right, well, the wise women came to believe that the womb is where they would carry our stories, or the stories of the village. You know, because, like I said, physically they could no longer carry babies there.

"They went from mourning the changes in their bodies to celebrating them because each change made way for something new. Plus, they wanted to express their joy because not all the women could or even wanted to hold babies in their bodies, but every woman could hold stories."

Mina used her hands to form an invisible baby bump over her stomach.

"Every woman holds *many* stories. And men and children too. The stories were something every human could have in common. The first celebration evolved into a great big outpouring of love for bodies and what they can do. Our bodies are miracles, Ayla."

Mina stopped.

"I know. I get that part," Ayla said, feeling defensive. "We do have bodies on Earth, just like you, you know." It sometimes sounded like Mina thought she was dumb.

"The bodies are the vehicles humans use when we're assigned here, Eemaside, to the ground," Mina said, "and they are really incredible. So we celebrate them. When we move on, we don't keep these bodies. When we leave them, we call that *shelling*. When we go spiritside, we just go back to being blobs of energy."

Mina moved her arms through the air like she was an octopus.

"How do you know that, Mina?" Ayla longed to feel the confidence Mina's voice indicated. "How do you know that we're really blobs of energy? Don't you think humans just die? Then get buried or cremated or whatever?"

"Our bodies die, Ayla," Mina said, nodding. "But our spirits never die. Spirits might transform, maybe enter a new body, but they don't die. They just keep going. And going . . ."

"How do you know that, though? Do the Mothers tell you that? Is it, you know, a *God* thing?"

Ayla felt like she was about to unlock one of the mysteries of life, a mystery that many people on Earth dedicated their lives to studying and, even then, never seemed as sure about it as Mina seemed now. Knowing exactly what happened to a person at death felt like an urgent matter. Ayla was desperate to know what had happened to Grandpa George when he died.

Mina's demeanor changed, like something startled her. She took a deep breath and looked intently at Ayla.

"Nobody needs to tell us," she said. "We just *know*, Ayla. There wasn't a time where we didn't know it. It's like we know our hearts are beating or our lungs are filling with air. Except it's not something we know with our bodies or even our minds. We know it in our hearts, or our souls, I guess."

Mina seemed to have so much more to say.

"How do you know something in your soul?" Ayla asked. She felt frustrated but was determined to figure this out. "Doesn't knowing happen in your mind?"

"Look, Ayla." Mina placed a hand over her heart, just as her mother had the night before, and then slid it down to where her stomach ended. "This space is heart and soul space. On Earth, they—or you—do most everything in head space."

Mina placed her hand on top of her head and let it rest there for a second.

"The tissue or cells that help you think, they also exist in this space." Mina motioned toward her stomach and chest again. "We use our minds too, but I guess you could say we do the same thing with our hearts and stomachs that you do with just your brains. It's from those places that we just *know* we are spirits. It's from those places that we celebrate our bodies. We celebrate this time we have to be human."

Mina reached for Ayla's hand and squeezed it. Ayla's need for answers faded as her body tingled all over. But as the tingly feeling faded too, she thought she felt something strange—an inexplicable new sensation stirred in her stomach and in her heart.

She felt like she was waking up after a long, deep sleep.

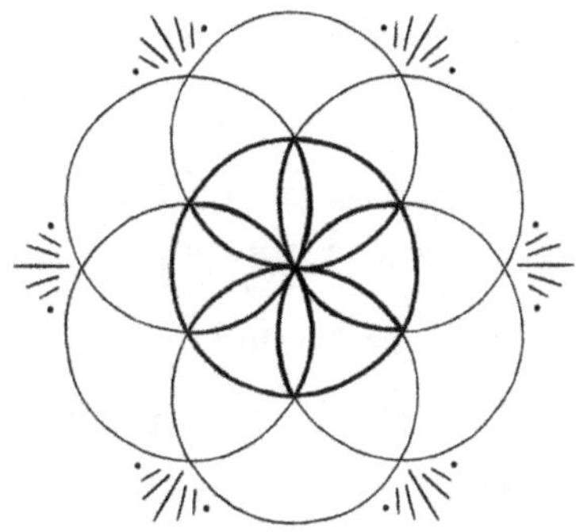

CHAPTER 15

As IT TURNED out, getting ready for the Embody Festival was an event in and of itself. First, Noor drew hot water in a bathtub and filled it with sweet-smelling salts, oils, and flower petals. She and Mina and Ayla gathered around the side of the tub in cushioned chairs and soaked their feet while sipping fruit-infused tea.

Mina explained that the process of getting ready was the first part of the celebration for the Embody Festival, and Noor told stories about her early festival memories. At her first festival with Bodhi, her skirt got caught in the door as she was leaving the house. It ripped in half, making her long skirt a short skirt. She didn't want to tell Bodhi what had happened, so she spent the entire night in the short skirt as if she'd planned it that way. He had no idea until he dropped her off that night and her skirt fell on the floor when he opened the front door.

My mom would love all of this, Ayla thought.

Once their feet were wrinkled like raisins, Ayla watched as Mina and Noor unpacked trunks of beautiful garments that looked a lot like Indian saris. There was a trunk for face paint and glitter and another for hair ribbons. Noor brought in a bowl full of freshly cut flowers.

Each of them selected their clothing after trying on multiple pieces. As it turned out, the sari-like skirts came in varying lengths. Mina and Ayla chose shorter skirts, in honor of Noor's first festival with Bodhi.

The fabrics were soft and flowy and felt like little kisses on Ayla's body. Noor braided the girls' hair and wrapped the braids around their heads. She added flowers and ribbons here and there. Once they were fully dressed, the face painting began. Noor drew three small gold-colored dots across the center of their foreheads. She then added three small stripes on each of their temples. The designs seemed random and even childish while Noor worked, but when she was finished and the girls looked at their reflections in the mirror, Ayla's jaw dropped open.

"We look like goddesses," she whispered.

"Yes! Gorgeous goddesses," Noor said. "Okay, now that you are done, I will leave you. I will be back, though, young maidens. I need to pull some things together for the festival."

She paused at the door and took one last look at the two girls. "You really do look beautiful." She smiled before spinning around and heading down the hallway.

"Okay, now give me your arm," Mina said to Ayla.

The girls were sitting in chairs knee to knee so Mina could add a few finishing touches to Ayla's face with makeup.

"My arm?"

"Oh, wait. Darn it! You don't have your mark of the flower. I'm sorry. I forgot about that. I guess we can't decorate it yet." Mina seemed more disappointed at this discovery than Ayla could ever be.

"My mark of the flower?" Ayla wasn't sure whether she should be disappointed too, or just supportive of Mina in *her* disappointment.

"This." Mina turned over her left arm and lifted her sleeve, revealing the small flower-like symbol that had held Ayla's attention since she first saw it.

"You know, I've been wondering about that," Ayla said. "I know I've seen it before—at home, I mean. And here, I see it everywhere. Doesn't your mom have one too? What is it?"

"It's the Flower of Life, Ayla."

"I don't know what that is."

"It's an ancient symbol. Some have spent their entire lifetime studying it here, and on Earth, and probably in other places."

"What does it mean? Why do you have it on your body?"

"It probably has different meanings to different people. We believe it holds the unifying code—for our universe, and yours, and all of them, really. It's a Universal Chronicle, I guess you could say. We put it on our bodies to remind us that we're all connected, like the petals."

Mina traced the petals on her arm.

"Wow." Ayla felt like she was falling under some kind of mysterious Flower of Life trance as she watched Mina's finger trace the symbol on her forearm.

"We get it once we've made the passage from childhood to womanhood or manhood. You know, for girls, when we've had our first moon." Mina winked at Ayla. "Once you're there, your body basically has the code, you know?"

"That seems so young to get a tattoo."

"Not everyone makes it permanent right away. Some never do. It just depends on your relationship with your body." Mina pulled out a sheet of paper from one of the trunks. It looked like a sheet of temporary tattoos.

"See?" Mina held the sheet of paper in the air to reveal several rows of the Flower of Life symbols. "A lot of us just use these for the festival. Would you like one?"

"Sure," Ayla said.

She watched as Mina figured out where to place the symbol on Ayla's arm.

"It goes on your left side, the receiving side, because you are receiving the code." Mina winked again. Her winks always made Ayla smile.

"Why did you get a real tattoo?"

"I just got it, actually, not long ago." Mina bit her bottom lip as she concentrated on her work on Ayla's arm. "It's not permanent, though. It will wash off eventually. But I do like seeing it there all the time.

"And for the festival, we decorate it. We use dots or other flowers and vines to symbolize different things we've done in our bodies since the last festival. Here."

Mina handed Ayla a makeup pencil and showed Ayla how to decorate her Flower of Life. The end result was stunning.

"And finally . . . these!" Mina reached into the trunk and pulled out a handful of silver and gold bangle bracelets. "We wear one for each year we've been in our bodies."

The girls sorted the bangles and put them on their arms.

"Well?" Mina held up her arms. She looked like Wonder Woman.

"Beautiful, Mina!" Ayla held up her arms. "And me?"

"I love it! You look incredible!" Mina's eyes sparkled. "Oh! One last thing!"

Mina went to a shelf in her room and grabbed a small wooden box.

"More?" Ayla had never worn so many pieces of clothing or jewelry at the same time in her life and could not imagine putting another thing on her body.

"Here." Mina pulled out a small brown bottle and took the cap off. The smell of roses filled the room. "Let's use rose oil. To raise our vibration!"

Ayla felt sure Mina's vibration could not possibly be raised any higher, but she loved the smell in the air and waited expectantly as Mina dabbed some of the oil on each of their wrists and behind their earlobes.

"Okay, my beloved maiden, Ayla of Earth, you are properly adorned," Mina said, giving her a tight hug and offering her an arm. "Let's go celebrate these exquisite bodies!"

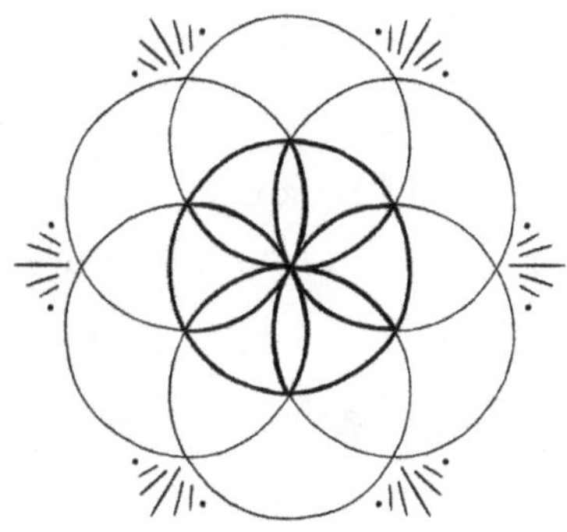

CHAPTER 16

THERE WERE TOO many scents in the air to identify just one.

Ayla smelled citrus at first. Then florals. Or was that rose oil? Then she smelled the scent of woods, maybe, like the wooded area of her neighborhood that was filled with pine trees.

All the colors, on every surface and all around, were deep, like the crayons in a brand-new crayon box. This was something she would miss when she returned home. Eema was so much more colorful than any place Ayla had ever seen.

The women wore crowns of flowers in their hair. Some men did too. Musicians were scattered throughout the hall playing flutes, guitars, ukuleles, and other small instruments Ayla didn't recognize. While they played their instruments separately, the sounds somehow came together in the most beautiful arrangements.

The sprawling room was lit only by candles. Down the center of the hall, a long table was set. Platters upon platters lay overflowing with food. There were fruits, cheeses, vegetables, meats, and pastries. Huge crystal punch bowls held a variety of drinks along the table. The food blended so well with the greenery and floral arrangements on the tables, it was hard to tell what was food and what was decoration.

But the most amazing thing about the space was the ceiling, which was made of glass. They could see the stars in the sky and enjoy the moonlight shining down upon them.

Ayla was mesmerized. She looked from table to person to flowers to musician, around and around and back again. It was magnificent.

And awkward.

Ayla had been to many birthday celebrations, family parties, and holiday gatherings. Nothing compared to this—not even her cousin's wedding reception, which was absolutely glamorous to start and a pretty crazy party scene at the finish. She didn't have words to describe how she felt. She was stirred by the sights and sounds, in awe of the beauty of it all, and yet uncomfortable.

It was similar to the way she felt at the dance she attended this year. It had sounded like it would be fun, and the gym was decorated beautifully with twinkle lights. The DJ played her favorite songs. But it was awkward. The boys in her grade didn't dance much, if at all. They huddled in groups, mostly hidden in corners of the gym. Girls on the dance floor and boys in corners. She remembered telling her mom how uncomfortable it felt, how it just wasn't fun.

"You're at an age where it can be hard to feel comfortable in your body, especially around people of the opposite sex," her mom said matter-of-factly.

"Oh, that explains it." Ayla laughed. "I think we've all been pretty uncomfortable around each other since the *video* we watched in health class at the end of fifth grade."

She and her mom laughed together, swapping memories of the days leading up to the *video*. Connor was relentless in his teasing. He tormented her and, for fear of making Grace and Amanda feel left out, teased them too.

In the end, the *video* wasn't a big deal at all. It was one of those things that sounded much worse than it actually was. All Connor's teasing did was add to the growing anxiety the girls felt over their changing bodies and potentially embarrassing interactions born from their curiosity about the possibility of sharing any part of their body with someone else.

How could she celebrate her body here and now? As much as she had enjoyed the afternoon, preparing for the festival with Noor and Mina, she felt completely out of place at the festival.

She poured herself a mug of something frothy and tried to find a place to sit down. If she was being completely honest, she was in awe of the ways in which all these different bodies occupied the space together. The bodies were old and young, reflected every shade of the skin-color rainbow, and came in all shapes. Not a single person seemed to feel self-conscious. Each of them had a space on the floor. Each seemed confident in the knowledge that they had every right to take up that space and to move around freely. It was the opposite of the dance at school, which ultimately felt like a breeding ground for humiliation.

This space and these people, in their incredible outfits, with their painted faces and flowers in their hair, with this dance, these decorations, and this food—it all added up to the ultimate celebration. Everyone and even everything looked so alive!

"Come dance with us!" Mina's friend Olivia yelled as she and Mina and their friend Zora tumbled toward Ayla. Olivia reached out for Ayla. When Ayla didn't immediately take her hands, Olivia spun around and went back to dancing.

Ayla watched as the three girls moved together, smiling and dancing like goddess sisters in a Greek myth. They looked so free. They were exquisite, just as Mina had said.

Olivia reminded her so much of her other bestie, Amanda, at home. In dance class, as Ayla concentrated on counting her steps and coordinating her movements with the music, Amanda made moving through each dance look effortless. She even closed her eyes sometimes!

Here, with her eyes closed, her arms twirling, and her hips swaying, Olivia didn't appear to be thinking at all. Her body had taken over. And the way she moved was truly remarkable. Her arms and hips swayed like paint strokes, creating art in the air around her. Olivia, Mina, and Zora formed a circle around Ayla, giggling and leaning in to kiss her on the cheeks. They smelled like flowers, and their faces shone like dew-covered leaves in the morning. Ayla felt her body wanting to join in, but she just couldn't let go. The girls formed a train, moving away from Ayla. Olivia motioned for Ayla to follow.

As Ayla stood up, so tempted to dance the night away with Mina and her friends, she decided to wander around instead. She made her way outside the large, overwhelming room and into a quiet corridor. She slid down to the ground and sipped her drink from a cross-legged position on the floor. The quiet was refreshing after being in a room full of music, conversation, and laughter.

Everything was done so wholeheartedly here. There were no wall-flowers. Nobody sat alone at the table. Everyone was all in. It was so different than home and what she was used to. Her friends, except Amanda, were mostly preoccupied with their appearances and fitting in, while the people here didn't even seem to notice themselves in that way. Nothing they did or wore made them fit in; they were just *in*.

Ayla had experienced tastes of that cell-deep knowing that she was accepted in her life; however, it wasn't a constant knowing. It was a sometimes knowing, not an always one.

Now that she was seated on the floor, she felt sleepy. She turned her arm over and traced the Flower of Life, as she had seen Mina do earlier. The tracing was like a meditation. She wondered if it would lead her to unlock the universal code.

Lost in her thoughts, Ayla was startled by a hushed voice she heard nearby.

"I think they're all gone now," the voice said.

Could that be Ishwa talking?

"How can we be sure?" said another voice, this one much deeper and unfamiliar.

"We can expect the tornadoes to stop. As soon as they do, we'll know it worked," the first voice said.

It had to be Ishwa. Ayla could feel the discomfort she felt around him in her body now.

"Does Noor know about the other . . . episodes?" the deep voice asked. He sounded worried.

"If so, I don't know anything about it," Ishwa said. "I don't think Bodhi has even had time to tell her since they realized some of the Chronicles were missing. I suspect most of the people around here couldn't comprehend the truth of what's happening. It all *has* to be because of the tornadoes. Bodhi told me there's a growing number of infants who won't stop crying. Nothing will soothe them. There's no power, so people can't see at night, and bad things are happening. Really bad things. Nothing like it has ever happened here.

"The biggest concern, though, is what should happen if the tornadoes continue to spread. We believe some have touched down in other areas and are moving this way—toward us."

Ishwa sounded scared, something Ayla would not have expected from him.

"And we agree with Seth?" the other voice said, sounding like they, too, needed reassurance. "That the tornadoes and what's happening in the South can be attributed to the chaos on Earth? The discontent among the people and planet there has made an impact here?"

"Even Noor and the rest of the Mother's Table agree on that matter," Ishwa said. "It's the only way to explain that degree of anger from our own planet. Eema has never cried out to us like this—with a natural disaster. Eema is definitely demanding our attention. What is happening here is well beyond the chaos happening on Earth.

"With all that has happened on Earth and the ways in which its people treat it and each other, it is a wonder that Earth is still spinning. The tornadoes had to have been activated by the pandemonium on Earth because the people on Earth are near implosion with their complete disregard for the land and each other. We know the Great Big Everything is connected—us, them, Earth, Eema, and everyone and all that is beyond. It is a logical conclusion that chaos anywhere would create more chaos throughout the skies. I hope, for our sake, the people of Earth will come to understand the impact of their unruliness. I hope they can activate the Star Within."

For the first time since she met Ishwa, Ayla felt a dash of compassion for him—but just a dash.

"And you think we've settled it?" the deeper voice asked.

"Yes, definitely. We erased the chaos. It can no longer repeat itself here. Not for now, anyway." Ishwa's voice was barely audible at the end of his sentence.

Erased the chaos? What did that mean? How could they have erased the chaos? Can anyone just erase chaos? This conversation was scaring Ayla.

"Well, we had to do something," Ishwa continued. "We had to take action. We couldn't just sit around and wait for N—"

"Ayla!"

Ayla turned to see Mina coming toward her. In the brief silence that followed, Ayla heard footsteps shuffle away. It had to be Ishwa and whoever it was he was speaking to.

"Where have you been? Out here? Are you okay? We've been looking for you."

Mina rushed like the wind toward Ayla and landed next to her, still sparkling with sweat and bliss.

"I, uh, well, I just needed some air—some quiet," Ayla said, trying to make a quick recovery.

She didn't know what to say. She didn't know how to explain what she'd heard or if she should even try to explain it. Maybe what Ishwa did was okay. Maybe it was right to erase the chaos—even though it made her uncomfortable to begin to imagine what that could mean.

She needed to stop thinking and say something.

"Is your mom here?" she asked.

"Yes, she's following me. What's really going on? You seem upset. Closed, even. I can't read you." Mina sounded concerned.

"Well, it's the dancing, I think. All the bodies. I'm just uncomfortable." Ayla was surprised by the words coming out of her mouth. Was that it? Was she really that self-conscious? Was that why she left the hall?

Mina was confused. "How did it make you uncomfortable, Ayla? It *is* getting warm in there, I guess."

"Hi there!" Noor said. She sat down across from the girls. Their knees almost touched, and together they formed a triangle.

"Are you okay, Ayla?" Noor asked. Her eyes raced around the corridor like she was looking for something she could smell but not see.

Ayla noticed her own palms were sweating. Seeing Noor, she was at a loss about what to do next. Tell her what happened? Not tell her?

"I guess sometimes it's just really obvious I don't belong here," Ayla said, looking down at her knees.

Then Ishwa bolted around the corner, giving Ayla a look that could have very well turned her to stone.

"Precisely," he hissed, not taking his eyes off Ayla. "You are one of many *things* that do not belong."

"Ishwa!" Noor raised her voice. She glared at Ishwa. "Leave. Her. Alone."

"You don't need her anyway, Noor. It's about time you realize that." Ishwa's eyes still did not move. Ayla felt like they were boring into her soul.

"Noor!" A familiar voice came from the direction of the hall. "Noor! We've been looking all over for you!"

It was Nell.

"We know what's missing," Nell said, panting as she reached them. Once she saw Ishwa standing with them, she appeared to regret having said what she did.

"What do you mean?" Noor asked.

"We know what's missing from the Chronicles," Nell said as Ishwa disappeared into the dark corner from which he came.

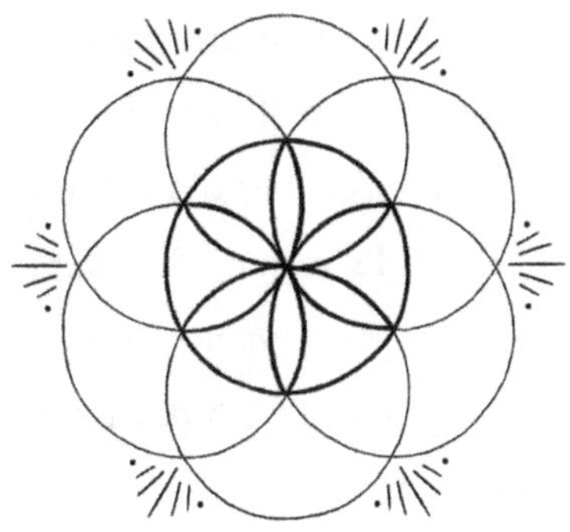

CHAPTER 17

As uncomfortable as she had felt while there, Ayla hated to leave the festival. It felt like being a character inside an actual painting, like the ones she had seen only in art galleries. The colors, the vibrancy, the smells, and the sounds of the joyful celebration were intoxicating. If the space Jeep didn't already float through the air, she would have floated back to the house herself.

She expected to spend more time with Noor and Bodhi that night. She wanted to tell them what she had heard in the hallway. Nell came back to their house too, though, with a couple others Ayla recognized but didn't know. And instead of inviting the children into the conversation as they usually did, the adults told them to go to bed. Mina looked nervous but tired, and Prem was lost in his thoughts. They went straight to their rooms, leaving Ayla alone.

Ayla tried to remember what she had heard Ishwa saying in the hallway. *Erasing the chaos. Eema demanding attention. The Great Big Everything. Taking action. The Star Within.* She considered going back downstairs to try to talk to Noor. She didn't want to intrude, though. They'd made it clear she and Prem and Mina were not meant to be included in their conversation. More than anything, though, she wanted to know what was missing from the Chronicles. It was catastrophic to lose even one of the stories held there.

Ayla sat inside her room on the floor as close to the door as possible and strained to listen. But the voices were too faint to hear anything. They must have closed the door downstairs in the kitchen. She pulled out her sketchbook and did her best rendering of a map of the United States. She drew little tornadoes over Texas and in the area her science teacher referred to as Tornado Alley, which was Kansas, Missouri, Nebraska, Iowa, and South Dakota.

What could be happening here on Eema? What could be so bad that it would make even creepy Ishwa nervous? Why were people turning on each other? What was the Star Within, and how could it help? What was the Great Big Everything?

Earth and Eema were connected. Who knew what else out there was connected as well? If two planets in different galaxies were connected, surely there were more. Ayla fell asleep as the questions continued to twirl like dancers in her mind.

She woke to a loud knock on her door.

It was morning, and she was still in her festival clothing, which carried a faint smell of the woods. The piney scent mixed with the florals was refreshing. As she reached for her doorknob, Noor opened the door from the other side and peeked her head into the room.

"We need to leave now for the Collective, Ayla. Can you be ready in a few minutes?" Noor handed her what looked like a homemade granola bar with a pleading look on her face. There were dark circles under her eyes and a new wrinkle in her brow.

"Of course!" Ayla said.

She would have agreed to anything. Even though she hadn't had a chance to tell Noor what she'd heard in the hallway, she felt she was hiding something, and it made her uneasy. She briefly wondered why she'd be allowed at the Collective now but had been excluded from last night's conversation. Perhaps another similarity between Eema and Earth was the seemingly uncertain space allowed for kids. It was not always clear when and where they fit in. Was that more soft space?

"It's about them, not you," her mother had told her countless times. Ayla could hear that voice clearly in her head. "Anything another person says or does tells you more about them and whatever it is that's going on with them than it could ever begin to tell about you. Give them the benefit of the doubt, Bug."

"Be present," her mother would whisper when she sensed Ayla's mind spinning off in multiple directions. *Be present. Be present.*

Ayla repeated this to herself as she prepared for the day. She was beginning to feel a little crazy with all the new developments that joined the already growing list of questions in her head. It would be such a relief to talk it all through with Noor. She hurried to get ready.

The ride to the Collective with Noor and Bodhi was silent. Ayla sipped a delicious berry smoothie while the two of them stared ahead. She went straight to the restroom when they arrived, and when she stepped back into the hallway afterward, she noticed the stillness and the silence surrounding her. It was eerily quiet.

She turned and walked right into Ishwa's chest.

"Oh good, it's you," he said. "What did you hear yesterday, Ayla?"

"What?" Ayla hated being caught off guard, and at first she really wasn't sure what he was talking about.

"I know you heard me talking to Pax last night when you were lurking in the hallway. I need to know exactly what you heard."

Ishwa's presence made Ayla's skin crawl. Or was that the burning sensation she felt when he was around?

"Pax? I don't know Pax, Ishwa. I don't know what you're talking about either. Please just let me go." Ayla tried to step around him, but he anticipated her move and blocked her way with his massive body once again. She sighed and looked up at him, feeling her confidence growing. She pulled her shoulders back, trying to gain some height, and looked directly at his face.

"What are you trying to hide anyway, Ishwa?"

Ishwa was alarmed by Ayla's sudden poise. He stepped back.

"Nothing," he said. "I have nothing to hide. Unlike you."

He turned and walked away. *Be present. Be present.* Ayla took a deep breath and continued repeating the soothing instructions. The words helped her feel less intimidated by Ishwa, at the very least.

She walked into the Screening Room, where the group sat around a huge round table. Noor, Bodhi, Nell, and most of the rest of the Circle were already seated. Ayla took an empty spot next to Noor and noticed there were only two other empty spots left. Ishwa and another one of those beings that wasn't obviously man or woman walked into the room together. Was that Pax?

"Ishwa, Pax, glad you could join us," Noor said with a hint of uncharacteristic sarcasm.

The two sat in the chairs that were left and, without communicating, scooted the chairs closer together. Ayla suspected they were trying to give the impression of a united front.

"As you have heard by now," Noor said, "we've discovered what happened when the Collective was broken into not long ago. We now know some of the Chronicles were stolen." Noor spoke slowly, clearly, and with a long look into each set of eyes around the table. "As you can imagine, this is devastating news. Again, I invite anyone here with information about the break-in to please speak up and share what you know."

Noor's eyes locked, once again, with the eyes of her cohorts one by one. Silence.

Ayla tried to stare down at her lap, but she couldn't keep herself from looking up intermittently at Ishwa and Pax. Pax squirmed in his seat and seemed to be trying to connect eyes with Ishwa while Ishwa stared straight ahead and sat as still as a statue. Ayla felt the tension in the room rise as the silence continued. The tension inspired a boulder in her chest, and its heaviness increased with every second that passed.

Ayla jumped when someone gasped, as if choking.

Noor spun to look at Nell. "Nell? Are you okay?"

"I . . . can't . . . breathe," Nell sputtered, her face losing all trace of color. "What . . . is . . . happening?"

"Who is doing this?" Noor yelled. "Everyone, clear the room!"

Ayla sat motionless in her chair. She watched as Ishwa shot a look at Nell and Noor that would freeze the sun. He sprang up, grabbed Pax by the arm, and hurried him out of the room. As the rest of the group fled the room, Ayla felt the tight boulder in her chest loosen. Nell began to breathe evenly again.

"What just happened?" Nell gasped.

"Someone was trying so hard to stay closed that they forced the air in the room to stop moving," Noor said. "And I think I know exactly who it was. I don't know what Ishwa is up to, but I know it's not good."

"I'm sorry I stayed," Ayla said softly. "I couldn't move either."

"It's okay, my dear," Noor said. "It would have been hard for you to move when Ishwa closed himself off in that way. That made it hard for everyone to breathe, let alone move. Nell is the most open of all of us, so she's more susceptible to that kind of deception. Anyway, I am glad you stayed. I think there is something you'd like to discuss?"

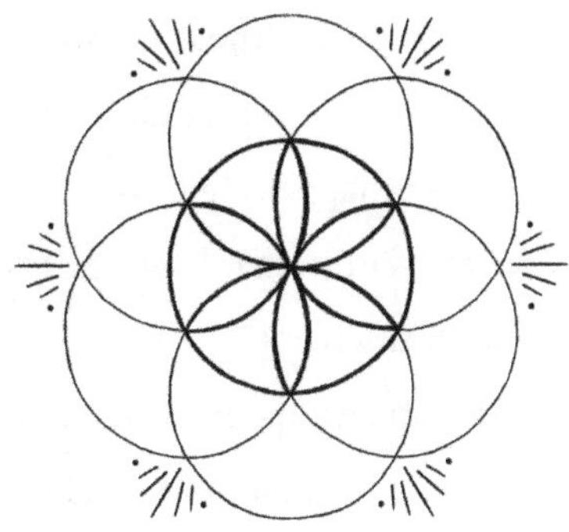

CHAPTER 18

Noor, Nell, and Ayla sat together in the Screening Room as Ayla shared everything she'd heard Ishwa say the night before. She hoped she hadn't left anything out—anything important, anyway.

"Based on what you've shared, Ayla, and Ishwa's recent behavior," Noor said, "I am confident he is either responsible for the stolen Chronicles or knows who is responsible.

"I had hoped Ishwa or someone—anyone—would come forward with more information, but I'm afraid we can't wait any longer. We must do something now to help save the people in the South. I'm concerned that if we don't determine what is keeping them from helping each other, we'll face the same dilemma here in the North, should we also get hit with tornadoes."

Noor's words sounded less like a song than usual. She sounded like she was trying to solve problems without a complete set of variables. Adding, subtracting, guessing at what could happen next, while also trying to figure out what was happening now.

"Noor, what is the Star Within that Ishwa mentioned?" Ayla asked. She wasn't sure she should interrupt Noor's thought process, but she felt like she had a gazillion questions. If she could only squeeze in one question, she chose this one. The Star Within sounded intriguing, like something she needed to know. "Ishwa said it was the only thing keeping the people from complete devastation. Maybe the Star Within is the answer. Maybe that's all they need?"

Noor nodded but kept her focus on the map over Ayla's head. "Well, hmmm . . . have you ever heard anyone say, 'We are made of stardust'?"

Ayla nodded, even though she couldn't actually remember hearing that.

"A large portion of the human body's composition comprises the same materials as a star. You are made of the same atoms as a star."

Noor stopped calculating and looked at Ayla.

"The Star Within is related to the *knowing* Mina shared with you. Remember? Here, we *know* we are spirits in human bodies, having human experiences in these bodies that we could not have as simple spirits. When our bodies die, we return to a spirit state, a spirit that is our own but also part of something bigger, a tremendous collective of all spirits, or one big spirit. This is true of all humans. Even you and the people on Earth.

"The Star Within is also a trait shared by all humans. It is the most concentrated presence of stardust in your body. Each of us has this, and because we each have it, it connects us to each other. We like to think of it as a guidance system, or maybe a map.

"On a very personal level, the Star Within tells us who we are. We believe it is at the center of the Flower of Life. That Star, made of the same stardust across all of space, unites us as humans. Some might even say it tells us who we are as a group of human beings."

"Who we *are*?" Ayla asked.

"We are one part of something much bigger, a bigger One," Noor said matter-of-factly. "A sliver of the Great Big Everything."

"So I'm more than just me? And you're more than just Noor?"

"Right. Me, you, Nell, Bodhi, Mina, Prem, your family, even Ishwa. Us. Together, we comprise one enormous One."

"Okay, so then how does that help? How would that help the people in the South?"

"When we see ourselves as part of the One, the Great Big Everything, we know we will always be supported by others, by each other, by the collective, or the whole. We cannot despair when we know we are not alone. Should those in the South lose sight of their place in the One, they may despair. Our knowing, or our trust in the Star Within, is what has always guided us at the Mother's Table. We see each other as another part of the big One first, then as individuals. If the people on Earth could see that too, if they had faith in it, they would stop fighting each other so fiercely. That would help stop the chaos on Earth and the tornadoes in the South."

Noor's eyes traveled back to the map, and Ayla sat very still, reminding herself to be present. To not let her thoughts run away from her.

"So, is the Star Within like God, but on the inside?" Ayla had to get in this one last question. It was something she had been wondering about anyway.

"You could say that," Noor said. "Some of the people on Earth say God *is* on the inside. I suppose God or the Star Within is much like an apple. The essence of an apple is always an apple. Each apple has skin, fruit, seeds, and a stem, but apples can be golden, red, green, sweet, or tart. The properties of apples change, but an apple is always an apple."

Noor took a deep breath before continuing.

"When it comes to God or the Star Within, Ayla, the only difference between people on Earth and people on Eema is that the people on Earth fight to prove they're right. Here, we are open. We are at peace with the possibility that there is more than we know or need to know. We are okay in the soft space of the unknown. Up until now, if we were to fight, it would be for each other. For the One. For the Great Big Everything. Here, everyone belongs, and we know that. On Earth, everyone is fighting to prove they belong, and that means whoever doesn't win the fight is left out."

Ayla sat in silence, trying to digest Noor's words, trying to imagine Noor explaining these same concepts to Grandma Ettie, like Connor tried to do. Grandma Ettie would lose her mind if she suspected God was anything but the God she had known since the day she was born and prayed to every single morning and night.

"Remember, Ayla," Noor continued, "some of it can stay a mystery. And even if we see this existence from different perspectives, God or the Star Within or any of the names you call it on Earth, the love we feel for each other as a result of this connection is the same love. Love is love is love. The knowing that we are connected so we belong together and to each other, that knowing is, quite simply, love. No matter how you name it, love is a constant."

Noor pulled Ayla close into a sideways hug and kissed her cheek.

"Now, you tell me something," she said. "What did you see in Eema's Chronicles? Why are our people turning on each other in the South instead of helping each other like your people do when natural disasters strike on Earth?"

Nell, who had been quietly listening this whole time while writing in a notebook, shifted in her chair to look at Ayla.

"I don't know, Noor," Ayla said slowly. "I have been thinking about what we have in common with you here. I haven't been thinking about what is different beyond the obvious. Can I see the Chronicles of the tornadoes? I think watching those would help me understand what's happening in the South."

"No, you can't see them, Ayla," Nell said, looking down at her notebook. "Those Chronicles are missing."

"What?" Ayla looked at Noor.

"Yes, I'm afraid Nell is correct," Noor said. "The Chronicles that could show us what happened when the tornadoes hit are missing. But let us confirm that to be sure."

Noor motioned to change the display on the screen. Nothing. Noor then swiped her arm through the air. Nothing.

"We have no trace of a single Chronicle for anyone in the South?" Noor seemed exasperated as she spoke her question into the air. She sighed and turned to face Nell and Ayla. At the same time, the door opened, and Bodhi peeked his head into the room.

"Can we come back now?" he asked.

"Yes. Come in," Noor said. "We were just talking to Ayla about what differentiates the response to natural disaster on Earth from the response observed in the South."

The group filed into the room and settled into their seats around the table. Noor motioned toward the screen, and it remained blank.

"Ayla asked if she could see the Chronicles to identify the differences. But we have nothing to show her," Noor said.

The room remained silent as all eyes watched the screen, waiting for something to play with each motion of Noor's arm, but the screen didn't even flicker.

"Ishwa, enough is enough," Noor said, breaking the silence. Her voice was loud and peppered with rage. She glared at Ishwa. "I know you know what happened to these Chronicles. We need them back. We need to know these stories."

Noor didn't blink as she stared at Ishwa. Ishwa stared at the screen. None of his body parts moved even a centimeter. He barely seemed to be breathing. Noor had suspected he would put every bit of his energy into staying closed, and it appeared he was doing just that.

"Ishwa!" Pax cried. "I cannot sit here and watch you do this. We are one! You are betraying our sisters and brothers! You are no better than the people in the South who are turning on each other. Tell them what you did!"

Pax stood up and threw his chair across the room, almost hitting the main screen. Ishwa turned toward Pax with fire in his eyes. Ayla's skin felt like it was melting off her muscles and bones, and Nell gasped again. Nell closed her eyes and after a few moments resumed breathing.

"I did nothing! Nothing!" Ishwa screamed, then spun around to glare at each person in the room. Everyone in the room looked from Pax to Ishwa to Noor.

"Ishwa, okay. You did nothing," Noor said. "Who did, then?"

Noor spoke as if she was questioning a small child, her voice taking a turn and overflowing with kindness.

Ishwa smirked. "Seth."

Noor looked taken aback but responded calmly. "Okay, what did Seth do?"

The temperature in the room continued to rise, and the expression on each face around the table transformed from curiosity and concern to fear. A tear inched its way down Nell's cheek.

"He erased the Chronicles," Ishwa said, a smug look on his face. "There are no Chronicles, nor will there ever be any Chronicles, for anyone or anything in the South."

Not a sound could be heard in the room. Nobody moved. In a split second, the air grew cold.

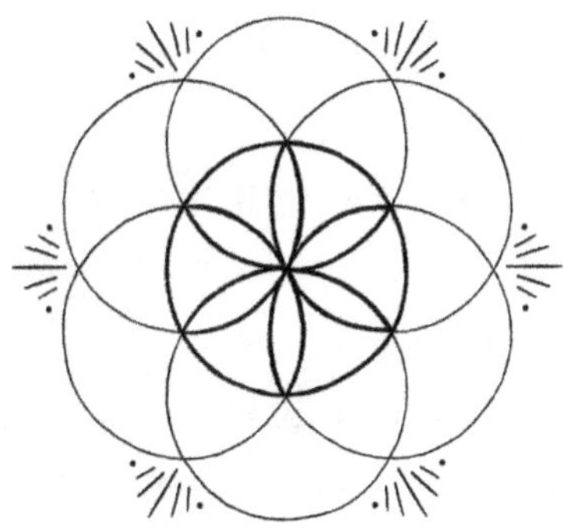

CHAPTER 19

THE TRIP TO the South was long, even in a space train—which, Ayla learned, was similar to an airplane but lower to the ground. The ride was smooth, and for much of the trip, Ayla stared out the window, watching the scenery. The land was less developed on Eema than on Earth, and the views out the window were absolutely breathtaking.

When Ayla wasn't staring out the window, she was nestled into the snack car with Mina and her dancing friends, Olivia and Zora. The Circle had asked the Medicine Woman and her daughter, who was Zora, to join them on the trip, along with a few close friends of members of the Circle. Most of the Circle members who had older children brought them along. Mina had wanted to invite Olivia, and Noor agreed, knowing Olivia was smart and strong and would be especially helpful.

Much to Ayla's surprise, Olivia was Seth's daughter. Ayla marveled at the way Noor treated Olivia as her own daughter, even knowing what Seth had done. But Seth had always brought Olivia with him when he was part of the Circle; even after he left, he didn't seem to mind when she spent time with Mina and her family.

Ayla couldn't wrap her head around the way forgiveness came so easily to Noor after Seth's betrayal. But Noor's next step was to move forward and find a solution to the problems at hand. She viewed all of the people in her community like she would anyone in her own family, still operating in a spirit of love for others, regardless of what Seth had done.

In the light of the train, Ayla noted yet again that Olivia was breathtaking. Although she was finding it less and less necessary to classify the people she met on Eema as anything but people, she was very much aware of and in awe of their physical beauty. The more she got to know these beautiful people and their wondrous ways, the more they seemed like spirits to her, just as Mina had described. Their bodies were merely vehicles, taking them from place to place. Maybe it wasn't even their bodies that were so striking to Ayla. Perhaps it was their spirits shining through their bodies.

Ayla tried not to look shocked when Olivia told her Seth was her dad, but Olivia knew. In some small way, she seemed to enjoy the fact that her father was the one who had erased the Chronicles. And while the space train carried them along, Olivia shared her father's story.

"My dad has been very open with me my entire life," she began. "When he was a child, his parents and grandparents kept secrets from him, and he vowed never to keep secrets from me. He told me everything."

Olivia stopped talking, perhaps waiting to see how Ayla would react to her declaration.

"He isn't ashamed of what he did," she continued. "He thinks he had good reason. I'm not sure what to think, but I want you to hear his story. I think he would agree it is important for you to know the truth of what happened."

Olivia took a long, deep breath before she continued talking.

As it turned out, Seth was the leader of a small group of insurgents in the North. It shocked Ayla to learn that anyone on Eema would disagree with the ways of Eema's people, given their kind and gentle nature, but apparently it was true that conflicts did occur on Eema.

Unlike most people Ayla had observed in the Chronicles, Seth's ancestors had reservations about the rules of the Mother's Table. First Seth's great-grandfather, then his grandfather, and then his father insisted that a Mother's Table was not sufficient to guide the people and the land. They believed that in order to make everything more equal, there should be a Father's Table too.

Had Seth's family not agreed to abide by the rule of the Mother's Table, even though they didn't approve of it, they would have been asked to leave. But they wanted to stay, and their commitment to contributing to the good of the Great Big Everything had not faltered, so they agreed to comply.

What nobody knew until now, however, was that Seth's great-grandfather originally settled in the South. He left there when the Mother of the South at the time scorned him. Ayla learned it was unusual for settlers to move between areas once they arrived. They typically stayed where they originally settled.

Seth's family was accused of hoarding resources—which, according to Olivia, was absolutely absurd because nobody hoarded anything on Eema. Hoarding wasn't even a concept known to the people of Eema, where the environment allowed for plenty of food, plants, and trees to grow. Everyone had more than they needed. There was more than enough to adequately feed, clothe, and shelter everybody.

Ever since he was a small boy, Seth had suspected there was more to his great-grandfather's story, but neither his dad nor his grandfather would answer the questions he asked. All Seth knew for sure was that leaving the South was an obvious source of pain for his family. Seth's grandfather passed the pain to Seth's father, and his father passed the pain to Seth. Seth felt it like it was his own pain.

Over time, as Seth's family refused to answer his questions, a small seed of fear took root inside of him. And in the absence of his family's stories, Seth wove his own stories about why his family left the South. He became suspicious that his great-grandfather must have done something terribly wrong. But suspicion was an unfamiliar feeling for anyone on Eema, and carrying that suspicion became a source of shame for Seth. Shame was another strange and certainly uncomfortable feeling on Eema, Olivia emphasized to Ayla.

When Seth was young, he didn't know how to handle his shame. He didn't even have a name for what he was feeling. He hesitated to talk about it with anyone outside his family because he didn't want to make his family uncomfortable. And he didn't feel he could trust his family because they refused to tell him the truth about their past. Shame was a burden he carried his entire life, and it made him feel like an outsider.

When Seth met Noor, Bodhi, and the rest of the members of the Circle as an adult, he finally began to feel less guarded. Time had passed, he had few living relatives, and he felt like he could open his heart a little and trust them. When he was asked to join the Circle as an advisor, mostly due to his technological genius, he felt he had finally redeemed himself and his family. An invitation to join the Circle was a high honor, and Seth was grateful for the opportunity to prove his worth. Of course, he was the only one who had ever questioned his worth, but he still felt he had to prove it.

Once Seth joined the Circle, however, he was introduced to the Collective Chronicles. Most people knew the Collective simply to be a building in town that housed artifacts from the past. The artifacts told stories the general public referred to as Chronicles. Only members of the Circle and their families knew about the actual Chronicles kept in the building. Many years ago, when the stories were collected on pages in books, the books were considered sacred texts, which were highly revered. Then it was decided that only the small circle of leaders, now known as the Circle, would know where the books were kept. Once the books were digitized and became the Chronicles, everyone outside the Circle forgot the books even existed. Even though it wasn't customary for anyone to watch the Chronicles, Seth was worried his family's stories would be accessed by someone in the Circle. He felt vulnerable. He was scared he would be rejected by the Circle if any of them learned the true story of his family.

After all this time, he still didn't know the real reason his family left the South. The fear of the unknown had haunted him his entire life. He'd thought about watching the Chronicles but knew he would have to be sneaky to do it, and he didn't want to risk getting caught. The only thing more powerful than his fear that his great-grandfather did something dreadful was his fear that someone in the Circle would learn before he did what his great-grandfather did and why his family left the South.

He thought his only choice, the only way to protect his family's story, was to remove himself from the Circle. So the last time the leaves turned, which Ayla guessed had to have been about a year ago, that's what he did.

Seth had been the Circle's expert in technology, and he'd wanted the use of technology to be more widespread. Noor didn't agree because she was afraid the broader use of technology would lead to less real connection among people. Once Seth left, she insisted any advances in technology continue to be used only within the Circle. Seth publicly criticized the Circle for keeping the technology to themselves, and a few other men who were also interested in technology formed the small group of insurgents.

The fears Seth carried with him seemed to infect the insurgents. Some of their families had only joined the community within the last year. They came with the understanding that this was a kind and innovative place that welcomed people from all over Eema. When they arrived and discovered that Noor had halted the use of technology, they were upset. They wanted to raise their concerns with the Circle but couldn't because the Mother's Table hadn't met in years.

After the first tornado hit in the South, Seth told the insurgents that he knew Noor and the Circle were keeping secrets from the community. This made the insurgents even more uneasy. Seth told them he would be a good leader because he would never keep secrets and would be committed to advances in technology as well. The insurgents felt comfortable with Seth and agreed he would make a good leader. They said they would do what they could to support him.

The members of the Circle never questioned Seth for leaving. He said another opportunity had been presented to him, and they believed him. One of Seth's gifts was his ability to appear open. It was a trick he'd learned as a child—to give the impression he remained open, even when he was closed. So, because Seth always seemed open, everybody trusted him. Throughout his entire life, nobody ever suspected Seth carried anything but goodwill inside him. Nobody ever knew the depths of his pain.

Once Seth left the Circle, he remained in close contact with Ishwa, who was still a member of the Circle, and eventually Seth told Ishwa his entire story. They joked that they would both be better suited to lead the Circle, though each regrettably acknowledged it was nothing more than a joke because only a Mother could lead the Circle.

Ishwa didn't tell the other members of the Circle about his friendship with Seth. In fact, he remained loyal to the Circle and to the Collective Chronicles until Ayla was called to Eema. Once she arrived, Ishwa feared her presence would bring misfortune to Eema. She was from Earth, after all, and the only thing he knew for sure about people from Earth was that no matter how smart or kind they were as individuals, they worked against each other in groups. They couldn't even agree on how to take care of Earth, their Mother. Ishwa feared Ayla's influence over Noor would lead to disaster. He did not want her to make a mess of things here on Eema.

Ishwa felt threatened by Ayla's presence. He had studied the connection between Earth and Eema for a long time and didn't think some young girl from Earth could help any more than he could. It didn't help that from the moment Ayla arrived, Noor, Nell, and Bodhi wouldn't leave her side.

Seth and Ishwa bonded over the fears each of them carried. To this day, Seth feared the Circle would learn something devastating about him and his family. He regretted not watching his family's Chronicles and learning the truth for himself. Olivia rolled her eyes when she said this. She thought her dad should have moved on from that by now. He just couldn't let it go.

When Ishwa told Seth about Ayla, Seth exploded. He didn't think it was wise to bring someone from Earth to Eema. Earth was a terrible place, and there was no doubt Ayla would cause trouble. Seth encouraged Ishwa to steer clear of Ayla and suggested they try to get rid of her before she caused any damage.

Seth knew more about technology, Earth, and the universe than anyone Ishwa had ever met. But what Ishwa didn't suspect was that Seth would take advantage of him and his access to the Chronicles and erase years of collected stories, just to make sure nobody ever found out about his own family's story, once and for all. Seth didn't really care what happened to Ayla.

Ayla felt uncomfortable knowing she had been Ishwa's target all along, and she deeply regretted that her presence made way for Seth to erase the history of the South.

Now that there was a new Mother in the South and the Chronicles had been erased, Seth had ensured there was no way anyone could go back and learn the truth about his family. He was relieved about this at first but started to feel sick shortly after he heard that Ishwa told the Circle what he did. He never meant to cause more harm and wished he would have thought more before he acted. He'd also shared with Olivia that he regretted erasing the Chronicles because now even he would never know the truth about his family.

By the end of Olivia's story, Ayla was baffled. Perfect, dreamy, beautiful Eema was at the very same time imperfect. This was a heart-wrenching realization. For the first time since her arrival, she felt so sad, she wasn't sure she could recover.

But at the same time, she also felt hopeful. For all the effort Seth (presumably) and Ishwa (definitely) had put into keeping secrets, it was Olivia, Seth's own daughter and Mina's best friend, who shared the innermost details of Seth's story. Knowing Seth, who had vowed never to keep secrets from his child, shared his heartache so openly with Olivia gave Ayla hope that something good could very well come of what seemed like a giant mess. It seemed like even though Seth himself had done something horrible, he really wanted to make things better.

She could hold on to that hope, she thought as the space train stopped.

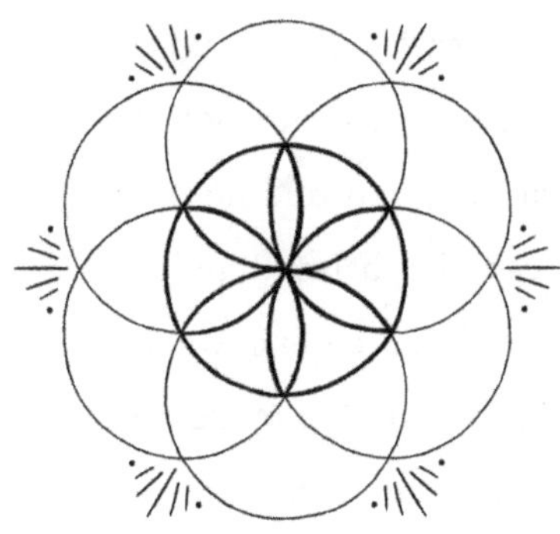

CHAPTER 20

THE AIR WAS thick outside the space train. It smelled like burning wood and stale wetness at the same time. Trees were splintered. Buildings had crumbled into pieces. Random remnants of objects, like clothing, shoes, and small devices, were strewn across the street.

Despite the destruction and debris, Ayla noticed the landscape was still lush here in the South. The greens were greener than at home, and the browns browner. Ayla admired the beauty she could see peeking out from beneath the damage, and that made it even more difficult to imagine the feelings of terror that must accompany the destruction here.

Ayla heard a child's cry nearby. Was the child asking for help, or just crying? She had seen pictures of destruction like this—photos in books and flashes of stories on TV—but never had she seen destruction so close that she could feel it, smell it, and touch it. She felt the typical reaction to such devastation: a sunken heart, a lump in her throat, and a sensation still new to her, one that could only come from seeing such a great deal of destruction right in front of her face. It was the same feeling she felt when her mom told her Grandpa George had *slipped away*. It stole her breath, her balance, and her sense of safety too.

A breeze blew overhead, adding a new mix of scents to the air. Some were rotten, like the whiff of mildew when she opened the washing machine after leaving her clothes in there too long—but worse. This stench was far worse. She gagged a little.

"Eema is crying," Nell said softly, placing her hand over her heart. She closed her eyes.

Ayla watched as Nell's body began to quake gently. Nell could feel Eema's pain.

"We hear you," Nell whispered. "We hear you, Eema, our marvelous Mother, our keeper, our land. We hear you."

Nell opened her tear-filled eyes and looked around, searching for more evidence of gloom in the air and on the ground. Ayla watched, in awe of the way Nell seemed so deeply rooted in Eema. Beyond the soil and the layers of ground beneath it, Nell's roots stretched down into Eema's core.

Ayla noticed the small crowd of people who had also disembarked the train and now gathered around them. They were looking around with fear in their eyes while stretching their arms and legs after the long ride on the space train.

"I'm glad we made it here safely," Noor said. "Thank you all for coming."

It was unusual for people to travel outside the area where they lived, Ayla had learned. While in spirit those who came were eager to help, the logistics were overwhelming. They weren't sure what to pack or how much they would need. They didn't know how to travel, let alone how to prepare for what they found when they arrived. Ayla had helped as much as she could, trying to heed her mother's voice in her head that begged her not to overpack.

They'd brought medical supplies, or what were considered medical supplies here. Zora's mom, the Medicine Woman, came along, carrying her most potent collection of oils and herbs. They'd brought clothing and stores of pickled food some of the families had put in jars to prepare for winter. They'd brought blankets, ropes, and flashlights. They seemed well prepared, as far as Ayla could tell, and it was quite a relief to finally feel useful.

Ayla thought back to the moments before the group had left the North to come here. As soon as Ishwa admitted Seth had erased the Chronicles, the room stayed silent for a long time. It seemed like hours—Ayla remembered her stomach started grumbling, and that had rarely happened since she arrived. After the long silence, Noor had been the first to speak.

"Well, okay then." She let out a deep sigh, looking around the room as if searching for a clue about what to do next. Her eyes locked with Ayla's. Ayla stared back, waiting to hear what Noor would say. Again, time seemed to stretch, and what was probably only a few seconds seemed like hours.

"Thank you, Ishwa," Noor finally said. "I'm glad to know what happened, even though I cannot be sure what it means that those sacred stories of the South were wiped from the Collective Chronicles. I'm disappointed Seth betrayed us."

Noor appeared to be studying Ishwa, perhaps waiting for an opening in his spirit. After a little more silence, Ishwa's body relaxed and his smirk faded. He looked concerned.

"I'm disappointed Seth betrayed *me*," Ishwa said, raising his voice at the end. "I wanted him to help me send *her* back where she belongs!" Ishwa turned and glared at Ayla.

"I understand, Ishwa," Noor said and turned toward Ayla. "Ayla, those of us who called to you, who brought you here, we believed you could help us. We watched as people on Earth, even those who normally would not have been friends, helped others in need after natural disasters occurred.

"At the time, we had noticed people in the South turning on each other. They have not been helping each other as people do on Earth, which is unusual. Our first instinct has been to look out for each other and to work together to solve problems.

"We were at a loss. You have studied our Chronicles, as we have studied yours. We are at a further loss now, without the Chronicles of the South to guide us. What do you suggest we do?" Noor gave Ayla a small, encouraging smile and waited for Ayla to respond.

Ayla's mind went blank. She didn't know what to say. She had expected Noor to send her home. After all, Ishwa wanted her gone, and she hadn't felt like much help at all since she'd arrived.

Then her body started to tingle, and her eyes closed on their own. The blank page in her mind began to fill with images of people—her and the others—traveling to the South. The images gave her hope.

"Well, if they will not help each other, then we must go there," Ayla said. "We must help them." Even though her words made perfect sense after she said them, she wasn't sure where they came from.

"And so we shall," Noor said, looking relieved and grateful for a plan of action.

As they had loaded into the car that night to go home and prepare for the trip, Bodhi winked at Ayla and whispered the word *intuition*.

And now, here they were.

"Ayla? Ayla? Can you take these, Ayla?" Prem's voice startled Ayla out of her thoughts and back to the moment at hand. Prem held out a pile of wool blankets, asking for her help in carrying them.

The sun was starting to set, and with limited daylight, they split into groups and began to search for survivors. A few members of the group stayed back to set up camp. Noor stayed with them so she could oversee the Communications Room since Bodhi and some of the other members of the Circle had stayed behind to guard the Chronicles. Noor wanted to check in with them.

Ayla welcomed the silence as she walked with Prem, Mina, Olivia, and Zora. She had observed that working in silence heightened her other senses and made her feel connected to the others. She was astonished, in fact, to discover how deeply connected to each other people were here without any of the electronic devices she enjoyed back home. Their connections didn't stem from cell phones they used to text and call or from apps they used to like and follow one another, but rather from that heart and soul space Mina had talked about. As far as Ayla could tell, they didn't need to send text messages or make phone calls to make plans. They acted like they were all operating with one brain.

Most of the people of Eema didn't know what they were missing when it came to technology. It had been agreed that only those at the Mother's Tables would use technology to communicate with each other, and only they even knew such technology existed. To share the news that there were people in trouble in the South would mean explaining there were ways for different regions to communicate. It would also mean explaining that for as long as that technology existed, only the Circle had access to it.

Noor wasn't completely opposed to sharing the details with her people; however, she had feared they were running out of time to make it to the South and didn't want to take the time to describe the advanced systems to everyone. Ayla had asked whether they would be upset to learn this technology existed and had never known about it.

The question had surprised Noor, but before she had a chance to answer, they were interrupted. Ayla was sure going to the South was the next best step to take, but she wasn't sure what to make of all the new information she'd been learning along the way. It was happening so fast, and the new information was jarring.

Prem, who had been leading the group forward, stopped walking. "Stop," he said. "Do you hear that? It sounds like someone over there is moaning."

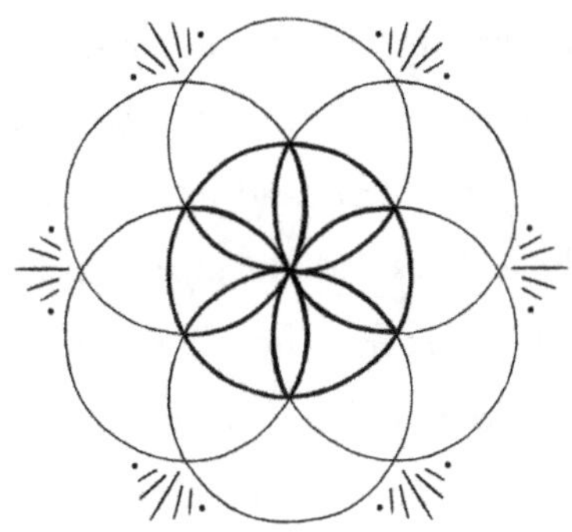

CHAPTER 21

Zora stepped away from the group and tilted her head to listen closely. Perhaps because she was the Medicine Woman's daughter, she seemed like one who saw far beyond what was obvious. Ayla would go so far as to say that Zora was downright magical.

For her entire life, Ayla had been intrigued by the idea of magic, but it was just that—*an idea.* Despite her mother's best efforts to convince her there was magic in even the most mundane details of life, Ayla knew magic was something that only occurred in fairy tales. Connor had introduced that idea to her early on with his insistence that for anything to be real, it had to be proven by science. Ayla didn't think it was worth arguing. She welcomed the simplicity of his opinion and laughed when he said in his best French accent, in response to his mother's arguments, "No proof, no exist."

But meeting Zora changed everything Ayla ever believed about magic. Zora was magical in every possible way. Her dark brown skin glimmered like little flakes of glitter were buried in her pores. She wore her dark hair on the top of her head like a crown. Her eyes danced slowly and soulfully at times and quickly and playfully at others. She smelled like a baked dessert fresh from the oven; wafts of vanilla and cinnamon emanated from her body. As soon as she moved or opened her mouth, she cast a spell on everyone around her. Her laugh was like birdsong, her smile like a warm embrace.

Zora reminded Ayla of her friend Grace back home in a way that made her miss her home less. She made Ayla feel like Grace was right there beside her. Also like Grace, Zora's most endearing quality was that she was completely oblivious of her effect on people. All she had to do was sit in a room without even saying a word, and she put everyone around her at ease.

Those were just some of her more obvious traits. But her most potent magic was hidden in her hands. On their way to the South, when Ayla had a painful stomachache, Zora placed her hands over Ayla's belly. Ayla felt a few rumbles, and then, within minutes, she felt better.

Perhaps it shouldn't have been surprising that Zora, the daughter of the Medicine Woman, would have a healing touch, yet everything about her surprised Ayla. Zora often seemed lost in her thoughts, yet she tracked everything that happened around her. She not only had eyes in the back of her head but also on both sides and even on top, and all those eyes were accompanied by a nose and ears. Nothing got by her. She took in everything.

Her magical hands could also shift the mood in a room from sad to happy. For example, the travelers had boarded the space train with a cloud of remorse around them, but Zora and her mother sat at the front of the train, holding their hands up with their palms facing the riders. Eventually, everyone's spirits lifted. Ayla had watched closely, and she could feel the air shift around her as the mood lifted in the space train. She had no trouble seeing why Mina adored Zora and was grateful for the close connection forming between herself and Zora as well.

The group followed Zora to a single wall surrounded by what appeared to be three other walls, now crumbled and lying in pieces on the ground. As they walked through the rubble, the moaning sound grew louder. There, at the end of the remaining wall, sat a small child. Her legs were covered in bricks and tattered pieces of drywall. A body with its head in the girl's lap lay in stillness next to her. Zora offered a slight smile as she knelt next to the girl.

"Hello," Zora whispered to the girl. "We have come to help."

Zora leaned in and listened at the mouth of the head in the girl's lap. She also watched the person's chest.

"This one is still breathing," she said to the group. "Come."

Without speaking, the group assembled around the body and began what looked like CPR. Zora moved the body away from the girl while reassuring her with gentle touches and loving eyes the entire time. She then placed a hand on each foot of the person, again seeming to transmute whatever was occurring in their body. Ayla watched in awe as the chest of the body rose higher, slowly but steadily coming back to life, breathing at full capacity. The eyes opened.

"Where is my daughter? Where am I? What happened?" the person asked meekly.

"I am Zora. This is Prem, Mina, Olivia, and Ayla. We heard you were hit by some big storms, and we came from the North to help." Zora's tender gaze appeared to put the face at ease.

"Thank you," the woman said, sounding the slightest bit stronger. "I'm Alice. I didn't think we would ever get help." Alice winced like she was in pain.

"Mama!" The small girl reached for her mother.

"Lucy, honey, we are going to be okay." Alice moved her body slowly and deliberately until she was sitting up next to her daughter.

The group, noting the sun had set, turned on their flashlights and began clearing the bricks and debris from Lucy's small legs. They learned Alice and Lucy had walked into town from their home a few miles away after the second tornado hit. Not long after arriving at this spot, the walls crumbled around them, burying them both in bricks. When Alice had finished digging herself out, a brick fell and hit her on the head.

They had been there for days, eating and drinking from a small ration of food and water they found nearby. Alice had faded in and out of consciousness while Lucy's legs remained buried. They heard voices and even cried out for help, but passersby kept walking. Alice said those who walked by were in a daze and seemed lost. She didn't recognize them.

It looked likely that Lucy's leg was broken, so Prem and Olivia built a small gurney from two boards they found in the debris. They covered her with one of the blankets they'd brought with them and carried her back to camp while Mina and Ayla assisted Alice. Zora led the way.

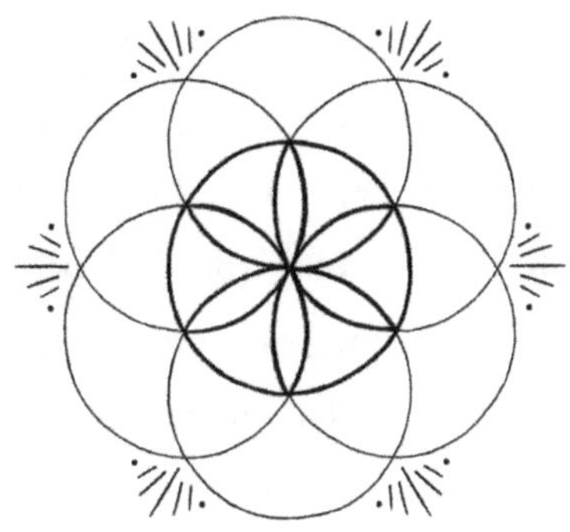

CHAPTER 22

The group followed a similar routine for several days. As people were found, they were brought to camp, where Zora's mother tended to their wounds. Then they were stocked with supplies and helped back to their homes. Lucy looked adorable in her little cast, although it was obvious the cast cramped the girl's spirit and style.

Ayla enjoyed living life by the rhythm of the sun and moon, waking at daybreak and resting when day and night traded places. The daylight seemed to last longer when they needed it to stretch. There were always enough hours. In the process of searching for people who needed help, she developed a deeper appreciation for human nature in general. The people rescued from the rubble quickly blended into the group that came from the North. It felt like they had all known each other entire lifetimes. The unmistaken heartfelt gratitude of the people here in the South made a powerful impact on those who came to help.

While everyone was sleeping on the second or third night, Ayla overheard Noor and Nell wondering how these kind people could have turned on each other in the face of destruction. They seemed to work so well together now. Once they returned to their homes, they moved toward helping each other rebuild what had been destroyed. It was hard to imagine them not helping each other from the start.

Ayla listened as the two of them reviewed stories they'd heard through the day about life in the South before the tornadoes. Nobody mentioned any kind of dissent between the people. On the contrary, life sounded peaceful here. Some shared stories of their horror at watching tornadoes destroy their homes and the utter dismay they felt afterward. They'd never seen or heard anything like it, and they said they hadn't known what to do next.

Ayla wondered if maybe they were in shock. Maybe it was natural for people to turn on each other after something so devastating had happened, especially if they knew no other way. Maybe this was one of those soft spaces where it wasn't clear what to do. Or wasn't there another term for it? Survival of the fittest?

Ayla fell asleep as the questions with no answers scrambled in her head.

Hours later, Mina shook her awake. "Ayla wake up—the Circle is convening! We have new data, and my mom wants you outside."

Ayla was so curious to hear the news, she fell out of her sleeping cot and didn't stop to pull her hair into a ponytail. Members of the Circle crowded into the Communications Room and gathered around a screen.

"We've drawn some conclusions since your departure," Bodhi was saying from the screen. Others stood behind Bodhi, including Ishwa, who had promised to help rebuild the lost Chronicles if possible. Seeing him made Ayla uneasy.

"As soon as you arrived and made contact, some storage space in the Chronicles lit up," Bodhi said, his eyes big with excitement. "New stories began to form and fill the Chronicles. People you haven't even reached yet started coming out of their damaged homes to connect with people. You've started a ripple effect across the South!"

For someone like Bodhi, witnessing history in the making was the only thing more exhilarating than studying history itself.

A ripple effect? *Wow*, Ayla thought, *it's been so long since I heard those words.* It probably hadn't been that long in Eeman time, but it seemed like a very long time since she had arrived here. She realized then how badly she missed her family, especially her mother. Ayla turned to watch Noor—her Eeman mother, she had decided—and loved seeing her face brighten at Bodhi's news. The Chronicles were filling, and the people in the South were helping each other now. Would it be time to go back to Earth?

"What do you think happened?" Noor asked excitedly.

"Well, we've been running scenarios nonstop," Bodhi said. "Our working hypothesis is simple." At this, his excitement seemed to fade. In fact, he seemed disturbed.

"Without the Chronicles to rely on," he said, "the people in the South had no collective history of devastation from time past. Further, as we know, nobody alive today has experienced any kind of devastation before," he said, looking at Ishwa, "and it is a collective occurrence that imprints the Star Within, informing us how to react the next time we experience something similar. No matter how long it has been since the imprinting occurs, it stays with us and is passed from generation to generation. We believe the people there were lost without the imprint of their ancient stories. Had the stories not been erased from the Collective Chronicles, they would have known what to do."

"I don't understand," Noor said. "The Chronicles were there when the tornadoes hit. They turned on each other immediately following the tornadoes. We didn't call on Ayla until then."

"It must be a glitch in the space-time continuum," Bodhi said, even more visibly disturbed. "We can't figure that out either."

"Wait!" Ayla jumped to the front of the group so Bodhi could see her from the screen. "None of you have experienced anything like tornadoes, right? I mean, you've never had those on Eema?"

Bodhi nodded. "That's right, Ayla. As far as we know, Eema has never known a natural disaster."

"Well, maybe it wasn't just the ancient history missing as a collective occurrence that caused them to respond this way. Maybe it was the tornadoes themselves, since they'd never experienced one before!"

Ayla's thoughts from the night before came rushing back to her. The humans she knew reverted to the most basic animal instincts under stress, just as Grandpa George always said: "Every man for himself!" That was it—that was the saying she couldn't remember last night.

"People in the South had never experienced the kind of stress that comes from a tornado," Ayla said. "Why would they know how to respond when it happened?"

Her mouth couldn't form the words quickly enough. "Every person we met here talked about not knowing what to do. There must be some other thing that makes us help each other, but I don't know what it is." Ayla stopped to catch her breath.

"Ishwa, when did Seth erase the Chronicles?" Noor asked.

"It was a long process, Noor," Ishwa said, seeming different now. "It didn't happen all at once."

"So, between the time the tornadoes hit and the time we learned Seth erased the Chronicles, stories were being wiped from the Chronicles?" Bodhi asked. "And then any trace of collective occurrence went too? With no history of tornadoes or natural disaster, there was nothing—*nothing*—guiding the people there, telling them what to do next. Is that it?"

"Right!" Ayla exclaimed.

Nell placed a hand on Noor's shoulder. "Noor, I don't think this is just about the people. I think this is about Eema too."

"What do you mean?" Noor asked.

"Eema is crying. The tornadoes were her cry for help. But her tears looked like betrayal to the people here. They forgot their connection to Eema. They didn't hear her cry."

Nell stopped.

"What do you mean, Nell? I don't understand." Noor looked confused, and the lack of sleep from the last few days was beginning to show in her usually bright eyes.

"The tornadoes felt like betrayal because the people here counted on Eema," Nell said. "To the people, Eema failed them by sending tornadoes. They lost faith in themselves and in each other when they couldn't access answers in their Star Within. They were lost."

Bodhi piped up. "Noor? Nell? There's more. It's the West. Wildfires are now spreading there."

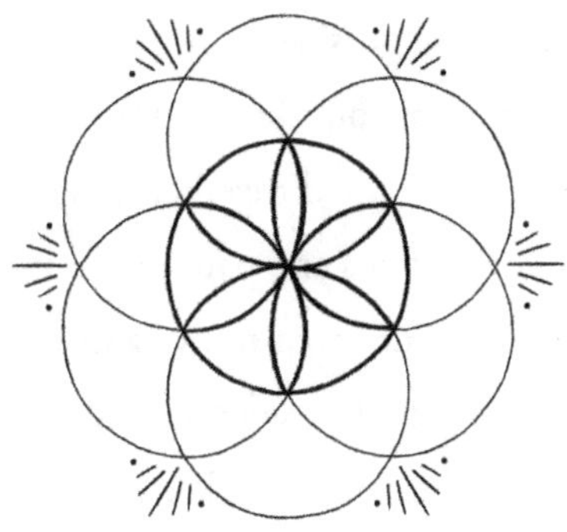

CHAPTER 23

THE RIDE BACK home went much more quickly than the ride to the South. *Why is it always true that the ride back is faster?* Ayla wondered.

Most everyone slept during the ride. Knowing their new friends were safe in the South and that the Mother there had been brought up to date on all of Bodhi's findings, the travelers were tired and eager to return to their homes. And now the members of the Circle knew there was a whole new problem to address: the wildfires spreading in the West. While everyone else in the travel group looked forward to returning to life as normal, the members of the Circle were impatient about having to travel when there was still more work to do.

"What on Eema do we have here?" Olivia asked as the space train landed. She spun around from the spot where she had been watching out the window and looked at Noor. "Noor, I think you need to see this."

Already, all the windows were blocked with curious travelers wondering what was happening outside.

When Ayla got a glimpse out the window, she couldn't believe her eyes. Several rows of people stood together, shoulder to shoulder. The customary bright, playful colors and patterns on their clothing provided a stark contrast to the furrowed brows and frowns on their faces. Ayla strained to see if she could recognize any of them. Some looked like they had been crying, and some looked angry, but the overall effect was that of a group who looked let down.

"I've never witnessed anything like this," Noor said. "What do you think is happening, Nell? They look miserable, even furious. Bodhi said nothing about any of this."

"The only way to know what is happening is to go and see," Nell said.

Noor nodded reluctantly. "Gather your belongings and let's leave the train," she said to the group. "We can come back for the remaining supplies."

The front row of people outside the train formed a wall, forcing the travelers to stay together once they disembarked. Beyond the last row of people, Ayla spotted Bodhi, Ishwa, and the remaining members of the Circle.

A man Ayla didn't recognize stepped forward.

"Father, what are you doing?" Olivia said, her usually light spirit growing heavy at the sight of the man, whom Ayla realized must be Seth.

"Excuse me, love," Seth said. He turned and locked eyes with Noor.

"Noor, all present here and now hereby demand that you step down as Mother of the North," he said. "You have failed us. You must relinquish your duties as Mother."

"What?" Olivia cried. "Dad, what are you doing? Please tell me this isn't happening!"

"Olivia, please be quiet," Seth ordered without expression.

"What *are* you doing, Seth?" Noor asked gently.

An androgynous figure wearing a hood shoved a piece of paper at her. "Here," they said.

Noor unfolded the paper and read it aloud. "Our Mother, Noor of the North, has deceived us. She and the Circle have been keeping secrets from us, lying to us, and spying on us right under our eyes. She has allowed an invader to live in our land. She cannot be trusted.

"Further, Ishwa betrayed us too. Both Noor and Ishwa should step down from their roles in the Circle and be punished for their misdeeds."

Noor looked up at Seth, dumbfounded.

Ayla felt how Noor looked. Was *she* the invader? She was shocked. This was not anything she would expect from the Eemans.

She looked around and saw that every person in every row of the crowd carried a slip of paper like the one from which Noor read. They were nodding in agreement with its demands. A quiet rumble started from within their rows. As it grew louder, it became clear they were chanting, "Go, go, go . . ."

"Seth?" Noor tried to get Seth's attention, but there was no way he could hear her over the chant. He stared ahead, still without expression.

"Seth!" she said again, with greater urgency.

Ayla was terrified. She studied Seth as he stood before her. He was very large, taller than Ishwa or Bodhi. He towered over Noor and everyone around him. He seemed strong by appearance, but in spite of his edge, he had a softness about him.

While in the South, Ayla had become better at reading people. They were so open there. She had expected the experience to be like hearing people's thoughts, since it seemed the people she met here could read her thoughts. But instead of hearing thoughts, she discovered she could simply feel the emotions and experiences stored in people's bodies.

Seth was wide open for reading, despite his large presence and obvious ill will, though Ayla sensed a wall around his Star Within. She felt his pain, his doubt, and his fear. She could now see his pain as a very deep well that also held the pain of several generations, just like the story Olivia told on their way south.

Ayla was so transfixed on Seth and his pain that she didn't realize pandemonium had broken out around her. Dust blew up from the street and into her eyes, and she flinched. She wanted to run, but before she could, she was picked up and carried away.

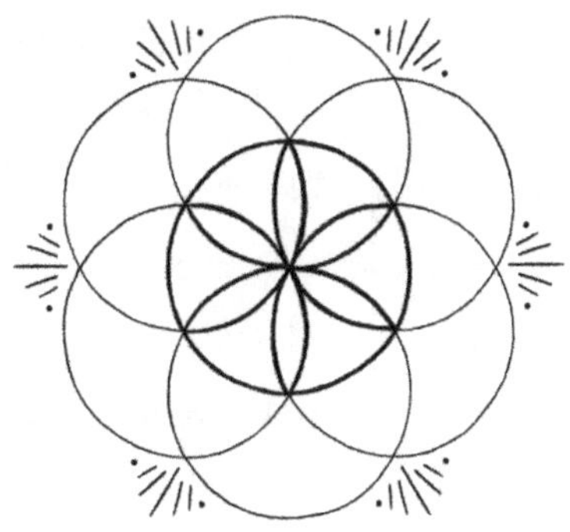

CHAPTER 24

Ishwa's body was more neutral now, and Ayla didn't recognize him at first. Much to her surprise, he had raced to the front of the group and scooped her up. Then he ran toward the Collective Chronicles, carrying her over his shoulder.

Ishwa carried Ayla into the building and straight to the Resource Room, where he set her down. One of the tables was heaped with food and fresh juices and teas, and Ayla realized she was hungry. She began to pick at the food and drinks as the room filled with the other members of the Circle.

Seth and those who stood with him followed them to the building and assembled outside. Ayla learned the Collective Chronicles had been declared a safe zone for the Circle and members of their family years ago. They had never needed the safe zone before, but they were grateful to have it now.

Olivia had decided to stay outside and try to talk to her father. She was distressed, and Ayla guessed she was also embarrassed—a feeling Ayla assumed would be unfamiliar to Olivia.

"Okay, what now?" Noor broke the silence in the room, looking around at each face. She was clearly rattled by the events. "I did not expect this at all, obviously, and I don't know how to respond. Perhaps I've exercised bad judgment. Stepping down, though? *Punishment?* I am unsure about those things. And why? Bodhi? Ishwa? Why did you not prepare us for this?"

"We didn't know," Ishwa said. "We saw folks gathering, and then we saw Seth, and then you were here. It happened quickly."

Something had changed in Ishwa. He seemed more open, but Ayla couldn't read him like she could Seth. He didn't make her uneasy now, though, which was good. But she was so confused by this change, she wasn't sure she could trust her instincts.

Noor took a deep breath and exhaled slowly. "Okay. I imagine that was as alarming for you as it was for me. And what about the fires in the West? This is all so much at once. I'm just not sure . . ."

"Noor?" Nell spoke up from Noor's side. "Let's eat. We cannot do anything well with empty reservoirs. Seth shows no signs of leaving, and we're safe here. I think we can take a moment to catch our breath and refuel. Look at all the beautiful food we have. It will be okay to take a few minutes to recharge."

The group ate mostly in silence. The situation with Seth and the others was on pause for now. Ayla was glad to be eating and feeling more relaxed as the food and drink filled her belly. Afterward, the children of Circle members who had made the journey to the South left to unpack supplies and clean the train. Zora and her mother stayed with the group and appeared to be managing the energy in the room, which felt nice. Ayla wasn't used to seeing anyone upset here, and it was strange to see them this way.

Noor, who was normally so calm and confident, looked like she was just as confused as Ayla. Mina and Prem looked tired. Bodhi was lost in his head somewhere, undoubtedly making nonstop calculations and speculations. She could tell he was anxious to power up the screens.

Then there was a loud knock from outside. Ayla felt the tension rise in the room. Everyone looked around with curiosity in their eyes.

"It's Olivia," Mina said.

How she knew that, Ayla didn't know.

Olivia asked to speak to the group and was welcomed into the room. She seemed at ease there, which surprised Ayla until she remembered Olivia had been there before. How long ago was that? Olivia shot her a little grin, as if she could hear her thoughts and was enjoying it. She had one of the slips of paper with her that Seth and the others had carried outside the space train. She unfolded it and began to talk.

"It doesn't really make sense to me," she began, looking down at the paper in her hand. "I wish he wasn't doing this."

"Whatever it is, it will be okay, Olivia," Noor said. She reached for Olivia's hand and gave it a squeeze. "Thank you for coming and for speaking to us. This cannot be easy for you either."

And then, as Olivia began to explain the group's demands, Ayla watched as Noor listened closely and without interruption.

Olivia shared that while the group had been away, Seth had made it his mission to talk to anyone who would listen to his complaints against Noor and what he was calling her *misdeeds*. He'd proudly shared this fact with Olivia when she went outside, and those gathered around him patted him on the back and cheered him on.

Olivia didn't recognize a lot of the people who were with him in the group because they lived on the outskirts of town. They were part of the greater community but chose to keep to themselves, so they weren't around much. They rarely attended festivals because they didn't understand all the celebrations and storytelling. They were content not to take part in everything the community did together.

Seth had told them about the Collective Chronicles. He told them the building they had always believed to be a simple museum actually contained the records of all that ever was, including their personal stories. He told them members of the Circle sat and watched the records, taking notes on what they saw and making decisions based on the records.

He told them about the tornadoes in the South too, which they hadn't known about, and how the people were lost there after the storms hit. He told them Noor and Bodhi had arranged for an invader to come all the way from Earth and help them—someone who looked like an innocent girl but had done nothing but cause trouble since her arrival. He said the invader had broken up long friendships, like his with Ishwa, and that now wildfires were spreading in the West because of this invader and the evils of Earth that she brought to Eema with her.

He didn't stop there. He also told the people he would make a better leader than Noor and that if they would help him make her step down as Mother, he would take over and make sure nothing bad would ever happen again. He assured them he would send the girl back to Earth and not allow any other invaders to come again. Finally, he told the group that Noor and Ishwa and anyone else who took part in deceiving the community should be punished.

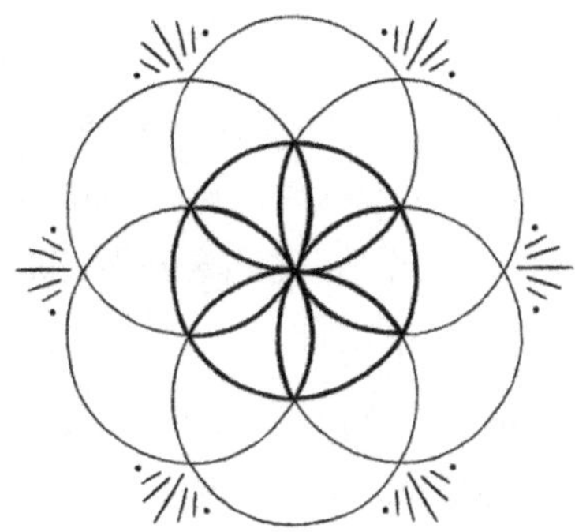

CHAPTER 25

SETH HAD SAID more, but Olivia stopped talking.

"Thank you, Olivia," Noor said when she sensed Olivia was finished.

Suddenly everyone was talking at once.

"Those things are NOT true!"

"What about him and what *he* did?"

"Punished? What does that mean?"

"This is outrageous!"

"He's senseless! He's always been senseless!"

"Who are those people? We don't even know them!"

"I never trusted him!"

"How could he?"

"He's the one who doesn't belong!"

"He should have stayed in the South in the first place! He never should have come here!"

They kept talking as Noor sat still, listening, and Ayla watched, horrified. It hadn't been long since she'd arrived, right? Not just days, but weeks—maybe a month? Of course, they didn't measure time at all here, much less in the way Ayla knew time, so she couldn't be sure. But she would guess she'd been there about three weeks. And never, in any of the Chronicles she'd watched or the interactions she'd witnessed, had a single Eeman shown any kind of outrage like she was seeing now.

Ayla was incredibly confused. Not much of what Seth told those people was even accurate. It sounded like he'd completely changed the story.

Olivia stared at her boots. Ayla wondered what she was thinking and whether she agreed with what her father said. Ayla knew she should go back to Earth, and she wanted to go back. She wasn't sure she had helped at all. She wanted to see her mom.

Suddenly Ayla remembered when her own mother, Helen, had been through something like this. One of her employees had been caught falsifying records. He was more like a peer, but he worked as a contractor in her department. It had been a nightmare for Helen and an intense time for Ayla's family—investigations into the records, the questioning of her mother's character because she oversaw the program, and even a lawsuit against the agency where she worked. Some local politicians made public statements, calling for Helen to resign from her position. Local parents were outraged.

It had taken a long time to piece together the truth, not so much because the facts weren't obvious but because once the public got involved, nobody wanted to wait for the facts. They just wanted to blame Helen and send the guy to jail. Once it was proven she had nothing to do with what he had done, nobody was paying attention anymore. They had moved on to the next big story.

Every once in a while, Ayla still heard rumors or jokes made at the expense of her mom. When she went to her mom with them, distressed by what she'd heard, Helen would say, "It's our culture, Bug. We're just wired that way. People like to have someone to blame when things go wrong. It's reassuring to be able to assign blame to someone."

Why? Why was it reassuring? Ayla couldn't remember.

And how could this be happening *here*? The Eemans weren't wired for blame or for rumors. These normally calm, peaceful people were protesting and shouting at each other. What was even happening?

She wanted to cry. She felt responsible for all of this chaos. Maybe there wouldn't be so much chaos if she hadn't come. Could she have brought the chaos with her? Was Ishwa right about that when he'd said it before? And if he'd wanted her gone before, why had he carried her into the Collective now? That was so weird. Was he protecting her now? For once, she wished there were more clear answers than there were questions.

"Ayla! What's going on up there?" Olivia tapped the side of Ayla's head, near her temple.

"I—I'm just thinking." Ayla felt unsure of herself, defensive. "But you knew that already, right? You probably even *know* what I'm thinking."

Olivia nodded, then said, "I'm going to get some air. Would you care to join me? It might even help clear your head."

The two of them slid through a side door, hoping nobody would see them. They walked outside and around toward the back of the building, passing the cedar trees where the Circle had met the day Ayla found out Noor, not Bodhi, was the leader of this community.

As they walked, Olivia jumped into the telling of a story she remembered about herself as a small child. She had been poking around in an old chest when her father had stopped her and told her never to go near the chest again. It was then that she first suspected her father was different than the rest of the adults she knew. She had never heard anyone snap at any child like he did that day.

When Olivia was finished with that story, she started a new story, and then another one. She talked quickly, like she had been holding these stories inside her body for her entire life and this was the first chance she had to share them. Ayla listened, watching Olivia as she spoke, still amazed by how much Olivia reminded her of her dear friend Amanda in her enthusiasm for stories and life.

Just as Ayla began to wonder if they should get back to the group inside, they rounded a corner, which allowed them to see what was happening in front of the Collective. Olivia stopped abruptly, in the middle of a sentence, and stared.

Two chairs were placed facing each other in front of the Collective. Noor sat in one. One of the people from the group outside the train sat in the other. Behind that chair was a long line of people. It looked like everyone who had greeted them at the train was in line.

"What's going on?" Ayla asked.

"Ayla, this is marvelous," Olivia said, speaking in a whisper. "It's a *Listening*."

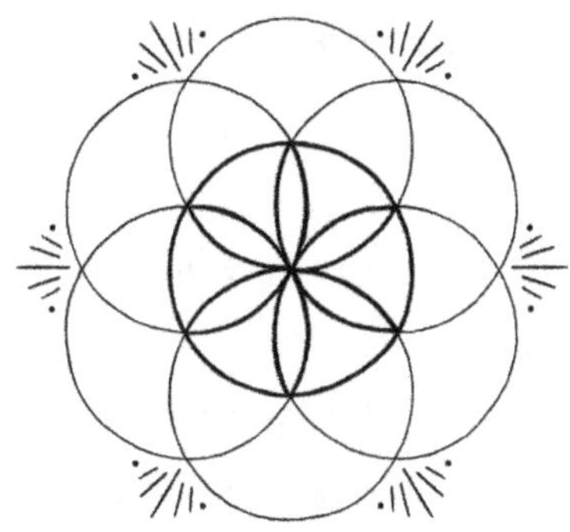

CHAPTER 26

Olivia pulled Ayla along as she walked closer to where Noor was sitting. She motioned for Ayla to sit next to her, and they settled in behind a tree not far from Noor but out of sight. If they were completely quiet, they could hear bits of what was being said between Noor and the person sitting opposite her.

Ayla whispered, "What is it, Olivia? What's a *Listening*?"

Olivia held her finger to her pursed lips like a librarian, indicating Ayla should stop talking. She pointed to her ear and leaned toward Noor.

Oh, right. Ear. Listening. Got it.

A woman with dark hair was speaking. "We have never felt welcome here, Noor," she said.

"You have never felt welcome." Noor nodded, tilting her head slightly to the left, just like Helen Stone did when she was engaged in conversation. Then she nodded again, as if telling the woman to continue.

Noor took in each spoken sentence like a bit of food. She listened, repeated what was said, and then, when it appeared she had swallowed the statement, she nodded and the person speaking to her continued.

"Do you think anyone is wondering where I am?" Ayla whispered to Olivia.

"They know you're safe, so no. You're fine," Olivia said. "Everyone is probably trying to see and hear as much of this as possible. It's been a long time since we've had a Listening."

Ayla realized it wasn't that hard to see what the Listening entailed. Noor was fully and completely listening as, one by one, the people who had gathered with Seth shared what bothered them. It might have been the most remarkable thing Ayla had ever seen. She recalled dinners at home where she and Connor talked over each other as their parents half-listened, also trying to have their own conversation at the same time. Grandma Ettie talked nonstop all the time. She barely stopped to catch her breath. She couldn't possibly listen with all the talking she did.

Her friends at home, Grace and Amanda, were both good listeners, but when the three of them were together, it was rare anyone completed a sentence without being interrupted. The topics of conversation changed more quickly than the weather in Michigan. Ayla tried to picture every person she knew at home, and as soon as she saw their faces in her mind's eye, she immediately noticed they looked distracted. Did anyone she know ever really listen?

When each person sitting in front of Noor finished what they had to say, Noor responded by saying, "Thank you. I believe you. I am grateful you shared this with me." She managed to show a genuine appreciation for what the person said while at the same time seeming not to take anything personally. She didn't stop anyone. She didn't ask any questions. She just kept listening. Nodding. Acknowledging. Thanking.

Each person stood and walked away from Noor visibly lighter. Some smiled. Some had tears in their eyes. Some hugged Noor. In a way, Ayla thought whatever it was the people said mattered less than the experience they had of being heard. She was in awe.

The Listening went on for hours, into the night, until each person had a turn to speak. Olivia and Ayla huddled closer together as the sun went down.

Olivia was absolutely enthralled with the process of the Listening, even though she couldn't hear everything being said. She barely moved her body as she watched. Every once in a while, Ayla watched Olivia watching the Listening. Seeing how the Listening held Olivia's attention made the experience even more special for Ayla. She knew she was witnessing something powerful.

When the last person finished and said good-bye to Noor, Noor closed her eyes and laid her hands, one on top of the other, over her heart. Ayla thought Noor looked like she was praying.

"Now what?" Ayla whispered.

"Well, I'm not sure exactly," Olivia said. "It looks like the crowd has dispersed. I don't see my dad. I think everyone must be going home."

Olivia turned to face Ayla, and Ayla noticed she looked tired.

"So, you don't see that happen very often?"

"No. Never," Olivia said. "The way I understand it, the Listening was one of the first things practiced at the Mother's Table. I've never actually seen one. I don't know if there have been any Listenings since I was born. Are you hungry?"

Ayla laughed. Olivia could move between subjects as easily as she danced.

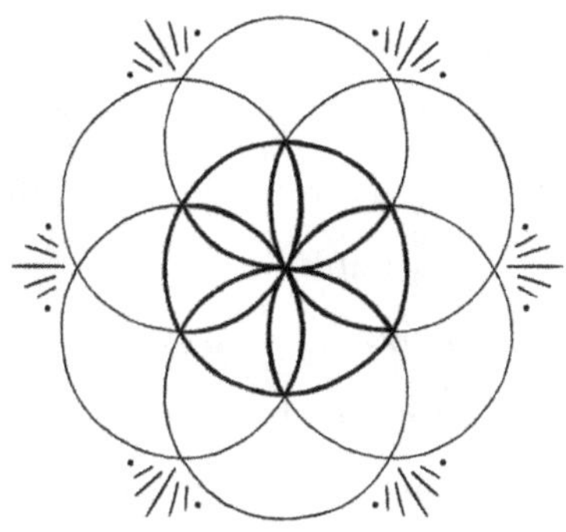

CHAPTER 27

Olivia had been right about the Circle. As Noor participated in the Listening, the members of the Circle had watched from various places in the building. Only Nell left the Collective, and that was to light candles at a nearby Mother's Table in honor of the courage it took for the community members to shed light on their stories by sharing them with Noor. Everyone went home after the Listening to eat and rest. Ayla slept deeply, glad to be back in her own bed, or at least her own bed on Eema.

She felt refreshed in the morning and, with a clear head, began to wonder what was left for her to do on Eema now that the tornadoes had stopped and the people in the South were working together to rebuild their community. Whatever was happening here with Seth and the community members who were upset, it seemed too daunting for

Ayla. Noor suggested they still needed her, but it didn't seem like Noor even knew what to do next.

The Circle was called back to the Collective Chronicles and Ayla joined them, hoping the group would figure out their next steps. Perhaps they would even figure out it was time for her to go home.

"What did the community have to say, Noor?" Ishwa asked. Ishwa's new, more peaceful demeanor was a welcome change. Ayla still didn't feel she could trust him completely, but she felt much less intimidated by his presence.

"Well, a few issues came up repeatedly," Noor said. Her eyes were clear, and she looked more refreshed than she had since the trip. "Outside of those issues, though, it felt like people merely wanted me to hear their stories."

Before anyone could ask another question or make a comment, Bodhi switched on the screen. The group watched in silence as a wildfire raged through a thick, beautiful forest.

"No people have been hurt, and no structures appear to have been damaged," he said. "But so far the fires in the West have burned acres and acres of magnificent trees and have displaced numerous members of the wildlife community."

Ayla could see by the expressions on the faces around the room that watching trees burn to ashes could very well be as devastating to the people of Eema as seeing people's homes destroyed by fire would be on Earth. Nell was in tears, whispering prayers to Eema and begging for Eema's mercy.

"Those trees," she said, her voice barely audible. "They are fully grown. They cannot be replaced. What a tremendous loss."

"Yes, Nell," Bodhi said. He rested a hand on her shoulder. "It is devastating to see what's happening."

"What can we do?" she asked.

"Maybe the best we can do right now is wait," he said. "We should know the extent of the damage before we do anything. We could try reaching out to our brothers and sisters in the West. We're also studying the patterns of wildfires on Earth. But, Noor, what do you suggest?"

"Hmmm?" Noor stared at the screen but didn't appear to be seeing anything.

"Noor? Are you okay?" Nell's eyes widened as she moved her attention from the screen to Noor.

"Hmmm?" Noor said again, turning to look at Nell.

"Bodhi! Call the Medicine Woman! Clear the room!" The force behind Nell's voice was surprising and out of character for the usually soft-spoken Nell.

Ayla rushed over and grabbed Noor's hand. Noor didn't even look at her. Her eyes were glued to the screen. She looked hypnotized.

"They want me to go," Noor whispered.

"Who wants you to go, Noor?" Bodhi's brow furrowed as he used a screen to call for the Medicine Woman.

"Them." Noor motioned toward the window. "Our community. Our people."

"I suspect her energy was completely drained in the Listening, Bodhi," Nell said.

Nell's transformation from a soft, tender being with tear-filled eyes to someone in command intrigued Ayla. There were so many sides to this person!

"What does that mean?" Bodhi asked as he crouched in front of Noor. He tried to look into her eyes, but she closed them. "I don't understand," he said. "She seemed so awake this morning. She was optimistic, hopeful. She said she learned so much from the Listening. Honestly, Nell, she was nearly euphoric."

Ayla didn't know what she should do. Bodhi and Noor had been such steadfast forces of calm and grace since she'd arrived. Now they appeared to be losing their minds right before her eyes. She left the room to find a cloth for Noor's forehead. A cool washcloth was her mom's trick for soothing any ailment.

When Ayla returned, the Medicine Woman was there, lightly rubbing oils on the back of Noor's neck. She was burning something that smelled suspicious. It looked like a bundle of dried leaves. She moved the bundle from place to place on Noor's body. Ayla watched in awe, noticing how Noor relaxed as the burning bundle of leaves moved over her body.

"Sage," Nell whispered to Ayla.

Ayla nodded, remembering that Grace's mom used sage to "cleanse her space" at home. Grace's dad teased her when he smelled the burning sage, so she tried to do it when nobody was around. Amanda, Grace, and Ayla giggled when they smelled it, and Grace's mom took that as confirmation it was working. "See, the air is already lighter," she would say with a wink. If Ayla squinted, she could see a resemblance between the Medicine Woman and Grace's mom. *What if we all have twins here on Eema?* she thought.

Ayla's lips formed a small smile, and she wondered if the walls of the room were slowly expanding. She could feel the heaviness lifting from her chest. It made her sleepy and awake at the same time. Maybe it wouldn't hurt to close her eyes for just a bit . . .

When Ayla opened her eyes, Noor was speaking in whispers to Nell and Bodhi.

"Whoa, what happened?" Ayla asked. She felt like she'd been sleeping for days.

"Hi there!" Noor said with a smile. Then she turned back to Nell and Bodhi. "It's been so long since we've had a Listening. Outside of my training, I don't remember ever conducting an official Listening. Not as the Mother, anyway. And I forgot one of the key details in opening that dialogue between the members of the community and myself."

It appeared that Noor was back, which comforted Ayla.

"What did you forget?" she asked.

"I think you would know it as establishing boundaries?" Noor said, smiling at her. "These would be energetic boundaries. I so badly wanted to hear what needed to be said that I left myself open and absorbed too much of the energy given off by those who came to share."

"What did it do to you?" Ayla imagined the energy moving around in circles, violating boundaries.

Noor broke out into laughter. "Yes! It does resemble that, Ayla!"

"With a firm but flexible boundary," Nell said, "Noor could listen without absorbing the feelings associated with the stories. The people who came had much to say. Some had carried their stories for generations. As they spoke, the emotions flooded out of them."

"And I held them all here." Noor put her hand over her heart.

"That was frightening, Noor. You have to protect that big heart of yours." Bodhi pulled Noor into his arms. "I'm glad you're back. Now we really have a lot to figure out!"

He turned his attention to the screen and the fires burning before his eyes.

Then, as if he had been waiting for his cue on the other side of the door, Ishwa burst into the room.

"Noor," he said, more loudly than he normally spoke. "Have you looked outside lately?"

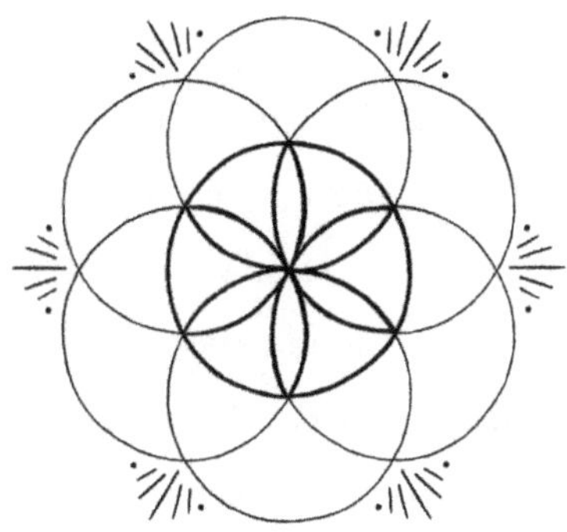

CHAPTER 28

Ishwa went to the window and motioned for the others to join him.

"Look—they're not finished." Ishwa pointed to a group of people who had assembled outside the building. Some held signs that read "It's time for the Mother to go!" Others were waving clenched fists in the air, chanting, "Go, go, go!"

"Noor, you never told us what they said at the Listening," Ishwa said. The fire had returned to his eyes. "What is going on out there?"

"Ishwa, calm down," Noor said. "We have already learned you do not make wise choices when you're angry."

She took a deep breath in, closed her eyes, paused, and then exhaled.

"I am not entirely surprised that the people have gathered here to express dissent over the Mother's Table," she began. "There are certainly issues we need to address as leaders of our community. For starters, those who live on the outskirts of town feel disenfranchised from the larger community—"

"Well, they could try moving closer into town!" Ishwa said. "What did you tell them? What promises did you make?"

"Ishwa, the point of the Listening is to *listen*," Noor said. "I said nothing. I looked into their eyes, I listened to their words, and I caught their stories. A Listening is not the time to respond with promises or to defend myself or the Mother's Table. Our Mother's Table has served us since the Mother of the First People greeted the New People when they arrived. It will continue to serve us. Let us now gather around this table and discuss what to do next."

Noor sat down and opened her notebook, preparing for a discussion. Ayla sat down but found herself squirming, preoccupied with her thoughts and memories of home. People were protesting the Mother's Table? How could that be? How could anyone object to this beautiful, peaceful, and apparently perfect place? What could they possibly be upset about? Was the air too fresh? The grass too green? The food too delicious? Were there not enough stars in the sky? As far as Ayla could tell, Eema was perfection. The First People and all the people who followed revered Eema, their town, and each other.

She had come here to help after the tornadoes hit the South, and she had helped in some way, but now what? The people outside the building looked like the kind of protestors she was used to seeing in the United States. They looked outraged, and she could not even begin to imagine why. She suspected it was time to go back to the chaos where she felt more comfortable—back to Earth. She couldn't imagine anything else she could do to help.

Noor cleared her throat. "There was never an indication they were in a state of discontent," she said, as composed as Ayla had ever seen her. "Did any of you pick up on that? Did Seth share that with you, Ishwa?"

"The only thing he ever said that even came close was that he thinks we need a Father's Table and that he thinks *he* should be the Father," Ishwa said, facing the window. "Quite honestly, I thought he was joking."

The room erupted in comments from everyone around the table. Noor put up her hand to quiet them.

"We have always had a Mother and a Mother's Table," she said, pursing her lips and coming as close to an eye roll as Ayla had ever seen from her. "It's not the Mother's Table that needs to change. It's them. They should appreciate how good we have it here. Life on Eema is bliss compared to other places—like Earth! We all know how bad it is to live on Earth. Right, Ayla?"

Ayla stared at Noor, willing herself to agree, but nothing came out. She felt, once again, like her world had been tipped on its side. Everything she had come to believe about Eema and even Noor was called into question in that moment.

"I—I don't know," Ayla stammered. "I'm sorry. I really don't think I can help you here. I think I need to go home now." She stared at her lap, pulling at a thread on her tunic.

"Finally!" Ishwa threw up his arms.

"If you leave now, I'm afraid you would not be ready," Noor said.

"Ready for what?" Ayla asked.

"Ayla, when you came here, we told you we needed your help. We suspected the chaos on Earth had spilled over, impacting us here." The kindness in Bodhi's voice melted Ayla.

"You are helping us see beyond what is obvious to us," he continued. "You are helping us navigate the gray area in that space. You are the reason we went to the South, and that trip made all the difference to us and the people there. Now there are fires in the West like never before, and we don't know what's next. And until calm replaces the chaos back on Earth, we are still in danger here. When you go home to Earth, we need you to help us there too. As we told you before, we just aren't willing to take the chance that all this chaos, moving back and forth between us, will end us all."

"Um, what?" Ayla said. "You think I can help you *on Earth*? Do you have any idea what's happening on Earth? Or how many people are already trying to make changes there? And how many people are resisting it? It's bananas. Noor is right—Eema is a far better place to live than Earth. How you think a kid from Earth could help you here is beyond me. I think you need to call on someone more powerful—probably even *older*—than me to help you out."

Ayla rolled her eyes at Bodhi. Yes, he was kind, but maybe he wasn't as wise as she thought.

"Listen, Ayla." Nell's typical softness had returned. "There is a reason you are here that is beyond even what we know now. Young people on Earth are more open than adults. As such, young ones can make the biggest impact. You *can* help us. When it's time for you to go, we will know it. *You* will know it. Your work here is not done."

Ayla felt her body relax as Nell spoke. *There's a reason I'm here. Young ones can make the biggest impact. When it's time for me to go, I will know it. My work here is not done.* Nell's words echoed through Ayla's body, filling her with resolve. As had become the routine on Eema, she didn't understand any part of what was happening with her mind but felt the rightness in her body enough to relax. To stay. To do her own listening and learning. To help in any way she could.

"Okay. Fine. I'll stay," she said. "I can't guarantee I'll be able to help you here—or back on Earth—but I'll do my best."

Ayla paused, thinking about Noor's words and her unwillingness to see that it may not be the people outside the building who needed to change but rather the people *inside* the building.

"I will stay," Ayla said again. "But just so you know, you may not like what I have to say."

Just then, a piece of paper flew into the room from under the door.

"What's that?" Ishwa hissed.

One of the members of the Circle leaned down to pick it up and read it aloud. "Dear Noor, Please come to my home tomorrow morning to discuss our terms. The people gathered outside the Collective will not stop their demonstration of unrest until we have spoken and reached an agreement. In peace, Seth"

"What?" Noor asked. "Why can't he just come here?"

"He wants *you* to go *there*," Ayla said. "You have to bend a little, Noor. You must go to him."

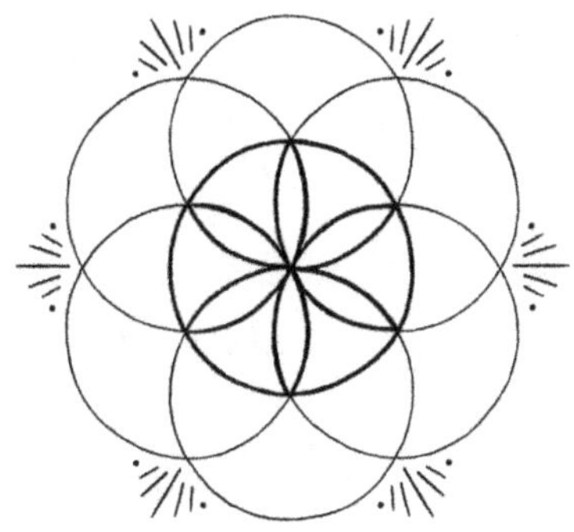

CHAPTER 29

Noor wanted some time alone with Ayla, and the members of the Circle wanted a break from all of it—the Collective Chronicles, the wildfires on the screen, the protestors, and even each other. Noor had made notes on the concerns voiced at the Listening so everyone could review them while going their separate ways for a lunch break. They would reconvene after lunch and make plans for Noor's visit to Seth.

Noor and Ayla ate together in silence.

"Well, Ayla, what else do you have to say that I will not like?" Noor asked after they finished eating.

"I . . . I . . ." Ayla struggled to find the words to describe what she was feeling.

"It's okay, Ayla. I want to hear what you have to say."

Ayla shifted in her seat, sitting up straighter. "Well, first, I think the idea of the Listening is cool, but I don't get why you didn't say anything to the people who shared their stories with you. Couldn't you have said something?"

"I—" Noor began.

"And then, what you said before lunch—with the Circle. You said *they* have to change—the people, not the Mother's Table. I mean, would it hurt for the Mother's Table to make some changes?"

"I—" Noor tried again.

"I mean, I love it here, Noor. I think it's perfect here. It's dreamy, like a fairy tale, even. It's probably even heavenly. You know how much I wish Earth had done things differently. I love Eema. Being here gives me hope that there are other ways for humans to treat each other. And it doesn't even seem like we're *that* far off on Earth. We *could* be more like you are here. But I don't know. I mean, well, doesn't it seem like *you* could stand to make some changes too?"

Ayla stopped talking.

"Are you finished?" Noor asked. "I wanted to answer your questions, but you just kept going. Can I say something now?"

She smiled hopefully at Ayla, who nodded.

"Okay, thank you."

Now it was Noor's turn to shift and sit up straighter. She cleared her throat and paused for a moment. Then she said, "The Listening is for listening. It's how we've always done it. Nobody here has ever—what do you call it? protested?—in such anger, as they are doing now outside the building. Not as far as I know. So, yes, I can see now that more must be needed from the Mother's Table. Something must come after the Listening."

Noor stopped, looking closely at Ayla, who again nodded.

"Ayla, the Mother's Table has worked since our community first formed. It has always been our way. When New People come here, they are given the opportunity to stay when they agree to our way. They know what they agreed to. If they are not content with the way we operate, they can leave.

"This is the way we protect our people and keep peace. It is the Mother's Way. It is probably why Seth's family left the South. Something about that way didn't work for them, and they were told to leave. And now our way isn't working for Seth. He probably needs to go before he causes further disruption. I will suggest that when I see him tomorrow. I will give him that opportunity.

"I am glad you love it here, Ayla. Bodhi and I are both glad. We are grateful you've had the opportunity to see our ways. We trust you will take what you've learned here and share it on Earth. We know you can help stop the chaos there, spreading the wisdom of our ways. Thank you for being here, and thank you for staying. And most of all, thank you for continuing to respect *our* ways."

Noor smiled again, taking Ayla's hand in hers.

Ayla had come to appreciate this point in their conversations. Noor's usual warm, tingly touch was reassuring. It made Ayla feel safe. And she wanted more than anything to feel safe right now because she found Noor's words unsettling. She waited for the peaceful feeling she normally experienced when Noor touched her to put her mind at ease. She waited. And waited. Noor's hand was ice cold.

"Do you understand, Ayla?"

As Noor spoke, Ayla noticed that her face looked normal and her voice sounded normal, but something was different.

"Noor, no—no, I do *not* understand," Ayla said. "Your words are empty. It's like you don't even care about *all* the people in your community anymore. And your hand is cold. It's never cold. You're actually creeping me out, Noor."

"Ayla . . . ?" As her voice trailed off, Noor stared past Ayla like she was invisible.

Ayla grabbed Noor by her shoulders and gently shook her. "I know you're in there, Noor. Listen to me. I remember the Chronicle about the first Mother's Table. The two women, the Mother of the First People and the Mother of the New People, they talked for a long time. They listened to each other. And then they responded to each other. They agreed on the ways *together*.

"When was the last time you did that? Mina said New People still come here and that a lot of the newest people are the ones outside right now. When was the last time you actually had a conversation at the Mother's Table?"

Ayla waited. If she was going to stay any longer on Eema, this place she had come to love, she decided she would defend the very things that made her fall in love with it. Like the Mother's Table. The beautiful landscape and the tranquility. The people and their reverence for Eema and for each other.

The way she had come to understand these things and the way they appeared to her now had shifted, though. And now Noor seemed to have slipped off to her very own brand-new planet. Had she taken in too much again? Did she need the Medicine Woman? Ayla had run out of things to say, so she waited, hoping Noor would pick up on her thoughts and respond. But how long could she really wait like this? What if Noor was permanently gone?

Ayla tried again. "Noor, come on. I know this is hard for you. You've been through a lot lately. The tornadoes, the trip to the South, the Listening, the protestors, the fires—now this meeting with Seth. When times are tough at home, my mom always says, 'You are stronger than all of this.' *You* are stronger than *this*, Noor. Your people need you. Eema needs you. Come on—where are you?"

Ayla searched Noor's eyes for a sign, for anything she could recognize as Noor.

There it was.

Noor's eyes filled with tears. "I—I closed, Ayla! It wasn't by choice. And I know now it was never a choice for Ishwa. We must just . . . close. Maybe when it's all too much? When we are made to hear what we don't want to hear?"

Noor shrugged, looking childlike in her wonder over what she just felt.

"I'm open now, though!" she said. "I'm back. You brought me back. Thank you."

Noor's skin tingled against Ayla's, regaining its warmth.

"I must remain open to speak to Seth," she said, looking eagerly at Ayla. "I need to know what happened in his past. I need to know why his family left the South, if it's even possible to know. I think that will help me reach him and convince him everything is better this way."

Better this way? Did Noor not hear a single word Ayla had just said? Does being closed make you clueless?

Ayla waited for the usual questions and doubts to take over her head, but instead, for the first time since her arrival on Eema—and maybe even for the first time in a long time—she saw the path in front of her. She had to make sure Noor was open when she went to see Seth.

"What about these books?" Ayla asked. She got up and walked over to the bookshelves behind the screens. "Don't these books hold the same stories as the Chronicles? Would they tell us what happened to Seth's family?" She cocked her head to the side to read the spines.

"Well . . ." Noor waved her hand in the air. "I hadn't thought of that. But yes. Okay, yes, there—that one there should tell us the story of Seth."

Ayla pulled the book off the shelf and handed it to Noor, who started thumbing through it.

"Ohhh, right," Noor murmured. "Mm-hmm."

"What? Does it say anything?"

"These books are formatted differently than the stories we see on the screen, Ayla. They're categorized by person rather than event. So, here, look here."

Noor pointed to the first page. Ayla read Seth's name and three others. She recognized Olivia's name, of course, because she was Seth's daughter.

"So, that's his mother?" Ayla asked, pointing to one of the other names. "And his wife? And Olivia's his daughter. Where's his father's name?"

"Oh, we don't record the fathers," Noor said, as if that should be obvious. She pointed to another page. "And look—see? I don't believe this is going to help."

Before Ayla could formulate a thought, let alone a response, she noticed the words on the page had changed. Noor flipped through the book and all the words on all the pages kept changing, as if someone was typing and deleting them right from a screen.

"How does that happen?" Ayla asked in awe.

"The first few pages are the facts. Those facts rarely change. It's essentially a list of the important people in Seth's story. Names may be added throughout his human life, but once a name is added, it cannot be removed."

"But no father? His father's name isn't recorded among the names of people who are *important in his life*?"

"Right," Noor said, again as if that were obvious. She may as well have added *duh!* on the end. She closed the book and set it on the table. "Only the mother and his life partner and their children, if he has a life partner and if they have children. The rest of the book can change depending on the choices Seth makes throughout his life.

"Our stories are always subject to change, sometimes by choice and sometimes not. His dissatisfaction with us now is most likely causing his story to change like this. He clearly does not know where he is headed next. See, I don't have the answers I sought, but this is still helpful information."

Ayla closed her mouth, which she just realized had been hanging open. She was in complete disbelief of what she'd just witnessed. No fathers? How was Noor so nonchalant about that, as if a father was not an important person in someone's life? Was Bodhi okay with that? Maybe helping Eema was going to be trickier than Ayla thought. Maybe they didn't really even know what kind of help they needed.

Just then, Bodhi burst into the room. "Noor! Ayla! You are *never* going to believe this!"

He ran to the windows and pulled open the curtains.

"It's *snow*!" he exclaimed.

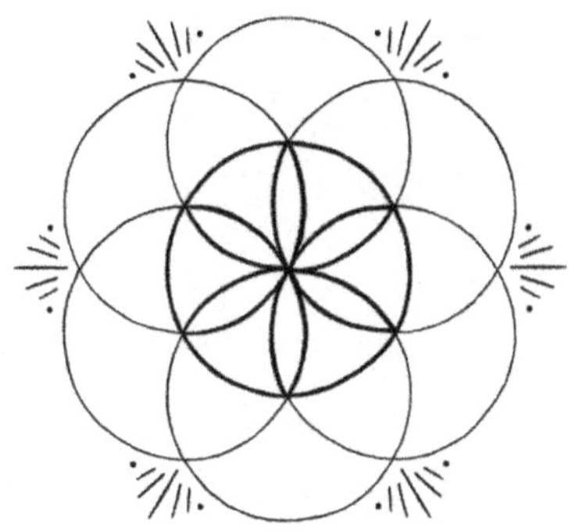

CHAPTER 30

Ayla watched as the members of the Circle filtered into the room and once again gathered at the windows. The windowpane was becoming a lot like the screens as the Circle observed from inside what was happening outside. Even though Noor had gone outside to listen, Ayla was now aware that nobody inside was engaging with those outside. They had even begun referring to the protestors as "the others."

Ayla peered around Nell's shoulder and noticed the people outside were already shivering.

"Don't they need coats?" Ayla wondered aloud.

"Coats?" Ishwa turned and glared at Ayla. "What on Eema is *coats*?"

"Ishwa, it's a *coat*! You don't know what a coat is?" Ayla folded her arms in front of her chest, rubbing her hands on her upper arms to remind Ishwa what a coat was.

Ishwa shook his head, sighed, and turned back to the window.

"What's a coat?" Nell whispered in Ayla's ear.

As far as she could tell, this whole situation was getting weirder and weirder. She couldn't believe these wise beings didn't know what coats were.

"It's a thing you wear," she said. "Like a blanket, but with sleeves, and preferably a hood. It keeps you warm. If they don't get some coats on their bodies, they're going to freeze out there." Ayla suspected Nell would be able to help.

Nell raised her eyebrows like she did when she was alarmed. "It doesn't snow here, Ayla. We have never needed coats to keep us warm. We don't even *have* coats."

"Okay, well, blankets, then? Or shawls? They need something!" Ayla was losing patience.

"Right!" Nell made some swipes on a nearby screen, and shortly afterward Olivia and Mina showed up at the Collective Chronicles to help. Ayla followed them to a room where there were piles of blankets. They cut several of the blankets into strips to make scarves and babushkas for hats.

Ayla surprised herself with her industriousness. It felt great to be accomplishing something so specific. She knew from living through many Michigan winters that cold could be dangerous. She worried that even these blankets and makeshift accessories wouldn't be warm enough, but she hoped Noor's visit to Seth would lead to a quick resolution so everyone would go inside.

As they worked, Ayla asked, "Mina, what do you think of the Mother's Table?"

"What do I *think* of it? Not much, I guess. It's like your government, if that's what you mean." Mina was concentrating intently on her cutting and forming.

"Do you think it could be a Father's Table instead? Or do you think you could have a Father instead of a Mother?"

"Whoa, whoa, whoa, Ayla!" Olivia said, holding up her hands. "We've always had a Mother's Table—it's just the way it is. Just because my outlandish dad is suggesting we name *him* Father and start a Father's Table doesn't mean we should actually do it!" Olivia shook her head and rolled her eyes.

"Right, Ayla," Mina said. "Plus, we can't just *make* someone our leader like that. They have to be appointed or born into leadership."

"*Born* into leadership?" Ayla was intrigued. "Like royalty?"

"I guess." Mina shrugged.

"So, then, are you next in line? Will you be the next Mother?" Ayla asked.

Both Mina and Olivia nodded.

"Wow, that's a pretty big deal!" Ayla slapped Mina on the back in congratulations.

"We'll see. That's a long way off. A *looooooooong* way off."

"So, wait," Ayla said. The thoughts in her head were beginning to spin. "If the Mother is appointed or born into leadership, then have all the Mothers come from the same family throughout time?"

"Yeah, more or less, I guess," Mina said. She held up a handful of makeshift scarves. "How'd I do?"

"Great! We should probably wrap ourselves up before we head outside," Ayla said. "I still can't believe you've never had snow."

Ayla tied a babushka and scarf around her neck, showing Mina and Olivia how to do the same.

"Nothing extreme here," Olivia said. "Our weather is smooth and calm—just like our future Mother." She winked at Mina.

The girls gathered their materials and headed outside. The air was colder than normal—just cold enough for the snow to stick to the ground but not so cold that anyone would be in danger of freezing anytime soon. Some of the people gathered outside the building stood with their necks bent back, squinting as they looked up into the sky. Giggles floated into the air as some tried to catch snowflakes on their tongues. They looked like a bunch of kids on a playground in the first snow.

Mina and Olivia looked at Ayla. Could they play too? Ayla nodded and took their piled blankets so they could twirl in circles, catching snow. She had to laugh as she draped the blankets around shoulders and helped the protestors adjust their makeshift hats and scarves. They nodded, smiled, and thanked Ayla but didn't seem at all concerned about the weather.

Watching Mina play in the snow, Ayla couldn't imagine her as the Mother. What would it be like to know that someday you would be the leader of your land? It had to be scary!

Mina didn't seem to mind. Ayla knew she would make a great Mother. She was calm yet playful. She was thoughtful and resourceful. She cared a lot about other people. She *loved* Eema.

"I *am* a little nervous," Mina whispered in Ayla's ear, sneaking up on her and catching her by surprise.

"Nervous about being the Mother?"

"Yes, I suppose. I've been in training my entire life, so I don't worry about not knowing *what* I'm supposed to do. It's more a matter of wondering *if* I could actually do it."

Ayla was surprised. Mina usually seemed so confident. "Why wouldn't you be able to do it, Mina? You seem competent to me. I think you'd make a great leader. A great Mother."

"I don't know. I don't think my mom really understands it yet, but I can see things are changing. My friends and I are well aware of that. What I've learned to do so far may no longer be the right thing to do by the time I become Mother."

Mina jumped back as a small snowball hit her in the shoulder. The girls spun around to find Olivia laughing so hard she fell to the ground.

"Snowball!" Olivia yelled through her laughter.

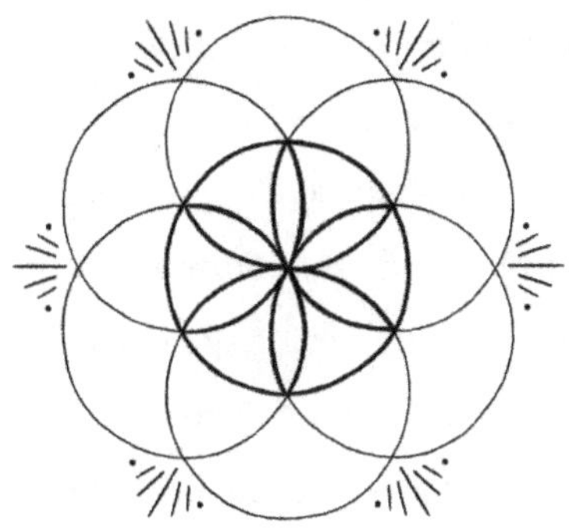

CHAPTER 31

The girls stayed outside, making sure everyone was warm enough, while the Circle met with Noor to review her notes from the Listening. Later, on the way home from the Collective, Noor and Bodhi shared some of what was discussed with Ayla and Mina.

Many of those who had stood in line to talk to Noor had arrived here in the last twenty years or so and had built homes on the outskirts of town. Rather than coming in large groups, like the first settlers did, they came alone or with just their immediate families. They seemed content for the most part, but some of what they shared indicated they'd suffered some confusion and pain during their time here.

These newer settlers, many of whom were now protesting, were contributors to the well-being of the entire community. They shared resources and participated in the civil ways of the land. But they didn't attend festivals or even the routine meetings held at the Mother's Table. With Noor, they shared they felt isolated where they lived and like they never fit in. The festivals didn't seem welcoming to them. They seemed the last to know news that impacted them.

The most disturbing issue that arose repeatedly in the Listening, Noor said, was that they didn't feel represented by their leaders in the Circle. She didn't understand how that could be possible and confessed it had been hard to hear that again and again. Everyone knew Mothers provided universal representation, she said. How could they not see that? Ayla noticed Noor continued to refer to them as "the others."

On top of what these "others" had been feeling about life here, Noor said, they also felt betrayed when they heard their leaders—Noor and the Circle—had kept advances in technology and other secrets about the Chronicles from the community. Additionally, they were in disbelief that while they felt shunned by their own community, an *alien from Earth* was not only welcomed but *invited* by Noor.

While Ayla hated the thought of making anyone uncomfortable, she did take some pride in being considered an alien. Connor would love that. She tried to listen closely to Noor and Bodhi but found it hard to listen without, at the same time, formulating her own opinions and responses to what they shared. Every now and then, Mina shot an urgent glance at Ayla.

This is exactly what I mean, Mina silently communicated to Ayla. She pointed at Noor's back. *How did she not see this coming?* Mina pulled her shoulders up to her ears and held her hands out. It was a classic gesture that said, without words, *What are they thinking?*

"But you said she should remain the leader," Ayla whispered to Mina.

"Right. But she needs to *wake up*!" Mina's eyes grew large, indicating an awakening.

When Ayla sank into bed that night, she welcomed the chance to finally be alone with her thoughts. She was learning so much more about her new friends on Eema now that they were in this predicament. It was interesting what you could learn about someone when they were in trouble. After everything Noor shared that night, it was obvious she still thought the "others" were in the wrong. She and the Circle had drawn up some Exit Options for the group that she planned to review with Seth. If the "others" didn't like it here, Noor still believed they should leave.

How would they leave, though? People on Eema weren't even used to traveling. This line of thinking seemed to conflict with the typically kind and loving nature of Noor and the people Ayla had met here, people who seemed likely to try to come to some type of agreement with these "others." Instead, Ayla saw Noor making no room for any reason she or the other leaders should compromise their principles or traditions for a group of protestors—people who could just leave if they weren't satisfied.

But what about new ways and other ways of living and being? Ayla thought. Didn't these people take pride in their commitment to finding new ways to do things? Who *were* these people—an unbending Noor and a Noor-abiding Bodhi? Could it be true that only Ayla, and possibly Mina, could see beyond the obvious?

Ishwa seemed inspired by confrontation. Why wasn't he arguing against Noor, even for the pure sport of it? And Nell, with her prayers for Eema—surely Nell could see Noor needed to at least consider being a little more accommodating. Now that Ayla was thinking about it, the rest of the members of the Circle didn't seem to have much of an opinion about anything. As far as she could tell, they basically did what they were told. Except for Ishwa. But something must have happened between him and Bodhi while the group was in the South. He was much more mellow now.

Ayla wasn't sure what role she would play in the visit to Seth in the morning. She was trying to see all sides of the story because she loved Noor and Bodhi, and she absolutely, positively supported the Mother's Table. She related to the protestors too, though, because she had always felt like an outsider at home too.

"I've never felt like I really fit in there, in my town," Ayla had whispered to Mina before bed. "Our leaders on Earth don't really look like me either. We have very few women in leadership or in our government. And most of the women we see in any kind of spotlight are skinny." Ayla sucked in her cheeks.

"Also, I'm young." She looked down at her lap. "Being young in America, it's like you don't have a voice. Adults have all these expectations and tests for us to take. We get ranked and graded, and it goes on and on, and we're supposed to just go along with it."

"Same here, Ayla," Mina said.

"No, Mina, it's not the same. You're involved in important things, and the adults here *listen* to you. It's more like you're all working together. In the US, adults and kids practically live in two different worlds. They have no idea what we go through. They have no clue how stressed out we are. They're too wrapped up in their own stuff."

"Hmm . . ." Mina paused. She appeared to be watching scenes of life on Earth straight from Ayla's mind. She nodded. "Okay, I see it. I get it now. We do have a lot of freedom here. We have a say in what we do and how we spend our time. Yeah, we're all working, or moving, toward the same . . . goal, I guess?"

The image of the young people of Eema working with the adults stayed with Ayla. She imagined what that would be like on Earth. What she saw in that possibility was comforting. She rolled onto her side, pulling the covers up to her neck and burrowing into the mattress. She fell asleep hoping the protestors were warm enough.

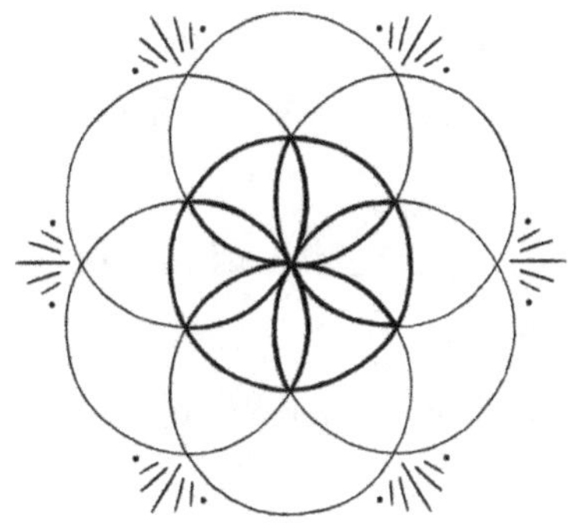

CHAPTER 32

Seth's house was the second Eeman home Ayla had entered since her arrival there. In shape and space, it closely resembled the home she had come to think of as her own, except instead of being sparsely decorated, Seth had displayed vibrant art on the walls and had piled interesting artifacts in the corners. Ayla didn't want to be rude by staring, but she was so enthralled by the art and piles that she couldn't take her eyes off them.

Upon closer look, it appeared Seth and Olivia had assembled little altars in the corners, similar to the ones Grace's mom had all over their home. In one corner, a small table was covered with a colorful cloth. On the cloth was a small collection of stones, a feather, a small wooden box with a heart carved into it, and a framed photo of a woman who looked like an older version of Olivia. Perhaps her mom? Where was Olivia's mom anyway? Near a window, another small table held candles, a few tiny blue glass bottles, and a bowl of small pinecones. Every little table was in some way an extension of the outdoors, right in Seth's home.

"What are you staring at?" Mina whispered.

"Is that—are those beads?" Ayla whispered back, tilting her head toward a piece of artwork on the wall over one of Seth's altars. Mina nodded her head, mildly annoyed by Ayla's fascination with Seth's home.

Olivia poured tea into mugs she said had been made by potters nearby. Once Mina, Ayla, and Noor had settled around the kitchen table, Olivia disappeared into the other room.

Noor and Seth talked while Mina and Ayla sipped tea. Noor told Seth how helpful Olivia had been on their trip to help after the tornadoes. She mentioned the fires in the West and the snow before Seth finally interrupted and shifted the conversation to the protest.

"I really appreciate your coming here, to my home," he said. He locked eyes with everyone at the table, just as Noor did in meetings with the Circle. *Is he trying to prove he has good leadership skills?* Ayla thought.

"Noor, I understand we find ourselves in a potentially uncomfortable situation," he continued. "I know the people who live here on the outskirts of town appreciated the Listening. They appreciated your openness and the opportunity to be heard."

"Well, it was a privilege to catch their stories, Seth. I learned a lot from the people who spoke with me. It's unfortunate they feel I am not an adequate leader." Noor pulled a stack of papers from her bag and laid them on the table.

"The Circle and I have met, and we want to make sure you and the others know your Exit Options," she said. "There are other places to go, not *that* far from here, that may seem more hospitable to you. As you know, I am committed to upholding the tradition of the Mother's Table, and that includes continuing my duties as the Mother, the leader of the North. You might be more content in another place, with another leader." Noor smiled, but Mina looked shocked, like someone had just run past and ripped her tunic right off her body.

What? Ayla looked at Mina.

Mina's typically pale cheeks had turned bright red. *I don't want Olivia to leave!*

Ayla didn't know when it happened, but she was now enjoying reading Mina's thoughts as if they were her own thoughts. It made communication between the two of them much easier, especially here at Seth's house, and especially around Noor.

Seth took in a slow, even breath and let it out slowly. He smiled back at Noor. "Noor, my family left the South many years ago and made a home here. I have no intention of leaving here now, and I would not expect the others to leave either."

Phew. What a relief. Mina's body relaxed.

"Well, okay then," Noor said. "We would never force anyone to leave. I know we can accommodate you here as long as you are willing to abide by our rules. It is not clear what you expect from us, though, Seth. Are you sure the others are not planning to leave?"

"No. We all want to stay. And you understand that your rules are our rules too, correct?"

"Yes! Exactly. I'm so glad you see it that way. And so your plans are to become more involved in the community? You will be joining us for more festivals? Participating in our Mother's Table gatherings? Is that accurate?"

"I believe so, Noor," Seth said. "We would like to participate—but not solely as members of the community. Noor, I am prepared to lead. I know we would be better off with me as our leader, with me as our Father."

"That is not an option, Seth," Noor said, shaking her head. "We have always had a Mother, and we will continue to have a Mother. No one has ever heard of a *Father* as a leader. The best you can do, perhaps as a principal player among the others, the people on the outskirts, is to better adapt to our traditions. You can model how it is done for the others. Once you are more enmeshed, I have faith you will come to love and appreciate what we have here, just as it is."

Now Seth shook his head. "Noor, your leadership has failed. You summoned an alien from Earth! With all due respect, Ayla." He glanced in Ayla's direction with a tense smile on his face.

"Under your leadership," he continued, "Ishwa betrayed you and the Circle. You are out of touch with the rest of the people here—people who have changed, by the way. Our circumstances have changed as well. We no longer want to stay safe and small within our borders. We want to explore."

Seth raised his voice as he continued.

"It is not reasonable that the most effective modes of transportation available are kept only for the use of the Circle. It is not reasonable that the most advanced forms of communication are reserved only for the Circle. We want to be able to travel and to benefit from the technology that is available."

Noor shifted her weight, sitting a little taller in her chair. "Seth, transportation and communication is limited for the safety of the people. The same is true all across our land. It would not be wise to share such advanced resources with just anyone."

"We are not just anyone, Noor. We are your people. And you are ours. We are each other's people. We are your sisters and brothers. And brothers are just as effective at leading as sisters." Seth's eyebrows shot up as he leaned in toward Noor. "What about a Medicine *Man*? Don't you think a man could practice medicine and be just as powerful a healer as a woman?"

Noor's eyebrows mirrored Seth's, and she leaned in until they were almost nose to nose. "Seth, medicine is practiced by *women*. Medicine Women have practiced here since before any Chronicles were even written."

"That limited line of thought—one that perpetuates what has always been done without consideration of other ways—that is exactly why we do not feel represented by you." Seth pulled back from Noor and slammed his hands on the table in front of him. "The others would feel better represented by me. At the Father's Table. Further—"

Seth was interrupted by a small animal that burst through the kitchen door. It looked like a little white wolf, and it knocked over one of Seth's altars and ran into the leg of the kitchen table, jolting the cups of tea. Then it stopped. After a moment, it hopped onto Noor's lap, sat down facing her chest, and looked up into her eyes.

Olivia burst into the room, yelling, "OH MY STAR WITHIN! PLEASE ACCEPT MY DEEPEST APOLOGIES! SNOW! GET OVER HERE—NOW!"

"What on Eema do we have here?" Noor leaned back as far as she could in her chair to avoid making any more contact with the small wolf than was necessary.

Seth smiled. "We also want to be able to keep pets in our homes, Noor."

"Pets? In our *homes*? Animals belong in the wild! They were meant to roam free!" Noor looked from the wolf to Seth and back to the wolf again.

"This is all my fault, Noor," Olivia said. She scooped up the wolf and cradled him in her arms. "I'm so sorry!"

"What is this? What have you done?" Noor picked up a small hair from her lap and examined it.

"Well, Olivia and I found this little guy under our porch a few weeks ago," Seth said. "He was wounded, and we've been taking care of him with the intention of releasing him back into the wild, as is our custom.

"He has been such a joy to have around, though, Noor. When Nahara moved on, it was like a piece of Olivia moved on too. Even knowing Nahara's spirit is here with us, we do still miss her. We have her art, and we do feel her presence, but it's just not the same. This little guy makes us laugh, like Nahara always did. He reminds us to play, like she did. Olivia takes great care of him too."

"I can't imagine life without him now." Olivia nuzzled her nose into the fur behind the wolf's ear. Ayla and Mina took that as their cue to jump to their feet and pet the wolf in Olivia's arms. He was basically irresistible.

"Oh my. Okay." Noor took a deep breath and exhaled slowly, looking from the girls to Seth and back to the girls again.

"His name is Snow," Olivia said. "I named him last night."

Ayla, who was known by her friends and family back home to make accurate predictions about what would happen next in an argument and who woke up that very morning suspecting Seth would be angry and confrontational while Noor stood her ground, stood in complete awe of the scene before her. Seth was calm. Noor was calm. Nobody was arguing. And Olivia's mother was dead! How devastating. And now a wolf was in the house.

She looked up, and Mina flashed her a huge smile. *Isn't this the best thing ever?*

Mina had told Ayla back when she arrived that nobody kept pets here because animals were meant to be wild. Some people, like farmers, kept animals on their land for work purposes, but those were not considered pets. Animals were never kept indoors.

Ayla's family had always had a dog or two, so she never noticed just how lonely a home could be without one until she came to Eema. She badly missed her own puppy, Apollo. Seeing Olivia and Mina giggle and coo over Snow made her miss Apollo even more. She couldn't resist giving Snow a quick kiss on the nose.

"So, is this your mom's art?" Ayla asked Olivia, pointing to the beadwork on the wall.

"Yes." Olivia blushed. She walked to the wall and buried her nose in Snow's neck. "She made the most beautiful creations."

"I can't believe she made that from beads. It's stunning."

Ayla stood next to Olivia, admiring her mother's handiwork. She was in awe of anyone's ability to create something from nothing. Olivia's mom had formed a row of intricate flowers out of beads that, from far away, looked like a painting. Ayla imagined her bent over, working with the beads, making them into flowers. It must have taken hours.

"Yeah, it sped by for her, though," Olivia whispered softly, as if seeing the exact scene Ayla had imagined in her head. "She got lost in it."

Through all of this, Noor had remained seated. Her eyes looked watery. "Girls. Okay now," she said. "Snow is darling, yes. But he is still a wild animal. And Nahara, yes. She was a woman of countless gifts. Seth, I am afraid I do not know what to say next."

She looked down at her bag, which was on the floor by her feet. It was glowing. She reached in and pulled out a small screen.

"Yes?" Noor said into the screen.

Bodhi's face appeared, looking strained. "I have some unexpected news, Noor. One of the others. A man protesting outside the Collective. He has moved on."

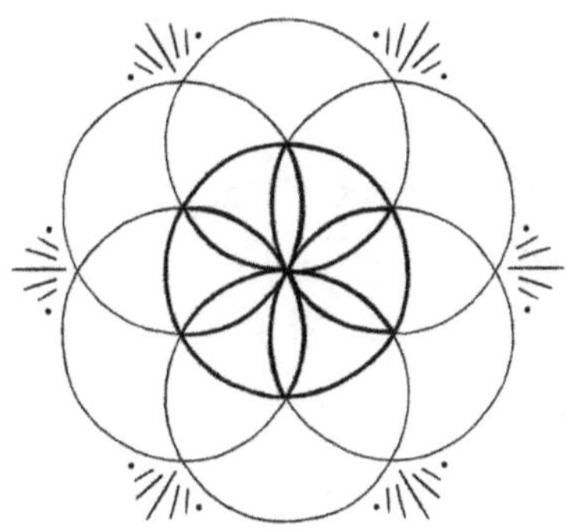

CHAPTER 33

Bodhi stood with Seth in the doorway of the Collective Chronicles a few hours later.

"Seth, you must convince them to go home," Bodhi said. "It's too cold outside for them to be out there like this."

Seth sighed, nodding. He hadn't looked up since hearing the news that one of his friends from the outskirts of town had been found outside the Collective that morning. They referred to him as a *shell.*

"This matters to them, though," Seth said quietly, still looking down.

On the way back to the Collective, Mina had tried to explain the shelling to Ayla in whispers. "It's when the spirit leaves the body. The body still remains, like a shell."

"So someone died?" Ayla spoke loudly.

"Shhh!" Mina said with her eyebrows raised. *I don't want Seth to hear us.*

Ayla raised her eyebrows in return. *Well, why don't you just talk to me like this, then? Without words.* The girls smiled at each other.

Yes, his body died, Mina replied. *His Star Within is visiting loved ones.*

How do you know that?

Ayla, we just know.

But how? What proof do you have?

Ayla, why is proof so important to you? We just know. It's what happens when a person shells their Star Within. The body stays. The spirit, the Star, moves on. Spirits still have a lot to accomplish even after they shell. I could just as easily ask how you don't know that.

"Mina, on Earth people *die,*" Ayla whispered. "We don't *shell our Star Within.* What you're saying sounds nuts to me. A lot of us think we know what happens when a person dies, but not everyone agrees. So your level of certainty is surprising, to say the least. Everyone on Earth is trying to prove how right they are about one thing or another. It's hard to imagine our entire planet agreeing on something. On anything! Plus, you're so calm about it. Someone *died*! Why isn't that a big deal to you?"

"Well, okay," Mina whispered back. "I think I can see where you're coming from. Moving on is a good thing, though. Our spirits don't love being contained by bodies. They want to be free. So, it *is* a big deal, but probably not in the way you're thinking."

Mina turned to look out the window, and the girls rode in silence back to the Collective. Once they arrived, they followed Noor inside.

The three of them settled into a room Ayla hadn't seen before. It was Noor's office.

Noor turned toward Ayla.

"Ayla, shelling is not feared here like death is feared on Earth," she said. "You won't see the same reaction to the shelling here that you would see to death there. You may even see some people celebrate that this man learned the lessons he came to learn. We celebrate when one of our people has the good fortune of moving on and shelling the Star Within. It means the Star Within is freed. It's a beautiful, honorable time in life." She placed a warm hand over Ayla's cool one, then looked up when the door opened and Nell looked inside.

"Noor, I'm afraid the others are reacting differently than is typical to this shelling," Nell said, speaking slowly, as surprised by the words coming out of her mouth as Noor appeared to be to hear them.

"Tell me more, Nell. I don't understand."

"They believe the snow took his body—his life—before he agreed to go. His soul never would have been able to imagine snow when he made his contract for this life. It could very well be true that this was not the scenario for moving on that he agreed to. They think the snow is Ayla's fault. They think it is part of a curse she brought with her."

"They think I *killed him*?" Ayla gasped. She felt her chest tighten.

"Ayla, no, that is not the way I would put it," Nell said. "Please understand it is rare for anyone here to move on for any unexpected reason. The others are alarmed, yes. But once the Medicine Woman confirms it was in his contract to leave at this time, everything will be fine. It's going to be okay."

Nell wrapped her arm around Ayla and pulled her in close. Ayla inhaled Nell's comforting, woodsy smell and closed her eyes.

"This is all a lot to take in," Ayla said quietly.

For once, her mind was blank, like all the thoughts that typically swam around in there finally collided into an explosion, and now only smoldering ashes were left. She noticed how strange yet refreshing it felt.

She kept her eyes closed and moved closer to Nell. Mina sat down on the small sofa with them, wiggling in next to Ayla. The girls sighed together, their eyes closed, and their bodies relaxed. They relished this moment of calm.

A while later, Ayla awoke to a fire crackling in a fireplace. She and Mina had inadvertently fallen asleep on the couch.

Ayla looked around, thinking about how this was the first time she'd been in Noor's office. One entire wall was lined with bookshelves. Pieces of artwork hung on the other walls. Ayla noticed some of the artwork looked like the flowers made of beads she saw at Seth's house. This space was perhaps the coziest she had seen in her entire life. It seemed to say so much more about Noor than her home, which held white walls and open space. This warm, colorful, quaint space *felt* more like Noor.

She realized her arm had fallen asleep and pulled it out from under Mina, waking her up.

"Hi," Mina said, yawning. "Where's my mom? Where's Nell?"

"I don't know. I just woke up."

"We must have needed some rest, eh?" Mina nudged Ayla with her elbow.

"That art—it looks like the beadwork Olivia's mom made," Ayla said, pointing to a piece on the wall.

Mina nodded. "My mom and Nahara were very close friends. They were inseparable. They met when they were pregnant with Olivia and me."

"Wow. She must miss her." Ayla couldn't imagine losing a friend like that. Losing Grandpa George was hard enough.

"You know when Seth said a part of Olivia left with Nahara?" Mina asked, staring at one of Nahara's pieces on the wall. "Well, sometimes I think the same about my mom. It's like part of her closed down after Nahara moved on—the part that would have seen how to help the others and make everything normal again."

Ayla watched Mina, knowing how hard it was to see her own mom change after Grandpa George died. Ayla didn't know how to help her mom, who sometimes seemed so empty, and she didn't always *want* to have to help. She was the kid.

"Mina, I'm scared," she said, wanting to change the subject. "I can't stand the thought that anyone would think I killed someone. This is too much for me. I'm just a kid, you know?"

"Ayla, you say that a lot. Here is something you need to know. On Eema, there's no such thing as *just a kid.* Sure, you don't have as much life experience as a human in a fully grown body, but you're still a legitimate human. You aren't inferior to a grown-up just because you haven't been in your body as long."

"I *feel* inferior," Ayla said, rubbing her eyes. "Especially here. Especially now. I don't even know why I'm still here."

"So, you'd rather go back to Earth—where you actually *are* inferior?" Mina smiled.

Ayla smiled back, shaking her head.

"Listen," Mina said, "you already know that when it's time for you to leave Eema, you will. Your life on Earth will be there waiting for you. I don't know *exactly* what your purpose is here, but I know we need you, and I know you wouldn't be here if you couldn't help." She patted Ayla's knee.

"It must be nice to just *know* all these things."

"It's not a special, secret gift exclusive to me, Ayla. You know all the same things I do. Your Star Within knows them. You just need to stop doubting yourself. Trust your Star Within! Now, let's go find Nell and my mom. I'm hungry!"

Mina and Ayla headed toward the Screening Room, where Mina suspected Noor would be with Nell. As they approached the door, they could hear yelling. They stopped outside the door and looked at each other, both hoping the other would know what to do next. Ayla couldn't remember hearing anyone raise their voice in such a way since she'd arrived on Eema.

"They want this! They believe in this! I AM NOT TELLING THEM TO GO HOME!"

"Seth?" Ayla whispered.

Mina nodded. "I think so," she whispered back.

Then they heard Noor, sounding just as calm as she always did. "I understand this is important to them, and you. I am not in any way suggesting any of this is unimportant. I'm merely suggesting that if, in fact, it is the cold and snow that caused him to move on before it was his time, they deserve to know it is dangerous to stay outside."

"Or you could step down, as they all want you to do, and I COULD TAKE OVER AS THE FATHER!"

The two girls looked at each other. "Seth," they both said, nodding in agreement.

"I am *not* stepping down." Noor's voice was firm and unwavering.

"I AM NOT TELLING THEM TO LEAVE!"

"Seth, I see that you are angry," Noor said. "You have every right to your anger. You do *not* have the right to speak to me that way. If you want to be a leader, show some compassion and ask your followers to go home so they can be warm and dry and can prepare for the celebration of their dearly departed friend's life."

As the sound of heavy footsteps moved closer to the door, the girls ducked into the hallway.

Seth blew through the door. "FINE!" he yelled, then spun around. "However! If you think for one minute we will back down from our demands, you are sorely mistaken."

Ayla and Mina waited for him to leave through the front door, then walked cautiously into the Screening Room. Scenes from the West were playing on the main screen. It looked like the fires had died down.

Noor stood watching the screens, her right hand laid over her heart. She jumped when she heard the girls approach her.

"Hello, sleepyheads," she said, smiling and reaching her arms out to them. She pulled them both into a hug. "How are you feeling?"

"I think we're just fine, Mom," Mina said, then pointed toward the door. "How about you? What's going on with him?"

"He's upset, obviously. It means a lot to him that the people from the outskirts trust him and are here supporting him and his claims that I betrayed them. He had hoped this morning's meeting would end differently. He's shaken by the shelling."

Noor looked tired.

"Well, what's next, then?" Ayla asked.

"Dinner." Noor smiled and again pulled the girls close for another hug.

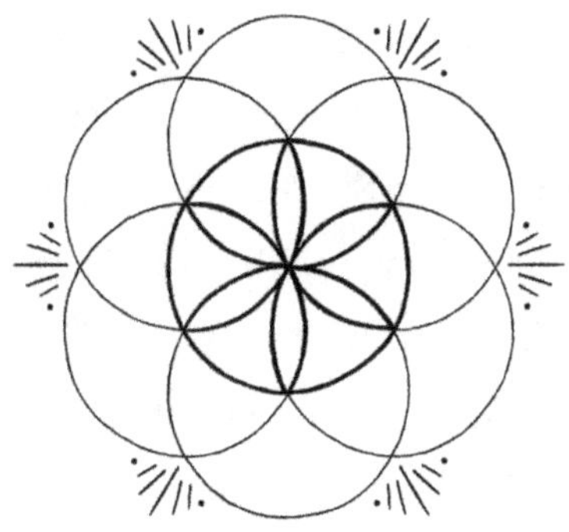

CHAPTER 34

AYLA FULLY EXPECTED a day similar to the last day she was on Earth. A dress code, a sea of sad people, homemade casseroles, and air so heavy it felt like it would crush her heart. Sure, the people on Eema believed the human body was merely a vehicle by which the glorious Star Within traveled. They believed their souls made contracts with Eema before they were born into their bodies—contracts that detailed the lessons they would learn, the people they would meet, and the terms of their shelling. Nothing had ever happened to prove they believed otherwise. But they must still be sad to lose someone they loved. There must be heartache. Despair. They must wonder what could have been. They must be grieving what they know will never be.

Nope.

As far as Ayla could tell, they wanted nothing more than to celebrate the fact that this man had moved on. Were they being insensitive? How did his family feel about all this? Wouldn't they be devastated? Hadn't Seth said that even Olivia wasn't the same since her mother died?

Aside from Grandpa George, Ayla hadn't known anyone who died. She'd heard stories from friends, though. She'd read stories of it too. She couldn't recall a single time when death inspired a celebration.

"That's just it, Ayla," Mina said, interrupting Ayla's thoughts. "We aren't celebrating death. We're celebrating *life*."

Mina grabbed Ayla's hand and pulled her out of the space Jeep. "You'll see. We honor life. We might even honor death too. But death is just a thing that happens. It's just another part of life, really. We're not celebrating *that*."

Mina dragged Ayla along as she spoke. They followed Prem into the same hall where the Embody Festival had been held—and the scene was quite similar. The room held beautifully set tables, music that stirred the soul, flowers, candlelight, and even a few people swaying to the music.

Once everyone had arrived, they took their seats around the tables. Noor and Bodhi and the rest of the members of the Circle sat at the front of the room. Seth was there too. Ayla saw a lot of people whose names she didn't know, but at this point most everyone looked familiar in some way. They were smiling, nodding, and hugging each other.

Several people, including Noor and Seth, spoke before the group. They talked about the gift of life in a human body. They talked about the Star Within and its deep desire to not be contained, to return to freedom. They talked about the space between life in a body and the shelling, where the spirit is set free. They talked about soul contracts and life lessons and the joy one could feel knowing they'd fulfilled their contract and moved on.

They spoke of their friend with pride, like he had won a prestigious award. They talked about how he made them laugh and how he was strong in mind, body, and spirit. His husband told a story about the day they met and how he carried him piggyback over a puddle of water. Songs were sung and drums were played. The delicious dishes of food contained all his favorites. Ayla saw smiles and laughter and very few tears.

Until the end of the celebration.

It started with a gasp from the husband, like his breath had left his body and he was trying to catch it. His eyes filled with tears that quickly ran down his cheeks as sobs took over his body. Their children's bodies shook as they cried too. Before Ayla knew what was happening, every single person in the room had joined hands, forming circles around the husband and children.

First there was a small circle. One of the women who joined that circle so closely resembled the husband that she had to be his sister. Their circle formed close to the husband and children, wrapping their arms around them and embracing them in a big group hug. A second circle formed a couple steps back from the first. They wrapped the first circle in a hug, then stepped back, wrapping their arms around each other's shoulders. Each group of people did the same until every person was held within a larger circle. The husband and children remained at the center.

Ayla felt her throat burning, then her eyes. Tears streamed down her face in full force. She tried to wipe one eye with her shoulder, since her arms were around Prem and Mina, and then heard Prem whisper, "It's okay. Your body was made to cry." He winked at her when she looked up. Ayla sniffed, hoping the tears would stop soon.

Every single person in the room was crying together. Arm stacked upon arm. Men, women, children, and those who didn't clearly fall into any of those categories. Old people, young people, and everyone in between.

"It's a *release*," Mina whispered in Ayla's ear. "We're releasing him with our tears. He touched each of us in his life, and we have carried him with us since. Now we return him. That will fully energize his Star Within."

Ayla faced forward, staring at the heads of the people in the circle in front of her. She was torn between wanting her tears to stop and wanting them to flow from her eyes forever. She could not imagine what it would be like to live a life where she could cry among friends and it would be okay—to cry openly, not just in her mother's arms and not just when she was a baby. She relaxed, noticing it was downright delightful not to try to hide her tears, not to suppress them, and not to be ashamed of them. She didn't even care that her face was a snotty mess, even though she definitely noticed it.

As the choir of cries slowed to a stop around the room, the outer circle separated. Two people stepped away from each other, creating a space between them. Then two people in the circle in front of them did the same. And so on, until a clear path was created from the outer circle to the inner circle.

Ayla caught herself wondering if the circles looked like a labyrinth from above. She strained to see their reflection in the glass ceiling above, thinking the whole scene must look amazing, but the room was too dimly lit. The sky was dark too. Ayla hadn't noticed before, but a light rain was falling outside, as if the sky was crying along with them.

Then one by one, each person walked to the center of the circle to acknowledge the husband and children with hugs and kisses and whispered words. Then they walked back through the remaining circles, down the path, and outside the hall. The first circle of people that had formed stayed with the family until the end to walk them out. The family was never alone.

Ayla stood in the outermost circle with her new Eeman family. She noticed Olivia with Seth. Ishwa with Pax. Nell with her daughters. Zora with her mother. Their tear-streaked faces glimmered in the candlelight. She was sure she had never seen such radiant humans. Not in movies or driving around town. Not at dance competitions or in school. Not on TV. These people were literally shining from the inside out. She was in complete awe.

"When we release our tears for him, our bodies are cleansed," Mina said. "The shine you see is the clear, collective light from all of our Stars Within." She kissed Ayla on the cheek. "Your Star is shining too, sister. Your light is big."

Again, Ayla's eyes filled with tears.

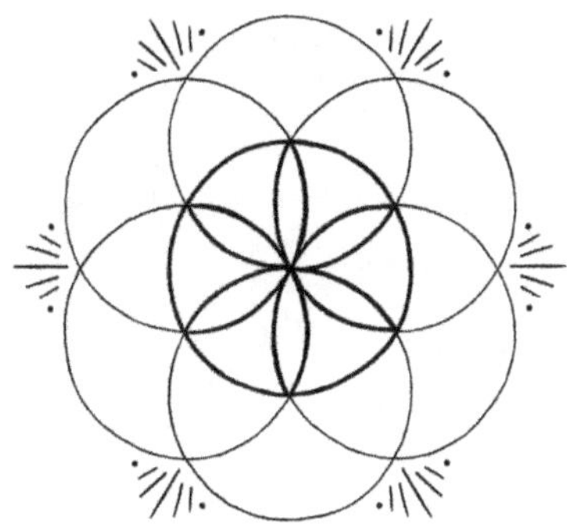

CHAPTER 35

EVERYTHING WAS QUIET around town for the next several days. For the most part, the entire community stayed at home. They prepared meals with their families, spent time with each other, and rested.

For Ayla, it was another strange yet now predictable time on Eema, where even with a sense of sadness, the air felt light. It felt like the celebration of life set the tone for the days to come. Where there was most certainly a loss, the community had also gained something in the face of that loss. Everyone had come together to celebrate a life well lived, and now they were interwoven more tightly, more closely, and more like one large garment instead of individual threads.

Noor explained to Ayla that, in large part, these were days of family reflection observed after a member of the community went spirit-side or moved on. These days were observed in this way so the shell's family wouldn't have to see everyone go back to their normal, everyday lives while their hearts were still so heavy from the recent loss of their loved one.

"It's just one way we can show we are all connected by acknowledging that their loss is our loss too," Noor said.

"I thought moving on was no big deal to you, though, because of the whole 'We're just spirits in bodies' thing." Ayla shook her hands in the air as she said it.

"Well, yes, we do acknowledge that we're spirits in bodies, and we do know our spirits are freed and continue to thrive once they leave our bodies. We know the spirits of those we love are still with us when they leave their bodies, but we do still feel a sense of loss, Ayla. We've only ever known them in their bodies, so when we no longer have them in their bodies, here with us, we still miss them when they move on."

Noor's hand rested on Ayla's knee.

"I guess I'm confused," Ayla said. "I thought you were okay with death. I mean, I loved the ceremony yesterday. I loved the way you celebrated—"

"*We* celebrated," Noor said. "You were there too."

"Right. I loved the way *we* celebrated. And wow, the thing afterward with the circles? I really loved that. It was beautiful. And when we were all crying together? I've never seen, and definitely never experienced, anything like that. I just thought that if you thought the spirits were still with us, you wouldn't be so sad when someone died."

"I believe our sadness might be different than the sadness you experience when a loved one moves on," Noor said, "but it is still sadness."

"How is it different? Isn't sadness just sadness?" Ayla wanted so badly to make sense of death here on Eema. She hoped to be able to share what she learned with her family at home. She knew nothing would be the same now that Grandpa George had died.

"Yes, sadness is sadness is sadness," Noor said. "But our sadness is born fully from love. When someone on Earth dies, your sadness is not only born from love, but also from fear."

"We wouldn't be sad if we didn't love the people who died," Ayla said.

"Right," Noor said. "When you lose someone on Earth, you're sad because you loved them. But, Ayla, fear also surrounds your loss on Earth. Most people on Earth are afraid of death. When someone moves on, you're afraid for them *and* for yourselves."

Noor paused.

"But we are *not* afraid," she continued. "We know death is the next phase of our growth. Death is actually a magnificent part of life! We know our loved ones are happy and well. We know we will be okay. Our sadness hums a different tune than yours. It is not better or worse. It is simply different." Noor swallowed, watching Ayla closely.

Ayla looked at Noor for a few minutes without saying anything. As had been the case so many times since she arrived on Eema, what Noor said didn't completely make sense to her in her mind but made sense in her body.

Noor perked up. "Yes! That is your intuition, Ayla," she said. "It is your Star Within! That feeling—the way you feel when something makes sense to you—that is resonance. Emotions resonate on different frequencies. It doesn't have to be logical for you to know it is possible. It feels right because even when your mind does not understand it, your heart and your soul know it is true."

"I can accept death as part of life, Noor," Ayla said. "That doesn't make losing Grandpa George any less painful."

"I know, Ayla Bug. It *is* painful. And pain is nothing to be afraid of either. On Earth, your people resist pain with so much might, you create even more pain."

"Okay, you lost me on that one, Noor."

Noor smiled at Ayla and patted her on the knee. "Ayla, picture your Grandpa George."

Ayla closed her eyes. "Okay."

"Now imagine you are back in the moment where your mom told you he had moved on."

"Okay . . ."

"What does that feel like in your body?"

Ayla noticed she had clenched her fists, her jaw, and even her shoulders. "It makes me tense all over! I was so scared when my mom told me he died. But I even thought, 'It's okay. Everyone is going to die someday.' I even knew then this was just part of his life."

Ayla wiped a tear from her eye.

"Ayla, this may be hard to understand," Noor said, "but much of what you believe about death, or anything, really, is a result of the story you believe about it. At some level, maybe in your brain or even in your heart and soul, you know death is okay. And yet the story you believe about death is a story that tells you death is not okay."

Noor placed her hands on Ayla's shoulders, gently applying pressure until Ayla felt her body relax.

"Really, I guess it would be more accurate to say that you fear the stories you know about death on Earth," Noor continued. "Those stories are passed on from generation to generation. You carry your mother's fear, and you carry Grandma Ettie's fear, and her mother's fear, and her mother's fear, and so on. You carry the fear of many." As Noor spoke, she placed her hand on her heart, then her stomach, as if showing Ayla where the fear she spoke of was carried.

She said, "Here, our stories about moving on have always been straightforward. A loved one moves on. We know shelling is a part of life and that the spirit leaves the body. It is free. We celebrate the life that was lived in the body. We hold each other through the sadness that comes from missing a person we loved. We hold each other as long as it takes."

Noor pulled Ayla into a hug as Ayla all but collapsed into her.

"I am certainly oversimplifying it," Noor said, "but for all practical purposes, death is far simpler than it is complicated. Truly, Ayla." She gently kissed Ayla on the forehead.

Ayla drew a long, deep breath and exhaled loudly. As Noor held her close, she felt every word Noor said sink into her body. Where she would have normally doubted the words as they were spoken, questioned their validity, questioned the woman speaking them, she doubted nothing now. Noor's words dropped like rain falls from the sky, dissolving into her skin, into her bones, into every cell of her body until the words and the ideas they represented were just another part of her.

"What do I do, then?" she asked. "How do I stop being afraid? How do *we* stop being afraid?"

"You write a new story," Noor said softly as a huge, warm smile spread across her face.

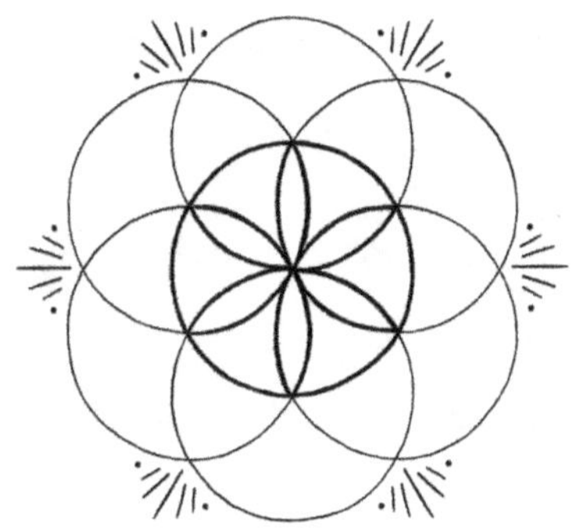

CHAPTER 36

Noor, Bodhi, Prem, Mina, and Ayla sat together in the family's living room so Noor could catch them up on what was happening. They all knew Seth had convinced the others to leave the Collective—to go home and stay there until further notice. Noor had just learned the Medicine Woman had determined their friend had moved on due solely to natural causes. He had fulfilled the terms of his soul contract as planned. Nobody understood it, but it was confirmed and not theirs to question.

This made the others feel less skeptical of Ayla and the snowfall. However, Seth made it clear when he contacted Noor after the days of family reflection that nobody had changed their minds. They still felt invisible in their community, and they still wanted Seth to be named Father and leader of the North. Noor said she would call a meeting at the Mother's Table, just like they used to do when New People arrived. But Seth said no way—it was too late for that.

"What about a trial?" Prem asked. "You could have a trial like they do on Earth!"

"Who would *be* on trial, Prem?" Mina asked. "Mom? Seth?"

Prem shrugged his shoulders. "Mom?"

Noor turned toward Ayla and studied her for a few seconds. Then she said, "Ayla, could you set that up for us? Could you make us a courtroom?"

Ayla objected immediately. The thought of building a courtroom or anything like it made her uneasy. She did not want to see Noor on trial. But as the five of them talked it through and it became obvious Noor wasn't going to give in, Ayla conceded and said she would help create a courtroom-like setting.

"It's more like a school board meeting, I think," she said, remembering a school board meeting she had attended with her mom as extra credit for social studies. "The Circle could be the board. You and Seth can speak. Then anyone who wants to speak would have an opportunity. There wouldn't be a judge, though. And I'm not sure how it would end without a judge." Ayla badly wanted this situation to be resolved.

"Okay, that sounds sufficient," Noor said. "I think we can work with that. It sounds a lot like the traditional Mother's Table, actually. We don't need a judge. We'll know what to do when the time comes to make a decision." Noor nodded as she spoke and continued to look at Ayla, but it was clear her mind was elsewhere.

Was it sufficient? Ayla felt like she was leading Noor to battle. If Noor stood in front of the others and told them they had to leave if they weren't willing to follow her orders, they might be outraged. And who knew what Seth would do with that kind of audience? He was so persuasive. Why was Noor being so unreasonable anyway? Ayla was scared and confused. And then she thought, *Maybe it isn't the gathering that scares me. It could be the story I'm weaving about the gathering.* Before the community had even had a chance to come together, Ayla had been writing an unfortunate end to the story.

"You will need to stay open, Ayla," Noor said reassuringly. "We will all need to stay open in order for this to work. I will not let Seth take over as our leader. Trust me."

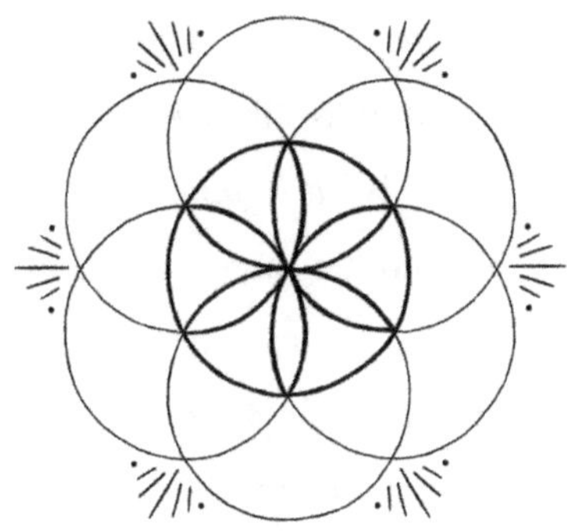

CHAPTER 37

INITIALLY, SETH SAID the meeting sounded too much like a Mother's Table. Noor assured him that both he and she would lead the meeting. She told him they would make sure everyone who wanted to speak had a chance to speak and that they would make all the decisions about how to proceed together, as a team. As soon as Seth agreed to meet in the way Noor suggested, Ayla began working on her plans to construct something like a boardroom. Noor had decided to hold the meeting in the hall where the community held celebrations, and as Ayla helped arrange tables and chairs in the room, Mina and Olivia walked in with armfuls of evergreen branches. Zora and her mom were behind them.

"What's going on? This isn't a party!" Ayla said.

The Medicine Woman smiled at Ayla as she pulled two small bundles of dried sage out of her medicine bag and handed one to Zora.

She lit each bundle with a match, then closed her eyes and sang a few words in a voice barely above a whisper. Although she couldn't hear the words, Ayla thought they sounded like a prayer.

Ayla mouthed to Mina, *What is going on?*

Mina smiled as Zora and her mom walked away with their burning sage. "They're clearing the space," she said matter-of-factly. "Normally, they would spend the whole day doing a much more elaborate cleansing ceremony, but my mom doesn't want to wait for that."

"And the branches?" Ayla nodded at Mina's arms.

Mina smiled her big, beautiful smile and said nothing.

"What is it, Mina? Come on! We need to get this room ready!" Ayla noticed how tense she felt compared to the way Mina and Olivia appeared, standing there with silly grins on their faces and their arms full of cedar tree branches.

"Right." Mina nodded her head. "Calm down. Deep breath in . . ."

"Don't use your yoga voice on me, Mina! Just tell me why you're carrying branches!"

Then Ayla felt herself soften. How could she not? Mina's playful presence helped her feel at ease.

"Yoga voice?" Mina glared at Ayla before her eyes softened, and she continued, "Okay, so, I know this is very un-Earth-like, and you may not like this idea. However, we believe in creating beautiful spaces here on Eema. So, we are decorating your boardroom."

Ayla rolled her eyes, then shook her head in disbelief. Olivia let out a giant roar of laughter and skipped off to arrange her branches. As if on cue, Prem walked through the door holding a huge wooden bowl filled with freshly cut flowers. He smiled slyly at Ayla, then turned toward his sister.

"Is she okay?" Prem asked Mina.

"She's fine. Everything's just fine." Mina winked at Ayla and then skipped after Olivia.

"Flowers too, huh?" Ayla said to Prem.

"Naturally." He smiled, balancing the bowl on his hip so he could reassure Ayla with a pat on the back. The gesture reminded her of Connor, which made her miss him—but just a little. Ayla appreciated the presence of a big brother, even if Prem wasn't technically her brother.

She felt much better once everything was in place. The room, she had to admit, was impressive. It felt warm and inviting, and it smelled like the woods. The flowers were subtle—not at all overpowering. The crew had tucked the stems into the cedar branches, which added a faint, sweet smell to the air and a dash of color to the room.

It was unlike any boardroom Ayla had ever seen and nothing like she imagined it would be, but she was happy with it. She couldn't help but wonder, *What if we put flowers in our boardrooms and courtrooms on Earth?* All the small touches the people on Eema added made a world of difference here. A universe of difference, actually. *The decorations make a universe of difference*, Ayla thought as she turned off the lights and closed the door on her makeshift boardroom.

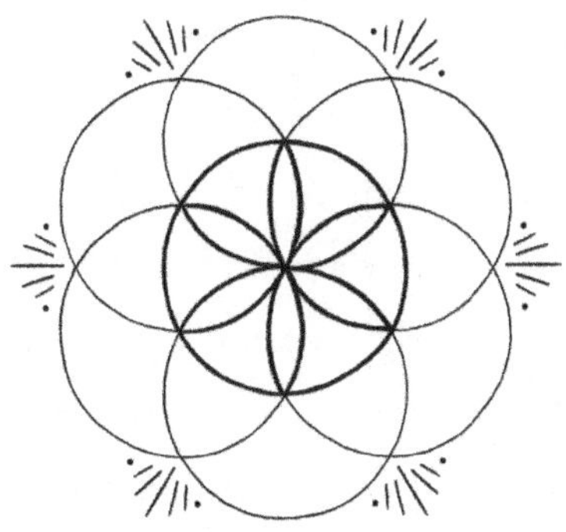

CHAPTER 38

The room was more crowded than Ayla expected it to be. As she looked around the room, she worried whether there would be enough chairs for everyone.

Despite the fact that this was the very first boardroom ever known on Eema, the community members appeared to be at ease within its walls. Ayla wondered if some of her anxiety about building a boardroom on Eema came from the stories she believed about them. *Maybe this won't be so bad*, she thought.

As the room filled, nobody seemed to have any trouble figuring out where to go. And when, in fact, they did run out of chairs, someone brought more into the room and placed them at the end of rows, as if they had always been there. Ayla let out a deep exhale, feeling less uneasy about her task yet no less uneasy about the situation and the future of this new place she had come to love like home. Noor gave no indication that she had changed her mind about not stepping down as Mother, and yet this morning she seemed less poised and more distracted than Ayla had ever seen her.

The members of the Circle looked as official as a row of angels dressed in tunics made of brightly colored fabrics with varying patterns could possibly look—which was not all that official, actually, at least not in the way Ayla understood the word. She noted the stark contrast between the attire of these ethereal beings and what would be worn in an official space like this at home. How many different shades of navy blue and gray could there be? Definitely not enough to even come close to matching the array of colors the people wore here.

As the members of the Circle whispered softly and laughed heartily together, Ayla's nerves began to calm. The love the people here had for each other was obvious. Even in the midst of this conflict, they seemed not to hold any ill will toward each other.

Ayla had done her best to create a podium where people could stand to speak in the front of the room. She'd placed it off to the side so the speaker could address both the Circle and the people sitting in the room. But she hoped nobody would fall into the podium, as it was made of one small table stacked strategically on top of another small table. She had laid a cloth over the two tables to conceal the table legs because Mina told her they were distracting. She noticed someone had lit candles around the room and that someone else, or maybe the same person, had set a table with fruit-infused punch and water. All she could do was laugh at this point. The people of Eema were determined to make everything look appealing and feel like home. They did it as effortlessly as they breathed, and Ayla knew she would miss it when she returned to Earth.

The members of the Circle stood, and what sounded like a flute began to play. Noor walked into the room, followed by Seth, who was followed by two boys who appeared to be about Prem's age. The boys looked familiar to Ayla, but she couldn't remember where she had seen them before. Since she hadn't known the boys were coming, she hadn't set chairs for them at the front of the room, so there was some shuffling to do before they could be seated. Once everyone was seated, Noor looked around the room. *Is she looking for me?* Ayla wondered as they locked eyes. Noor pointed to the podium and shrugged. Ayla nodded eagerly.

Noor walked to the podium, as Ayla had directed her to do when they discussed the setup the day before. At first, Noor had objected to the podium because it went against the spirit of the Mother's Table, where everyone was equal. Seth, on the other hand, loved the idea of a special place for him to stand in front of the room. Noor agreed to the podium after speaking to Seth. She appreciated his approval, which annoyed Ayla. But she decided to keep her opinions out of the situation because, after all, she wanted to be helpful and didn't want to disappoint Noor.

Noor welcomed everyone and thanked them for coming. She looked around the room, locking eyes with as many individuals as possible and nodding at each of them with a small but genuine smile. It still felt a little awkward to lock eyes with Noor, but Ayla couldn't get past how good it felt to be acknowledged in that way. Then Noor invited anyone who wanted to speak to form a line. Seth would speak when they were finished, and Noor would speak last. What would happen after that was still unknown. Ayla hoped Noor would find a way to make the others feel welcome here and to convince Seth she should remain the Mother and the leader. Still, the knowledge that Noor resisted the idea of making changes, even though it seemed like it was time for change, made Ayla uncomfortable. She knew nobody would get hurt because there was no violence on Eema, yet she hoped everyone would be okay.

Ayla sat in awe of the ways the people spoke and how they were heard by those in the courtroom. One by one, they came to the podium to speak, each of them moving gracefully and speaking eloquently. There were no outbursts of anger. There was no interrupting. Everyone listened like they cared about how the speaker felt. It felt like everyone in the room was part of one big family.

The phrases that each of the people used made them sound like the daughters and sons of social workers, just like herself. They said things like, "When I heard the technology had advanced past what we've been able to access, I felt angry," and, "When Noor didn't make any changes after the Listening, I felt betrayed." *Could all these people just know these ways of speaking naturally?* she wondered. She thought of all the times she and Connor lashed out at each other with words and how each time her mother corrected them. "Ayla, try saying this: 'Connor, when you take my toy from me, I feel angry.' Use feeling statements."

Use feeling statements. How many times had her mother said that?

Noor nodded, smiled, and listened. She didn't seem defensive. Oh, how Ayla hoped she was *really* listening. There must be a way to make everyone happy *and* keep her in the role of Mother.

Seth, on the other hand, had a harder edge than usual. Ayla couldn't read him at all. He radiated heat from his body and his eyes. He definitely *felt* angry. He made Ayla nervous.

Just about everything said at the podium had been shared with Noor before, either at the Listening or by Seth. Some expressed disappointment because nothing changed immediately after the Listening. Some said they were scared about the weather patterns spreading across the land and wished they knew more. Those speakers glared briefly at Noor and at Ayla before moving on. Was that for emphasis? Or were they holding back outbursts?

Ayla tried to take it all in like Noor, without reacting or taking anything personally. But she found herself struggling to do that. A few times, she tried to catch Mina's eye, just for reassurance, but every person in the room was listening so intently, she had no choice but to do the same.

She was relieved when the line of speakers began to dwindle after lunch. *Pretty soon this will all be over*, she thought. They'll finish up, Seth will say his piece, and Noor will wrap it all up.

But then some of the people who lived in the city stood up and began to form a line behind the others who remained. *That* made Mina turn toward Ayla. Up to this point, the only people who had spoken to Noor at the Listening or had stood up to speak at the podium were people who lived on the outskirts of town. Those in the city were considered Noor's people.

What? Mina mouthed. She looked alarmed. Her mouth hung open.

Ayla shrugged. Maybe they wanted to speak out in support of Noor?

It seemed like several more hours passed as the people from the city spoke. They were unhappy too.

For the most part, they shared that they were shaken by Ishwa's betrayal of the Circle and were surprised to learn there was so much they didn't know about their community. They wanted access to more technology, to transportation, and to the Chronicles. They wanted to see the stories the Circle had seen. They wondered if there were ways to predict surprising weather patterns. They seemed as relieved as the others were to speak openly about their issues—but they did not want Seth to be their leader.

"Perhaps a viable solution would be for the others to vacate the outskirts of town?" one woman said. "Maybe we could build a Center for Technology there instead." Ayla felt the tension rise in the courtroom. *This* was unexpected. Did Noor have any idea this would happen? Probably not. Ayla wished she could disappear.

With each person from the city who spoke, Ayla began to think maybe life wasn't so bad on Earth. At least she *knew* the problems on Earth, and at least there were people already working to fix them. But this took her by complete surprise. It no longer seemed likely that Noor would be able to wrap this all up tonight.

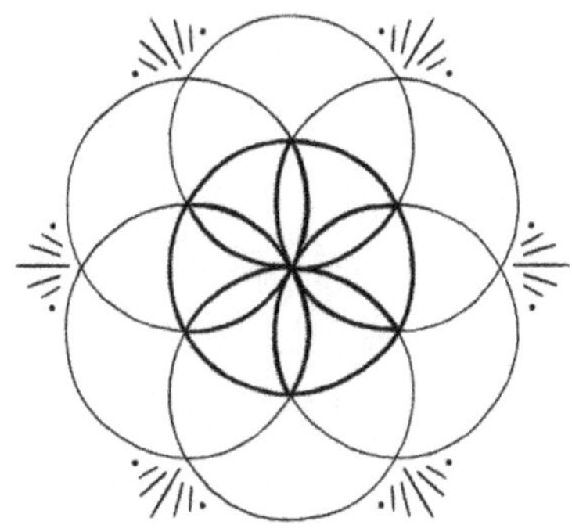

CHAPTER 39

"WHAT WOULD YOU suggest I do?" Noor asked loudly. She and Bodhi had been talking in whispers since dinner ended, which felt like hours ago. The whispering part of the conversation must have ended.

At the sound of Noor's raised voice, Ayla, Mina, and Prem stopped what they were doing and stared at each other. They waited.

"I don't know, Noor." Bodhi's deep voice had a whole new vibration at this volume. "You heard the same concerns I heard today. I don't think the answer is for you to do nothing, though."

The kitchen door swung open, and Noor stormed through.

"Stop, Noor!" Bodhi came out after her.

She stopped and turned slowly. She looked like she had been crying. "This has never happened," she said. "I don't know what to do!"

"Talk to us, Mom," Prem said.

Noor dropped into a chair and spoke to her family. As Ayla suspected, Noor had been surprised when the people from the city spoke up at the meeting. She had not expected any of them to speak, and she felt like she had let them all down.

She shared that as they spoke, she had sensed Seth was glad to hear from them at first but then grew frustrated when they said they didn't want him to be their leader. She knew he was getting angrier and angrier because she could feel the heat coming from his body.

"I really believed this would end with the others leaving," she said. "I thought the rest of the community was content here. I had no intention of making any substantive changes to the way we live."

"And now, Mom?" Mina asked, biting her lip. "Don't you think now we could make some changes?"

"Where would it end?" Noor asked, throwing her hands in the air.

Mina and Prem shrunk into their chairs.

"It wouldn't hurt to enhance our use of technology, Noor," Bodhi said.

"You only say that because *you* want to enhance technology," Noor said, pointing her finger at Bodhi. "You aren't thinking about what's best for the entire community!"

Who is this person? Ayla had that same feeling she got when a character she loved in a movie turned out to be different than she expected. She didn't recognize Noor.

"What do you think, Ayla?" Noor spun around to look at her.

Ayla was shocked. She didn't know what to say next.

"Ayla, you are here because you can see beyond what is obvious," Noor said with a slight hiss. "What am I missing?"

Ayla took a deep breath. She wanted to choose her words very carefully. She had come to love Noor with all her heart, and yet she couldn't understand why Noor was so resistant to change.

"Well," Ayla started, "as the Mother, don't you think . . . well . . ."

"Yes?" Noor said, her voice softer. "Keep going, Ayla."

"Well, I think—I mean, don't you think, well, maybe it *is* time for a change?" Ayla longed to make a strong statement but could only ask another question.

"Is that what you would suggest, then?" Noor's voice rose again. "That I give in to their demands?"

"Well, I mean, obviously, you are the Mother and I'm just a kid, really. From Earth, too, so there's that. Change isn't always about giving in, though . . ." Ayla's mouth couldn't keep up with her thoughts. She silently pleaded for the right words to come out.

"I'm sorry," Noor said, noticing Ayla's angst and knowing she should put her at ease. Then Noor slowly looked around at each member of her family, holding each person's expectant gaze.

"I'm scared," she finally said. "I want to do what is right and best for everyone. It's my job to protect our people. I'm afraid advances in technology would be dangerous for all of us. I also know now there are many people in the community who would like to see Ishwa suffer in some way because of the way he betrayed us. I can't think of anything we could do to increase his suffering beyond the suffering he has already created for himself."

Noor wiped her eyes.

"It's okay to cry, Mom," Prem said. He walked over to his mother and put his arm around her. Then he looked up and winked at Ayla.

Everything is going to be okay, Ayla thought, her spirits rising.

"Maybe everyone who is unhappy should just leave?" Noor asked, presumably to the ceiling. "I never should have agreed to this. I should have insisted on a Mother's Table!"

What? What is she thinking? I thought she'd moved past that ridiculous idea. She refuses to change. She's holding too tightly! Ayla was trying to remain quiet, but even her thoughts were too loud. Mina and Prem looked at Ayla expectantly. *Say something!* they urged her with their thoughts.

Why me? Ayla wished someone else could reach Noor.

She will listen to you. It was Bodhi. Ayla knew she couldn't let him down too.

"Noor," Ayla began, "I know it seems like your people would be safer if everything stayed the same here. As long as things stay the same, you know what to expect, right? You could continue to protect them, as you always have.

"And I can see how you might think it would be easier for those who disagree with you to leave, rather than make any changes here.

"But, Noor, the truth is that, as the Mother, as the head of the Mother's Table, when your family or your people or, you know, your community? When they're unhappy or don't agree with you, you can't make them leave the Table. They belong here. You need to actually make *more* room at the Table. So everyone has a spot. Even the people who disagree with you.

"And maybe you *do* need to serve something different at the Table now. As the Mother, you are really the only one who can make sure everyone has what they need."

Ayla stopped. She waited for Noor—or anyone—to say something. Anything.

"Thank you, Ayla." Noor forced a slight smile. "I hear you. All of you." Noor's eyes met each of theirs. "I have heard enough now."

She stood and walked out of the room.

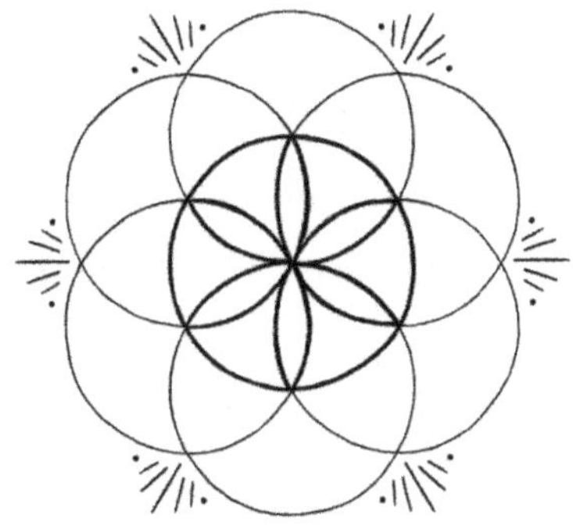

CHAPTER 40

The next morning, Ayla sat next to Mina and Olivia in the boardroom and watched as Seth walked in, whispering to the two boys who accompanied him.

Mina nudged Olivia with her elbow. "What's up with the two boys?"

Ayla remembered when she was worried yesterday about not having chairs for the two boys who had unexpectedly arrived with Seth. If only *that* was her biggest concern now. Noor hadn't spoken to any of them that morning, not at home or on the ride to the boardroom. As soon as they arrived, she'd disappeared. Ayla was now beside herself with worry over what she had said to Noor. Mina assured her several times that she had not overstepped, that Ayla had said exactly what Noor needed to hear.

It seemed Noor was the only person here who wasn't truly ready for a change. None of her family members could understand why she was so determined to keep things as they had always been, and none of them felt like they could reach her.

"I need to tell you something," Olivia whispered to Ayla and Mina. "Come here."

She grabbed the girls by their hands and dragged them to a corner of the room.

"My dad did something," she whispered, her voice barely audible. "Something bad."

"Something *else*?" Mina whispered back.

Ayla felt her chest tighten. "What did he do?"

Olivia grabbed them by their hands again and dragged them out the door. She stopped in the hallway, looked over her shoulder, and whispered, "Those two boys are my dad's assistants."

"*Assistants?*" Mina and Ayla whispered together.

Olivia nodded, then looked over her shoulder. "He said he needed assistants too, because Noor brought you two to the meeting at our house."

"Okay, that might be *weird*," Ayla said, "but why bad? Having assistants doesn't seem that bad to me." She was trying to remain calm, but a sick feeling was rising in her stomach.

"They had to compete to be his assistants," Olivia whispered.

"Compete?" Mina said loudly.

"Yes! Shhhh! Mina, it's even worse than it sounds. He made them *fight* for it." Olivia's eyes began to fill with tears. "It was awful. It happened during the time of reflection. There were about seven boys who wanted to compete." Olivia wiped her eyes with her sleeve. "They fought each other. They *hurt* each other."

"I don't understand, Olivia." Mina's voice had a hint of panic. "I've never heard of such a thing!"

"I know." Olivia's chin dropped to her chest. She stared at the ground.

Ayla was confused. She didn't know what to make of what Olivia shared, and she knew she would never be able to make sense of it with her mind. She *felt* terrible, though, and that was all she needed to know.

"One of the boys who fought was hurt pretty badly," Olivia said. "My dad wouldn't let them call the Medicine Woman. He hasn't spoken a word to me since the fight. It's so hard, watching him whisper to those poor boys when he won't even talk to me." Olivia let out a deep sigh. It sounded like she had been holding her breath for days.

"Does anyone else know? Anyone from town?" Mina asked.

"No. He told us all not to tell anyone. I've never seen anything so shocking in my entire life. It was worse than watching my mom's spirit leave her body, which completely shattered my heart—but *that* was beautiful. Hard, but truly . . . wonderful." Olivia bit her lip in an attempt to stop her tears.

"This was unspeakable," she continued. "I can't comprehend why he would want them to fight each other—to cause each other pain." Olivia looked at Ayla, as if expecting Ayla to know the answer to her questions. It was strange for Ayla to see Olivia, someone usually so full of life, looking deflated.

"I don't know, Olivia," Ayla said. "On Earth, you know, that kind of thing happens all the time. Maybe not like this, exactly. But people fight. They hurt each other. I think it's about wanting to be powerful." She was having a difficult time speaking. Her chest was so tight, she was struggling to breathe.

"Powerful? He didn't look powerful, Ayla. He looked weak." Olivia sounded like a person whose optimistic view of her life had shifted from hope to sadness.

"Well, maybe it's about control, then. He wanted to *look* powerful. He wanted to show himself in control." Ayla reached for Olivia's hand and gave it a light squeeze.

"They're starting," Mina said, wrapping her arms around the girls. "I'm so sorry, Olivia. So, so sorry."

They walked back inside, and Ayla sank into her chair, wishing she could disappear. She longed for Earth, her true home. She knew the time was near. She could feel it, just like Noor said she would. She had pictured a gentler departure, though. From the looks of it, she could very well be violently ejected from Eema, and soon.

Ayla held her right hand over her heart and closed her eyes. *If you are in there, Star Within, God, Great Big Everything, Great Mystery, That Which Has No Name—Whoever or Whatever is listening, please help Noor stand her ground. Whatever that looks like. Please help her. Please help these wonderful people not ever know the ugliness we know on Earth. Thank you.*

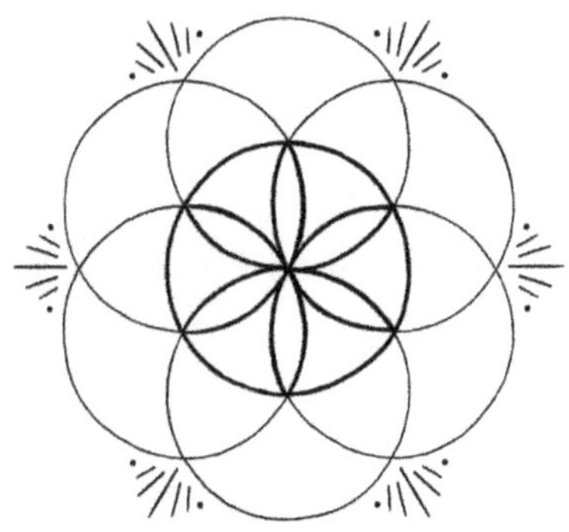

CHAPTER 41

Noor was at the podium, thanking everyone for returning for a second day of discussion. She thanked everyone who had spoken the day before. Then she thanked Seth for giving her the opportunity to see that change was indeed needed.

Ayla began to panic. *Oh no! What is she doing?*

"I have taken your words, all your words, to heart," Noor said. "I am grateful to have heard what you've shared here. After giving your words my full attention, I have decided it will not be necessary for Seth to speak here today. He will not need to speak in order for us to move ahead."

"What? I have a right to be heard!" Seth growled, bolting up and out of his seat. Everyone in the room shrunk into their chairs, as if trying to hide from Seth. The two boys on either side of him lurched forward, sticking out their huge, muscled chests.

"Yes, and so you shall be, Seth," Noor said. "As the Father of the North, you will be heard."

An explosion of voices filled the boardroom. Noor held her hand up to quiet Seth and the crowd.

"Seth, Circle, fellow community members," Noor said, her voice raised but still calm. "I am stepping down. I will no longer serve as the Mothe—"

"No!" Ayla cried, interrupting Noor. She shot up out of her chair and ran to face Noor as quickly as she could. Ayla felt her blood boiling and her heart racing. She had spent her entire stay on Eema trying to shrink, trying to stay as small as possible, trying to take up as little space as possible, and trying not to be noticed or heard. Her own roar echoing through the room startled her. It almost stopped her completely.

"YOU SIT DOWN!" Seth screamed at Ayla. "YOU HAVE DONE ENOUGH! YOU WILL BE GONE SOON! DO NOT SAY ANOTHER WORD!"

"Ayla, I think Seth is right," Noor said quietly, calmly, her words hitting Ayla like a stun gun. "I think you have said enough." Noor looked around the room and continued quietly, "A good Mother makes room at the Table. It is time for change. It is time for a new leader at the Table."

"No, Noor, you can't," Ayla said, pleading with Noor. "You need to stay."

"Ayla, it is too late. You said so yourself. This is what must come next for my people and me." Noor sounded like a robot. Ayla searched her eyes and found no sign of the gentle, compassionate woman she had come to love as her very own mother. Noor was worse than closed. She seemed to have left completely.

Ayla grabbed Noor by both her arms, squeezing maybe a little too tightly. "I came here to help," she said. "I didn't think I could help, but now I know I can."

Ayla glared at Seth. "We've had Fathers on Earth, where I'm from," she continued. "We have a very long history of Fathers as leaders."

Ayla looked around the room. The fear and confusion she felt was reflected back to her in the faces she saw before her. She paused, remembering to try to meet as many eyes as possible before continuing.

"I know you're scared." She stopped, smiled, took a deep breath. "Our Fathers on Earth, in my own country, they have done their best with what they had and what they knew. I think they always wanted to protect us in some way.

"But instead of peace and love like you have here, they have used violence in the name of protecting us. They have hurt others, and they have hurt their own people. They have even hurt themselves.

"So, well, it just hasn't been good enough to have Fathers as our only leaders. We know we can do better. There have been many times throughout our history when other people, people who weren't the Fathers—regular people, just like you and like me—have spoken up and wanted change, just like you are speaking up now.

"They are speaking up now too. On Earth, a lot of people are upset about the way things are. They feel left out, and they are hoping for change. But many of our Fathers have turned their backs on us. They aren't listening to *all* of us. They only listen to the ones they *want* to hear. It makes us feel insane. People are saying and doing things you cannot even imagine."

Ayla took another deep breath and tried to remember to look at everyone like Noor always did. To include everyone with her gaze. To be a leader. Like a Mother.

"Mothers never stop listening," she said. "Even when they think they've heard enough, they still listen." Ayla paused. She looked at Noor, who looked as surprised as Ayla was to find herself still talking. *I can't stop now*, she thought.

"I know from life on Earth that change is hard. Sometimes the people in charge, the leaders, they fear change as much as we fear that things will never change." Ayla paused, wondering if she was even making sense to these people. "That is usually the best time for change. Change is okay. It might be hard, especially at first, but it *is* okay. It's okay."

Ayla was looking directly at Noor at this point. She took Noor's hand in hers and flinched when she noticed Noor's hand was as cold as ice.

"It's okay, Noor," Ayla whispered, staring into Noor's eyes. "I did say it was up to you to make more room at the Table. But Noor, I never, never thought *you* would go! It's a Mother's duty to make more room at the Table, but she doesn't leave the Table. Your job as Mother is to stay at the Table. To keep listening." Ayla paused. She felt the warmth returning to Noor's hand. She felt her own hand begin to tingle.

"You can't go," she said to Noor, her voice getting a little louder again. "Eema is the peaceful, beautiful place it is because of *you*—because of Mothers."

Ayla looked at Seth, but only briefly because she was afraid he would cut her off while she was still speaking. She wasn't sure how much more she had to say.

"We need Fathers too, of course," she continued. "Fathers are important. But Mothers are the fiercest yet gentlest and most noble leaders. Mothers make everything work. Mothers make everything *flow*. I see that here.

"Please don't make the same mistake we made on Earth. Eema needs you, Noor. Eema needs all of its Mothers."

Ayla caught a glimpse of Nell out of the corner of her eye. She was smiling and nodding, keeping the beat to Ayla's words.

Seth lunged toward Ayla.

"ENOUGH OF YOUR NONSENSE! YOU ARE A DISGRACE TO EARTH AND TO ALL OF YOUR FATHERS! YOU DON'T BELONG ON EEMA! YOUR WORDS MEAN NOTHING HERE!"

Ayla ducked, and Seth fell into Noor, knocking her to the ground. By that time, almost everyone had jumped out of their seats. The members of the Circle pulled Seth from Noor. Bodhi rushed to make sure she was okay.

"Enough out of you!" Ishwa hissed at Seth, his nose an inch from Seth's nose as he pinned him to the ground. The two boys lunged toward Ishwa, which caused a few boys in the crowd to run to the front of the room.

"He's dangerous! He hurt us!" one of the boys from the crowd yelled, pointing at Seth. With the help of some of the others, Ishwa and Bodhi shielded Seth from the crowd with their bodies. Seth's followers stared at him. Ayla expected them to look angry or afraid, but instead their faces were blank.

Half the courtroom erupted into a quiet chant, quite the opposite from the one yelled outside the Collective not long ago. "Stay, Noor. Please stay! Stay, stay, stay."

"YOU SAID YOU WERE GOING!" Seth roared from behind the bodies shielding him. "NOW GO!"

"Go, go, go," Seth's followers chanted, as if coming to life again. They pumped their clenched fists at Noor.

"Stay!"

"Go!"

"Stay!"

"Go!"

The chants continued, getting louder and louder.

Then, *gonnnnnnnnnnnnnngggggggggggg*. *Gonnnnnnnnnggggggggggg*. *Gonnnnnnnnnnngggggggggggg*.

Three clangs of a gong reverberated throughout the boardroom. Ayla felt the vibration hum in her chest. All heads spun around, looking for the source of the sound. Nell stood at the podium, holding a small gong and padded mallet.

Mina's huge eyes found Ayla's. *How on Eema did that little thing make such a big sound?*

"Nell?" Noor looked at Nell in disbelief.

"*Enough!*" Nell's typically soft voice pierced the courtroom.

The room grew so silent that Ayla could hear Mina's stomach gurgling. The girls looked at each other, their eyes wide with anticipation.

"Eema is *angry*!" Nell spoke with a ferocity Ayla hadn't yet seen in her. Her normally deep brown eyes were overtaken by a deep golden color. Her eyes looked like the eyes of a wild animal. She glared from person to person, lingering longer when she came to Seth, then Noor.

The room was completely still.

"Eema feels we have let her down," Nell said. "The stewardship she needs now is not confined within the body of a Mother or a Father. There is no right body in which to guide our people. It is what the body holds, the Star Within, that determines a leader's potential.

"We have reached a point in time where our needs are many, and for each need a different person will lead, depending on their gifts. We must come together. We all have a place at the Table. We must work together. Because our dear Eema, our original Mother, who has held us since our inception, is looking to us now to hold *her*." Nell's voice was deeper now. She sounded like a different Nell, and she held everyone's attention as if they all knew that she was about to say something important.

"Her sister, the *Mother Earth*"—Nell's voice softened as she met Ayla's eyes—"is in trouble. We believe that Earth's turmoil is spreading across space, across galaxies, and all across the plains in the sky. We believe that all of us—here and on Earth—are in grave danger. Eema is counting on us to overcome this petty foolishness."

Nell pointed her finger out and around the room.

"We must pull ourselves together and prepare our sister Ayla to take the light, our light, Eema's Star Within, back to Earth, to show its people that our light reflects their light, the light they have forgotten. This is how we will help Eema and Earth heal. This is how we will help each other heal. This is how we will save Eema and Earth."

Nell closed her eyes and inhaled as if she was trying to suck every trace of negativity out of the room. She exhaled, then inhaled. Exhaled, then inhaled. Every person sat in complete silence. Some closed their eyes along with Nell. Ayla felt the very air molecules in the room shifting. She felt the cells in her body shifting too. It felt as if each cell was repairing itself in some way. She felt more rejuvenated with each of Nell's long breaths.

"What, then? What do we do?" Noor spoke softly. She looked at Nell with the eyes of a bewildered child who was tired of trying, who was desperate to know what to do next.

"First, you don't give up. Ayla is right, Noor. You cannot leave your people. You cannot leave the Table." Nell's voice had softened, but she was still more resolute than Ayla or anyone in the room had ever seen her before. The strength she so carefully held within her could no longer be contained. It was now clear she had been a force of power all along.

"But she stepped down!" Seth cried.

"Second, you stop arguing, and you do not, under any circumstances, resort to violence," Nell said, ignoring his words and focusing her golden eyes on Seth. She looked from one of Seth's boy assistants to the next.

They and Seth looked at the ground. A small snort exited Seth's nose.

"Our Mother Eema is our highest teacher," Nell said. She pointed toward the ceiling, and Ayla imagined a ray of light shooting up from her pointed finger like a lightsaber. Nell looked around the room, meeting the eyes of Ayla, Mina, Olivia, Zora, Prem, and each of the young people. "Every piece of her whole has a role in sustaining her. The sun provides light to us. And we, in turn, have our own sources of light—our own light bringers."

Ayla felt a surge of warmth pulse through her chest. With it came a sense of knowing that she and the others, her peers, were the light bringers to whom Nell was referring. *A light bringer? No pressure there*, she thought, catching Mina's smile.

"The ground holds us," Nell continued. "It is from the ground that our roots have grown. These roots, bound in Eema, are like our Mothers and our Fathers." She looked from Noor to Seth. "Both are essential to our growth and well-being.

"From now on, our fathers' names will be written in our Chronicles."

Ayla couldn't be positive, but it looked like Seth's body might have relaxed a little.

"From the moon to the stars to the flowers on the ground and the birds with their songs, each piece has a significant part," Nell continued. "No part is small. And each piece has a season. It is part of a cycle. In the winter, we rest. In the spring, we bloom. In the summer, we play. In the fall, we release what no longer serves us. We live, we die, we repeat. Together, we are to each other what the light, the roots, the moon, the stars, the flowers, and the birds are to Eema.

"The Table shall forever be round, like a circle, with no end and no beginning. There is no head of the Table. There shall be Mothers, Fathers, Solunas, and Young Ones at the Table. We will all have a part, and we will all work together. We will draw from the very First Ways of the past, from our beginnings until now, and again we will create New Ways to live and be together." Nell raised her eyebrows and looked around, her eyes returning to their original deep chocolate brown color.

"Any other questions?" Nell said, softly as ever, with the kind of smile a mother gives her peaceful, sleeping baby at the end of a long day. Ayla looked around and noticed a huge smile on Noor's face. She no longer seemed defeated. In fact, she looked absolutely radiant. Noor's smile was contagious. Ayla tried to hold back a giggle of delight. She really wasn't sure what any of Nell's words would mean for the people here, and she had no idea what a Soluna was—there would be time to figure that out—but she felt so light that she thought for sure she could fly if she tried.

The entire room breathed a deep sigh of relief with Ayla. Somehow, in some way—a *new way*—Nell had transformed the room from a place of despair to one of hope. Her presence was powerful, but it was her words, like medicine, that seemed to soothe the souls of those who were present. Ayla blinked, sure she saw thin rays of light beaming out from the tops of everyone's heads and into the heavens. Where the people here seemed to have been splitting and falling in different directions, Nell had managed to mend the divisions and reunite them. Even though what happened was as real as the breath in Ayla's lungs, it felt like Nell had waved a magic wand over the entire room. It was alchemy. Nell's spell stopped the chaos. The universe, the multiverse, all of space and time was altered when Nell spoke.

Could it be that simple? Ayla wondered. *Can a person simply speak a new way into being?*

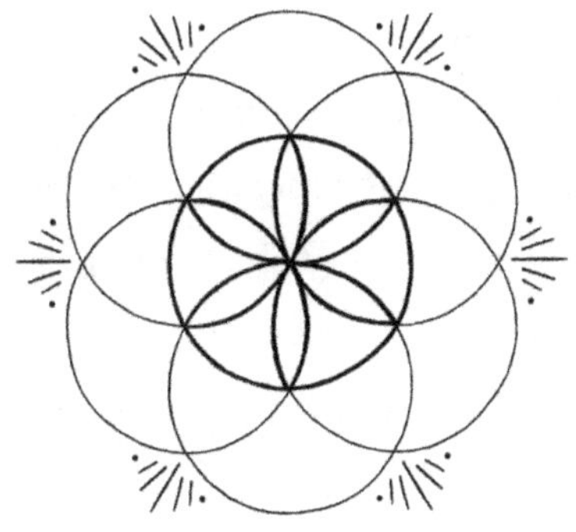

CHAPTER 42

WITHIN A MATTER of days, Nell's directives began to take form. Everything happened quickly. Nell insisted her orders for how to proceed came straight from Eema. The Mothers from all four directions welcomed the suggested changes and immediately began working to form their new Circles. The Circle in the North expanded with new members. Noor stayed on as Mother, and an advisory committee was formed to determine whether the Circle would benefit from the addition of a Father. Noor thought Seth could help the committee if and when he was ready. Representatives were appointed from all over the town *and* the outskirts. A few Young Ones were also added to the Circle and would eventually form their own Circle and act as advisors to the adults.

A few people in the newly formed Circle focused on technology and travel, and some jobs were dedicated to listening and making sure the needs of the entire community were being met. A few men began to study medicine under the Medicine Woman. Some people were even assigned to research pet ownership. Ayla marveled at how quickly the changes were embraced. It was as if the possibility for change was right there all along, just waiting to be welcomed.

Almost instantly, the technology team distributed devices that looked just like cell phones. These made communication between everyone much easier. The Circle began sending out polls, seeking feedback from the community, and the technology made it possible for the opinions to be tabulated and returned to the Circle instantly. The few who still had reservations about the changes in technology were paired with others who helped them learn how to use their devices. Nobody looked back and wished things could stay as they always had been. Nell knew that after what had happened, the people realized nobody could be truly content until *everyone* was at peace.

Mina was asked to help coordinate the changes being made from the Screening Room at the Collective Chronicles. Her main role was to watch the Chronicles and report anything notable to the Circle. Ayla watched with Mina and helped where she could. She thought a lot about her first meeting with the Circle and the days she had spent at the Collective Chronicles with Bodhi. She didn't look taller and she probably wasn't taller, but she *felt* taller. She felt bigger, like she now took up more space. Mina seemed different too. Taller? Bigger? There weren't any distinguishable physical changes, but she was definitely more obvious now. Mina had developed a *presence.*

Ishwa was around a lot, also helping to facilitate all the new changes. He was different too. Maybe smaller? Ayla struggled to find the words to describe what she observed. So much of what she was seeing was like everything else she had witnessed on Eema. The most obvious indicator of change was the way she felt. Ishwa *felt* safer when he was around.

Even so, she bristled when it was just the two of them in the Screening Room one afternoon. Mina had just stepped out, and Ishwa stepped in.

"Oh. Hi, Ishwa," Ayla said with reluctance when she saw him.

"Hello, Ayla," he said, swiping his arm in front of the screens. "I need to check in on the West. Watch for more wildfires."

"You know," Ayla started, feeling bold but still not entirely at ease, "I don't know a whole lot about wildfires, but I think they are relatively normal."

"Yes," he said, nodding as he scanned through scenes of the landscape in the West. "You are right about that. But these wildfires were different, Ayla."

"And different is . . . scary?"

He turned toward her and smiled. "Yes. Different *can* be scary."

Ishwa gazed at Ayla, making her a little uncomfortable. She waited.

"Listen, Ayla," he said. "I was wrong about you. I was afraid. I didn't think it would be safe to bring you here, and I thought you were trouble. I made a mistake, though, and I caused more harm to my community than I think you ever could have caused. We are repairing here, and I know you will return home soon. But before you go, I want you to know that I am sorry. I am sorry for the way I treated you."

Ayla didn't know what to say. *I am sorry. I am sorry. I am sorry.* Three short words. And yet hearing them made an enormous impact on her. Before she could speak, scenes from the Chronicles ran through her mind. Arguments, fights, wars. She recognized some of the quickly moving faces. Some were from books and movies she had seen. Another was Connor. Her parents. She had witnessed many conflicts in her short life.

"Ayla? Are you okay?" Ishwa moved closer to her.

"I—yes," she stammered. "I'm okay. The Chronicles, my Chronicles, from Earth—they're running through my mind. And . . . well, I remember lots of arguing and fighting. But I don't remember hearing *I'm sorry*. Not much, anyway. The way you said it, well, it means a lot. Thank you for saying 'I'm sorry.'"

"I mean it, Ayla. I regret what I did." Ishwa paused as if he wasn't sure he wanted to share more. Then his face softened, and he continued, "I was always very judgmental of Earth and the choices your people made. You all seemed foolish to me."

"Foolish?"

"Yes, foolish. Vicious. Unreasonable too." He shrugged his shoulders, as if what he said should be obvious.

"Okay, I think you made your point," Ayla said, raising her eyebrows.

"I now see I can be foolish too. I can't remember a time in my life when everything felt so unpredictable. Uncertain times cause people to act in uncertain ways. I see that now, and I do hope you will forgive me for my behavior." His voice was even, calm, and quiet.

"I do, Ishwa. I do forgive you." Ayla smiled at him, still not believing this man who once intimidated her could now seem so mild-mannered.

The surprises were endless on Eema, and in these moments when what she believed to be true about someone or something was proven otherwise, it seemed that *every* space had the potential to be a *space between*. In every aspect of life, there appeared to be a right and wrong, and sometimes those were obvious. But sometimes there was something else, a different category, that was not at all obvious.

Ayla thought back to the moment when she met Ishwa and he made her uncomfortable. And she thought of him now, when he seemed so harmless. Ishwa hadn't really changed at all. Between the space where she first met him and now, when she understood him better, was simply a man who cared about protecting his people and his home. That's all he ever was.

Seeing him in this new light, Ayla felt like she could relate to Ishwa. She even felt a deeper connection to him because she knew that even if she made mistakes along the way too, she would do whatever was necessary to protect her people and her home—just like Ishwa did.

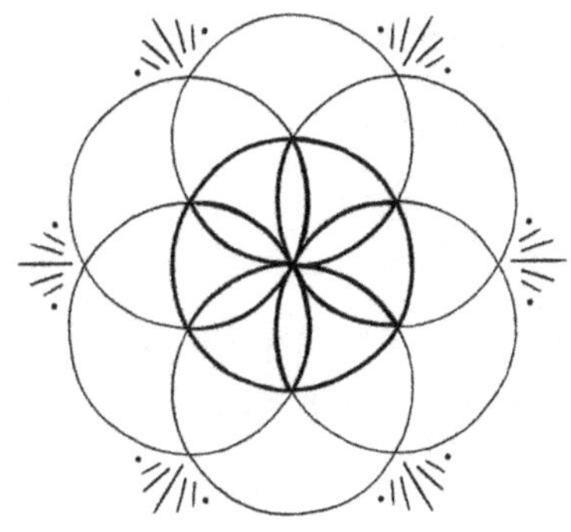

CHAPTER 43

BEFORE TOO MUCH longer, it was time for Ayla to start preparing to return to Earth. She tried to sneak into Noor's cozy office at the Collective whenever she could. Noor and Nell would drink tea and speak in whispers while she and Mina did the same in another corner of the room. Often, the four of them talked together.

Ayla made notes and sketched, trying to recollect everything she had experienced on Eema in order to etch it into her brain, her body, and her soul. She thought about all the different people she had met and how she had been struck right away by all their different skin tones. There were no "majority" or "minority" shades of skin color here, like there were at home, but there had been the "insiders" who lived in town and the "others" who lived on the outskirts. Those differences had not been apparent to her when she first arrived.

"Those are the differences you will need to continue to seek, Ayla," Nell said, reading her thoughts. "The differences that are not immediately apparent. To see what really needs attention, always look beyond what is obvious."

Ayla knew her new friends and family were counting on her to continue helping them when she went back to Earth, and more than anything she wanted to be helpful. However, she couldn't imagine trying to explain what she had learned during her time away to people in her town, let alone in her state or her entire country. *If only they could see all I've seen*, she thought. *Then they would understand.*

She turned to a blank page in her notebook to take more notes. She was determined to listen closely to Nell and Noor, to capture everything and to ask only *some* questions—her most important ones. But Nell was reluctant to explain much to Ayla before she returned to Earth, despite Ayla's long list of questions.

"Eema called on us to look beyond what was obvious," Nell said to start. "It was time to establish a new sense of order here on our planet. Noor, as our Mother, struggled to see we needed to make changes here. She wanted to keep our rules and traditions intact so she could protect us, as she and all the Mothers always have. Once the tornadoes hit in the South, she became overwhelmed and disoriented."

Nell stared intently into Ayla's eyes as she spoke, seeming to gaze beyond her eyes and maybe even into her soul.

"Seth knew that Noor had lost track of the needs and desires of the people here," Nell continued, "but he tried to replace her with something that would have been very much the same—himself. A new leader, only a Father instead.

"We have outgrown that whole approach to leadership and organization here on Eema, and I suspect that maybe the same is true for you on our sister Earth. But that will be for you and *your* Circle to determine."

"*My* Circle?" Ayla said. "You do realize my country doesn't really value the opinions of Young Ones like you do here, right?" Ayla kept telling herself to stay calm and to stay open, but she could feel her anxiety mounting.

"When you go back, you will need to keep looking for solutions that aren't obvious, Ayla," Nell said. "You will need to look for *other ways*. It seems overwhelming now, we know, but it will be okay. You won't be alone.

"Just remember that what is best for everyone is not as obvious as it may have seemed in the past. Your capabilities have evolved at such high rates on Earth. Faster than your bodies, your minds, or your spirits. Issues, problems, and even people have become more complicated. There are multiple layers, and sometimes conflicting needs. Your solutions will be found in the space between all or nothing. Insisting on only one fixed and rigid way of operating is an outdated approach to problem-solving.

"Earth needs you, Ayla. Eema needs you. *We* need you."

Nell's words felt heavy to Ayla, but at the same time they were laced with hope. With her whole heart, Ayla wanted to believe she was capable of doing whatever it was she would need to do once she returned home, even though it was not at all clear what that would entail. She was caught between the struggle to do what was best and not knowing what the best even was. It made her squirm in her seat.

"What if I need help? How will I contact you?" she asked, shifting her body so she would be closer to Mina.

"Place your hand over your heart," Noor said. "Imagine the light glowing from your Star Within. Then imagine my light, or Mina's, or Nell's, or whomever you need, and speak to us. The light connects us instantly. We will hear you."

Ayla wanted to believe it was that simple.

Nell affirmed Noor's words. "Ayla, your light connects you to the light within any and all spirit energy—the energy that is contained within human bodies. Remember? Anytime, anywhere, you just need to ask."

"So, does that mean I could talk with Grandpa George too? Since he is spirit energy now?" Ayla wondered if she was pushing it. Her curiosity was getting the better of her.

"Yes, you can talk to him too," Nell said, smiling reassuringly and nodding her head.

"Wow." Ayla paused to take that in. "Okay. So, here's another question. The Solunas? I think that was the word you used. I hadn't heard it before, and I've been wondering about it. You said Solunas are part of the Circle now—what are those?"

"I'm a Soluna," Nell said with a smile, flecks of gold shining in her eyes. "I am neither a man nor a woman. I am both. I am a person of the masculine sun and the feminine moon—a *Soluna.* When I was small, I decided to call myself a *she*, and that is how I've always identified."

Ayla remembered that when she first met Nell, she couldn't tell if Nell was a man or a woman. The same had been true for some of the others she had met. Between the baggy tunics they all wore and the array of hairstyles—things that normally served as clues about a person's identity at home—Ayla didn't always know who was man or woman or boy or girl on Eema. Now that she thought about it, none of that even mattered here.

"Nell would never tell you this, Ayla," Noor said, putting her arm around Nell and squeezing her close, "but Solunas are highly respected and revered here on Eema. They have the gift of extreme and constant openness. Traditionally, each Mother has had one trusted Soluna who served as counsel to her. I have been fortunate to have Nell by my side."

"Wow. Solunas sound incredible. So, can they see into the future or something?"

"Solunas are wholly in tune with nature and its signals, so, yes, in a lot of ways they know what is coming. They know what Eema wants us to know," Noor said. "And because they have both masculine and feminine attributes, they can see all aspects of life from both perspectives. Their wisdom is limitless."

As Noor spoke, Ayla noticed Nell's cheeks growing pink.

"Nell's extreme and constant openness allows her to speak to Eema, to animals, and to trees, plants, and flowers," Noor continued. "She can communicate with just about anything! And actually, her openness is what made it possible for her to find you. She recognized *your* openness and picked you to come and help us." Noor paused and gave Nell another squeeze.

"Eema gave us Solunas in these limitless bodies as a symbol of *all that is possible*." Noor patted Ayla's knee and nodded at Nell, who then began to speak.

"Ayla, we went one way here on Eema by choosing leaders who are women, and you went the other way on Earth by favoring leaders who are men," Nell said. "On Earth, you fight and fight over who is better at what, a man or a woman. I'm afraid we were headed toward a similar path. Whether a person is a man or woman does not determine whether they will make good leaders, though. Leaders aren't defined by their bodies or shades of skin."

Nell smiled at Ayla, and Ayla's entire body tingled with warmth.

"None of our most significant virtues are obvious to others, because they come from within us," Nell continued, gazing into Ayla's eyes. "The blueprints are there—in your light, in your Star. Solunas know this, and our androgynous bodies were meant to serve as a reminder that we, as spirits, are so much more than our bodies. The gift of extreme and constant openness ensures that we Solunas never lose touch with the human potential that lies within." Again, the flecks of gold shimmered in Nell's eyes.

"Imagine if we all knew how powerful we are," Ayla said dreamily. "And it came from right there within us. I thought it would come from somewhere else. Somewhere outside of me." She looked toward the ceiling.

"Ayla, do you know what is most amazing about humans?" Nell said, speaking slowly. "Each of us *is* born knowing. We may not all appear to have a Soluna's body, but all humans are given the same spirit gifts as Solunas at birth. These gifts are written into us by the stardust from which we are formed. These are the gifts of unconditional love, infinite belonging, inner knowing, openness, and connection to all that is."

"But *how*?" Ayla was caught between wanting so badly for Nell's words to be true and not being able to comprehend how they could be true.

"Humans forget," Nell said, her golden brown eyes filling with tears. "Our lives are littered with disappointments and misunderstandings. Our brains deceive us with stories that betray our hearts and take us away from the truth, from our birthright—these magnificent gifts."

Ayla stared at Nell, wondering how she, young Ayla Stone from Michigan, could be as powerful as Nell. But that is what Nell was telling her was true, that *she* had the power of a Soluna at birth.

"Ayla, the only thing that matters now is that you stay open and return to Earth with the knowledge and faith that you carry the gifts of a Soluna," Nell said. "You *are* a Soluna. You are *everything*, all at once.

"When the snow fell, Eema told me the Solunas are here to help lead the way out of chaos. I didn't know that before. I didn't know why I was born this way or why I must live with the burden of openness. It is painful to feel so deeply, to see so clearly. I trust Eema, though. I know you can trust her too. And you can count on her—and her sister, Earth—to help guide you along the Soluna's way."

Ayla was stunned by Nell's words. *The Soluna's way.* Love. Belonging. Knowing. Openness. Connection. She closed her eyes, hoping the words—and the way—would seep into her very being. She knew it would take time to settle into her body. It could take a very long time.

She had one more question. It was the one she was most nervous to ask. The one she dreaded. The one she almost *didn't* ask but knew she would regret not asking if she didn't at least give it a try.

She opened her eyes. "And Noor?" she began.

"Yes?" Noor was all warmth and honey again. She seemed unburdened—peaceful—since Nell had given her directives. She was no less strong, and was maybe even stronger, after all she had been through.

"What happened?" Ayla asked. "How did you ever think it would be okay to make the others leave instead of answering their call for change?" She asked the question and then held her breath until Noor spoke.

"It is really very simple, Ayla," Noor said. "Despite my best efforts to stay open, I was actually closed. I had been for a long time. Since my dear friend Nahara moved on. In fact, I could no longer see what was in front of me, let alone that which was not."

Noor looked from Nell to Mina, both of whom looked back at her with so much love, Ayla could feel it in the air between them.

"I don't understand, though," Ayla said. "You have always been open. I have felt the warmth in your hands. How could you have closed?" She felt her eyes burning with fresh tears. It was surprising to learn what she thought was true might not actually be true.

Noor placed a hand on each of Ayla's knees and looked her directly in the eyes. "Ayla, remember the degrees of openness we talked about when you came here?"

Ayla nodded.

"When Nahara crossed over, I opened to a degree I had not yet experienced. I felt like my whole being was broken open. As the Mother, though, I could not afford to be broken in that way. I had to force myself to bounce back quickly."

"Mom!" Mina interrupted, stunned by her mother's words. "You always tell us to be okay with whatever feelings we have! How could you make yourself bounce back?"

"I know, dear one," Noor said, reaching out to tuck a few strands of Mina's hair behind her ear. "Mothers have immense responsibility, though. I did not think I could afford to sacrifice time to take care of myself when my people needed me. I thought I had to prove to everyone I was strong."

Mina sighed and fell back into her seat. "You *always* tell me to take care of myself first. This is outrageous."

"I know. And I mean that," Noor said as she turned back toward Ayla. "Listen, Ayla. This is really important, because when you return to Earth, you will have just lost your beloved Grandpa George. You are open now, and again your challenge will be to stay that way.

"As I watched Earth's history, I saw how events like the death of a loved one initially opened a person to feeling at an immense capacity.

The death of a loved one is one of the only occasions in which a human on Earth allows him or herself to really, truly *feel.* You don't give yourselves enough time, though. You close back up quickly. Sometimes you shrink even further into yourselves. You become *more* closed than you were before.

"I spent my entire life with the confidence and security of being open. I believed nothing like the closing that happens on Earth could ever happen on Eema, especially to me. I did not even notice myself closing when I tried to get back to work after losing Nahara. I was so focused on being a good Mother that I put all my energy there. I stopped allowing myself to *feel.* Feeling is the pathway to healing, and I never healed.

"And so, yes, I was open *enough*. You saw me drifting back and forth, in and out, and I was always partly open. But I was mostly closed." Noor drew in a deep breath and looked from Ayla to Mina.

"I had no idea," Mina said.

"Nobody did, my dear." Noor smiled. "Once I began to close, the gate to my Star Within became impenetrable. My Star could no longer serve as my guide. I lost my way."

"So, by the time the chaos from Earth reached you here," Ayla said, "you were out of touch with yourself, the people here, and pretty much everything?" Ayla could see her own mother's struggles in Noor's words. Helen Stone sometimes appeared to be fighting to stay open when she really wanted to close down. To shut everyone out. Perhaps staying open would be hard for her too.

Noor nodded, looking past Ayla's eyes straight to her soul. "It will not always be easy. You are right about that. You, too, may weave back and forth between being open and closed when you return home. Try to remember us, though. Remember everything you learned while you were here. Remember that we love you and we believe in you and we are counting on you to *stay open.* Above all else, remember that rules or ways that don't support and uphold everyone end up supporting and upholding no one. You helped me see that, and I am eternally grateful."

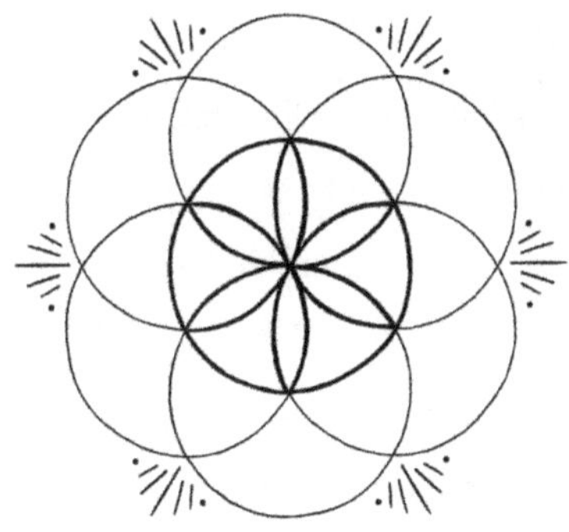

CHAPTER 44

"I'M NERVOUS," AYLA said, sure that every cell in her body was shaking.

"Why? Why are you nervous?" Mina smoothed Ayla's hair as she arranged a crown of flowers on top of Ayla's head. "You know everyone attending. We just want to bid you farewell. It will be fun!"

They were sitting in the family's living room one last time, together with Noor, Bodhi, and Prem.

"No, not about that," Ayla said. "Well, I guess I am a *little* nervous about that. I'm more nervous about traveling, though. What if I can't get back to Earth? Or what if I explode or something?"

Ayla adjusted the crown. It was making her head itchy.

"You won't explode," Prem said, rolling his eyes and shaking his head.

"You can get back," Bodhi said, looking at a screen as he talked. "We already ran all the scenarios. We checked the equations. As it turns out, it's perfect timing." He swiped his finger here and there, then held up the screen as proof.

Ayla shrugged her shoulders. She wanted to believe him. "Okay, that makes me feel better, I guess? Thanks, Bodhi. But another thing is, what if nobody remembers me?"

"Ayla, they won't even know you left. It's like"—Prem snapped his fingers—"no time has passed."

"I guess that scares me too." Ayla felt like she was about to throw up.

"What do you mean?" Mina stopped fussing with the crown and looked at Ayla.

"It scares me that I've been here for what feels like a long time, but no time has passed on Earth." Ayla threw her hands in the air. "If I tried to pretend this never happened, I could, you know? I could pretend I never came here to Eema. Nobody would ever know."

"*You* will know," Noor said. "You are forever changed. Your family and your friends will notice changes in different ways too. They will sense something has shifted in you, a little like a slight change in hairstyle. Something about you will seem different, but they won't know what it is. And only you will know why. This is like any other significant journey. Nobody even needs to know *what* changed or *why* you changed. They love you however you are, Ayla Bug."

"You know, I never asked you this," Ayla said, "but I've been wondering: how do you know to call me that? Only people really close to me have ever called me Ayla Bug."

Noor flashed Ayla her warm, soothing smile but didn't say anything. It wasn't a direct answer, but it was enough to satisfy Ayla, who knew she would miss seeing Noor's smile.

"You already know all the answers you seek," Noor said and then winked. "Look beyond what is obvious."

It was the kind of wink that indicated a secret shared between two people, but Ayla didn't know the secret. She still had so many questions. She wondered what would happen now that nobody would be there to answer them.

She fidgeted with the elastic band in her leggings. It was good to be back in her own clothes, but her leggings weren't as soft as the pants she wore on Eema. The material felt foreign to her now that she had worn something so different. She felt altered too.

"Remember, take your time," Noor continued. "Take as long as you need to absorb all you have experienced here on Eema, Ayla. There may be things you will never know for sure. Not anytime soon, anyway. Try to be okay in the soft space—in the mystery."

"It's time to go!" Bodhi stood up suddenly, still looking at his device, and motioned for the others to join him.

Once they left the house, they saw many of their friends were already heading to the creek. Olivia, who was coming from farther down the road, ran to catch up to them. Snow, her wolf pup, was nestled in her arms.

Ayla was happy to see her. "Hey, you! How's your dad?"

"He's good. He's *really* good. He's getting a lot of help. The Medicine Woman is working with him, and he meets with someone from the new Listening Circle almost every day. I think it's helping him. He had a lot of . . . stuff? Congestion?" Olivia waved her free hand back and forth over her chest and stomach a few times. "It's been stored inside him for so long—clogging his Star Within, I think he said. There were outdated stories stuck in there, left over from his family and from losing my mom. Stuff just stays stuck in there, I guess. It can be cleared, though. He's working on that." Olivia shifted Snow to her other arm, and he licked her face, which made her giggle.

"You know, as bonkers as he went," she said as Snow continued lathering her face with his tiny pink tongue, "I think he just wanted to be *heard*. To be seen for who he is, not who his family was—or what he thinks they were. He lost it, though. It was bad. I was scared." Olivia pulled Snow away from her face. "Stop it, Snow! I'm trying to talk."

She continued, "I think he'll be okay, though. I really do. I know he's looking forward to maybe being a Father. And to joining the Circle again. The *new and improved* Circle." Olivia winked, then held Snow up in the air like a dance partner and spun around in her own little circle a few times before running off ahead of them.

"Later, loves!" she called back to them, her voice trailing as she ran away.

"I'm glad Seth's okay," Ayla said.

"Me too," Mina agreed.

The two girls fell into step, each of them remembering their first walk up the same hillside they were now descending. It seemed like so long ago, and certainly a lot had happened. Yet in all the ways Ayla's arrival on Eema seemed like ancient history, it also seemed like she had only arrived yesterday.

"Look!" Mina squealed. "It's *beautiful*!"

Ayla had been so lost in thought, she was surprised to see they had made it to the creek. It was just ahead, glistening in the sunshine. The trees all around them were bare. A small structure, like a trellis, had been built of thick birch tree branches. It stood next to the creek. Fresh-cut wildflowers were tucked into arrangements and placed into the branches. It looked like a much smaller version of the Embody Festival, only outside. And there was no punch.

A few people sat off to the side, drumming on small drums they held in their arms.

"It's dreamy," Ayla said. She told herself to take it all in, to savor every last bit of rich, delicious beauty and every last heartbeat of love pulsing through the air. She never wanted to forget what it felt like to be on Eema. It was like she imagined heaven would feel.

"Are you ready?" Noor asked.

Ayla nodded. "I think so. I mean, I guess so." It was much different this time. This time, she knew she was about to travel across space and time, back to Earth. She didn't even remember the traveling part from last time, it had been such a surprise.

"Okay, I think Zora and the Medicine Woman are ready too." Noor looked at Bodhi, who nodded, slipping his device into his tunic.

As Ayla approached the trellis with her new family, all the people formed a circle. Zora stood under the trellis ahead of them, next to the

Medicine Woman, her mom. The family stopped just outside the circle of people. Mina and Ayla stood together, holding hands. Prem stood behind them, and Noor and Bodhi stood in front of them.

Noor pulled her children into her arms—the two children who once grew in her body and her new child, who had traveled all the way from Earth. Bodhi wrapped his arms around them too. *Group hug?* Ayla thought to herself, smiling. In her mind, she could hear her parents' voices, and Connor's too, shouting *Group hug!* as they all fell into each other's arms.

When they finished hugging, Ishwa and Nell, who stood side by side, stepped away from each other to let the group of five enter the circle. They looked like a wedding procession, walking from one point in the circle to the other, until finally they stopped in front of Zora and the Medicine Woman. Noor and Bodhi stepped aside so Ayla and Mina could stand directly in front of the Medicine Woman.

Do you take this woman to be your wife? Ayla thought.

Mina held back a giggle and let go of Ayla's hand.

"Thank you for answering our call, Ayla," Noor said, more to the rest of the people in the circle than to Ayla. Ayla heard whispers of affirmation and thanks uttered from within the circle.

"Your presence was a tremendous help to us, and we are grateful." Noor looked directly at Ayla this time.

"We present you with this," the Medicine Woman said to Ayla. She pulled out a small leather bundle, presumably out of nowhere, and held it in her hands, her palms facing up. Zora leaned in and untied the bundle. As the sides of the little package fell open onto the Medicine

Woman's hands, Zora pulled a round piece of metal from inside. She reached for Ayla's hand and placed the metal in Ayla's palm.

Ayla held the piece of metal in front of her face so she could see it better. It was about the size of a quarter and felt about as thick as any coin. It looked like it was made of copper. A small Flower of Life was etched into both sides of it. Ayla smiled when she recognized the flower.

"Please accept this symbol as our gift to you," the Medicine Woman said. She spoke slowly . . . soulfully. Her words brought tears to Ayla's eyes.

"This gift represents the Flower of Life," the Medicine Woman said, "which holds the universal code for all universes—your universe and our universe. The code is transmitted to you in the language you understand best. In your language, the code translates as *love*. It is love that binds you to your universe and all of us to each other."

The Medicine Woman pointed at the flower. "This gift is etched in copper to represent you, who, like copper, are a conduit for change. May this gift remind you that we are bound beyond what is obvious, beyond human logic and understanding, woven together with spirit magic and mystery, since the inception of the Great Big Everything and until infinity."

The Medicine Woman reached back into the bundle. "This is *lavender*, for healing," she said. She placed a small pinch of lavender in Ayla's palm.

"And this is *sage*, for cleansing." She placed a miniature bundle of sage in Ayla's hand.

"And these." The Medicine Woman placed three stones in Ayla's hand.

"This is *rose quartz*." She pointed to a smooth, pale-pink-colored stone. "When your heart falls into sleep, allow this stone to awaken it to the love that surrounds you."

She pointed to a clear, whitish, hard-edged stone that looked like a tiny glacier. "This is *selenite*. It will connect you to your Star Within, and to all the Stars Within."

Then she pointed to the last stone, a smooth, whitish-gray one. "And this is *moonstone*. May it remind you of us on Eema. While we are many moons apart, you can carry this stone with you. It holds the peace, calm, and harmony you experienced on Eema. It will help you sustain these qualities at home, on Earth." The Medicine Woman held Ayla's hand in hers, using her opposite hand to close Ayla's fingers around the new treasures she held.

Ayla closed her eyes and placed her bundle of treasures over her heart. "Thank you," she whispered.

Nell spoke next. "As you know, Ayla, we on Eema called upon you for help, and you came. We appreciate your openness, your wisdom, and your support through the challenges we faced. Although we must part ways now, your work here is not yet done."

Nell gazed so intently into Ayla's eyes, Ayla swore she could feel her soul tingling. "Ayla, you brought your Earth knowledge to us and helped us clear a pathway to healing our land. As we continue to heal here, you must take the gifts you received from Eema and help heal Earth."

The Medicine Woman placed her hand over Ayla's heart. "*You* are a Medicine Woman now. *This* is your medicine. Let it be medicine to Earth as well." Ayla tingled from heart to head to toe.

"Me? Are you sure? I know we've been through this. I know I even went along with it. But it seems so much more real now. I am *really* just a kid—just a girl—on Earth. I don't know . . ." Ayla's lip began to tremble.

"Ayla." Noor lowered her voice to a whisper. "We have absolutely confirmed that the tornadoes, the wildfires, and even the snow we experienced here on Eema are directly related to the chaos you and your people have been experiencing on Earth."

Noor paused as Ayla's eyes filled with tears.

"No, that can't really be true," Ayla whispered.

"Yes, Ayla," Noor said. "It *is* true. The unusual weather patterns combined with the hopelessness the others were feeling here, and you know what happened then. It is all connected. It started when the Earth could no longer contain its chaos, and it spilled over. Chaos rippled out of Earth, into your galaxy, and beyond, all the way to us.

"What is happening on Earth is indeed affecting us here, Ayla. Every little ailment, every bit of stress, every strain of discontent—each of these things starts a ripple. From person to planet to galaxy, the ripples dance far beyond what we can even begin to imagine."

Ayla stared at Noor as she spoke. *How can she be so calm? These findings are catastrophic!*

"We should be okay now, for a while at least," Noor said. "You helped us, Ayla. And because we were able to reel it in here with your help, there shouldn't be a ripple back to Earth. You have also kept Earth from catastrophe. We are all okay.

"But you cannot waste any time upon your return to Earth. There is still work to be done to stop the chaos entirely. Ayla, please know you are not alone. There are others—others like you. Some have even been to Eema, as you may recall, and some have not. They are waiting for you. Together, you form a powerful clan of Solunas."

Noor's smile soothed the feeling of dread that was rising in Ayla's chest as Noor spoke.

"You are all open, and you see beyond what is obvious," Noor continued. "You know the answers lie somewhere between what, at first sight, appears to be obviously right or wrong. You see all the space between. You are *light*. You are all you need. You will inspire change on Earth, and you will oversee its healing."

Ayla took a deep breath in. It sounded phenomenal, but this was a lot to carry with her on a quick trip from one planet to another.

"Remember and trust in the gifts with which we are all born," Noor said. "You are and always will be loved unconditionally. You have and always will belong. You know all there is to know. You are open. You are connected to all that is, ever was, and ever will be."

Noor pulled Ayla into her arms for one last hug. Ayla felt her body relax as the warmth from Noor's body spread over her.

Noor whispered, "You are it. You are everything. You are the Medicine Woman and the Mother, a Soluna. You are the whole Circle. The Great Mystery. The Star Within. You are a part and the sum of all the parts of the Great Big Everything. Go. Listen. Inspire. Heal." She whispered the words over and over, like a song and a prayer in Ayla's ear.

Mina, Prem, Bodhi, and Nell joined Zora and the Medicine Woman to form a circle around Ayla and Noor. As Noor kept whispering, Ayla absorbed each word, letting each one descend into her body, just like she would swallow a spoonful or capsule of any other kind of medicine. As the rest of the people who had gathered together formed more circles around them, Ayla imagined the medicine words traveling all about her mind and through her body, turning her doubt and fear into love.

Once all the circles were formed around them, a path was made for Ayla. Noor and Mina walked Ayla to the edge of the creek. Mina lifted Ayla's flower crown from her head. Except for the small medicine bundle she held in her hand, Ayla looked exactly like she did the day she arrived on Eema.

Noor handed her a stone and motioned for her to drop it into the water. It was all happening as quickly as a sprint and as slowly as a seed grows into a flower, and all at the same time. Ayla took a deep breath. She wanted to stay *and* she wanted to go. She knew it was time to leave Eema, though. She nodded at Noor and Mina.

"Farewell, our dear Ayla, bringer and bearer of all that is light and right. Farewell, Soluna." The Medicine Woman's soft good-bye was barely loud enough for Ayla to hear.

"Thank you all," Ayla said through her tears. "I will not disappoint you. I just want to say that . . . you can count on me. I don't know how yet, but I *will* show Earth the Soluna's Way."

Ayla smiled, meeting all the faces looking toward her with a nod, one by one. She dropped the stone into the water and imagined its ripples extending beyond the creek, beyond this spot, beyond Eema, and into space, all the way to Earth. She watched the ripples in the water until her vision was blurry. Finally, she closed her eyes.

Ayla didn't need to open her eyes to know she was home. She felt it. She knew everything was different and, at once, the very same.

The End

ACKNOWLEDGMENTS

I offer my heartfelt thanks to my editor and dear friend, Christianne Squires. Christianne, you took Ayla and me by our hands in the very beginning and walked this path alongside us, every step of the way. It was a privilege to work with you. Thank you.

I am grateful for those who asked and listened as Ayla's story unfolded. Your eagerness to read a book like this one kept me going. A huge thank you to my early readers. I sincerely appreciate your insight, feedback, and, most of all, your support.

When I set out to write this book, I hoped for the opportunity to collaborate with others, and that hope was fulfilled. Thank you to my meticulous book formatter Ines Monnet for your efforts and for inviting proofreader Callie Walker and book designer Carole Chevalier to join our team. Thank you all for bringing your own unique magic to this process and for helping me bring *The Soluna's Way* to life.

This book wouldn't be possible without my closest advisors: James, Alexander, and Sophia Oginsky. Thank you for answering my endless questions with such clarity and depth. You are and always will be my greatest teachers and guides.

Daniel, thank you for everything. Your support of my work and my words means the world to me. I'm so lucky to be doing this life with you.

Thank you to the indie authors and artists who came before me, showing us all that anything is possible at this point in time.

And finally, a deep bow of gratitude to all the Mothers—especially Mother Earth, the Medicine Women, and the Solunas among us. Thank you for sharing your wisdom. May we listen, may we learn, and may we heal.

ABOUT THE AUTHOR

Author photograph © Christina Kafkakis

Anna Hodges Oginsky is an award-winning author as well as a workshop and retreat facilitator. Since she was a little girl, she has loved reading and writing stories. She believes in the healing power of storytelling, and in her work, she uses writing, art, meditation, and yoga to help children and adults express the stories they hold in their hearts.

The Soluna's Way is Anna's debut novel.

She lives in Michigan, USA, with her husband, their three children, and their labradoodles, Henry and Ollie.

Visit her at www.annaoginsky.com or on Instagram @annaoginsky.

To continue your adventure with Ayla, visit www.thesolunasway.com to download a coloring page created especially for you, dear reader. Be well, be light, and enjoy!

CPSIA information can be obtained
at www.ICGtesting.com
Printed in the USA
JSHW030229031020
8420JS00004B/16